FOREVER and ever

EVA SIMMONS

Copyright © 2023 by Eva Simmons

All rights reserved.

No portion of this book may be reproduced in any form without written permission from the publisher or author, except as permitted by U.S. copyright law.

This novel is entirely a work of fiction. The names, characters and incidents portrayed in it are the work of the author's imagination. Any resemblance to actual persons, living or dead, events or localities is entirely coincidental.

Published by Eva Simmons

Editing by Kat Wyeth (Kat's Literary Services)

Proofreading by Ellison Lane (Kat's Literary Services)

Cover Photography by Rafa Catala

Cover Model David Bodas

Cover Design by Eva Simmons

Formatting via Atticus

ISBN: 9798352068045

Playlist

Situations – Escape the Fate
Keeper – Reignwolf
Trauma – NF
Self Sabotage – Abe Parker
Sorry – Nothing but Thieves
Rose Tattoo – Dropkick Murphys
Something Loud – Jimmy Eat World
Monday – The Regrettes
I Think I'm OKAY – Machine Gun Kelly, Yungblud, Travis Barker
This is What Falling in Love Feels Like – JVKE
Lydia – Highly Suspect
Lost in the Moment – NV, Andreas Moss
Figures – Jessie Reyez
All the Things I Hate About You – Huddy
Record Player – Daisy the Great, AJR
Anthem of Our Dying Day – Story of the Year
Niki Fm – Hawthorne Heights
MakeDamnSure – Taking Back Sunday
The Death of Peace of Mind – Bad Omens

Pain – Jimmy Eat World
Put You Through Me – Arrows in Action
All I Wanted – Paramore
Making All Things New – Aaron Espe
All That Really Matters – ILLENIUM, Teddy Swims
Hurt for Me – SYML
Sparks – Coldplay
Hold On – Chord Overstreet
Only One – Yellowcard

You can find the complete playlist on Spotify.

For love worth holding onto through the messy parts.

Prologue

Noah

Love at first sight is bullshit.

Everyone knows this. Even an idiot like me, who has a history of tripping over his heart every chance he gets.

Been there.

Done that.

I learned my lesson and now I'm over that kind of optimistic thinking.

At least, I was. Until right now, standing here, scraping my jaw off the floor after witnessing what just walked into my dressing room without knocking.

She's a dark goddess in a black tank top and low-rise dark gray jeans. Her skin is laced in tattoo ink, and she's sparkling in piercings. She's by far the most beautiful chick I've ever seen, looming in the doorway like a pit of vastness I'd like to swallow me whole. And she's staring at my hardening cock because I'm one hundred percent buck naked.

"Nice dick," she says, her spiky eyelashes flicking as she looks up at me with a feisty smirk tugging at her bright red lips.

I'd like to see what else her sassy mouth is capable of, but I grab my jeans off the chair and slip them on instead. Because I'm a gentleman. At least, until a woman asks me not to be.

"You don't believe in buttons?" she says when I don't fasten my pants all the way.

I reach for the bottle of bourbon sitting on the table and take a healthy sip straight from the bottle.

"No point." I take another drink and relish in the burn of alcohol fresh in my throat. "They'll be coming off again soon enough anyway."

I wink at her, and the dark goddess rolls her eyes. But not in a way that tells me she's irritated with my comment, more like unimpressed. Like this is what she expects. After all, I'm the drummer for Enemy Muse, the biggest rock band in the country. This is exactly what she should expect from a guy like me.

Her expression proves she's not naïve.

I walk over to a table in the corner and pull a hair band off my wrist to tie my blond hair into a bun on the back of my head. Picking up a razor blade from the table, I scrape together a line of white powder, feeling her eyes on me the whole time. I make three nice little rows guaranteed to send me into a black hole where I don't need to think about what a fucking mess my life is.

"Want some?" I hold a straw out to the hot-as-fuck chick still standing in my doorway, but she shakes her head.

"No thanks." Her eyes narrow the slightest, and I don't like that she seems like she's trying to read me. Maybe she's even judging me, but if so, she doesn't say shit.

I lean over and snort a line up my nose until my brain starts to tingle. The air gets fuzzy, and there's a slight ringing in my ears, dulling out the voices in my head. Just how I like it. The blurrier my thoughts, the less I have to live with them.

"Fuck." I drop the straw and sit on the couch in hopes it will hold me in place as my body starts to vibrate.

The dark goddess doesn't move as I blink her back into focus. She's pulsating—or maybe it's my brain. There's one of her, then three, then one again, as I find my bearings. Once she's clear, I notice her eyes are still fixed on me.

She's not a groupie, or she'd be working her way across the room already instead of staring at me like I'm the most unimpressive piece of rock star trash. But damn, I wish she was. Because even though her eyes are a gavel casting judgment, everything about this chick makes me want to peel off her layers and see how far her ink goes.

"I should leave," she says, like somehow it just occurred to her that she walked into my dressing room without knocking and is now just staring at me.

"Not staying for the party?" I kind of hope she will, even if she seems a little uptight about what I just stuck up my nose.

After all, I'm a *rock star*.

Fucking deal with it.

It's either I numb the pain, or I let the demons in my head loose. And if I go for the latter, there's no coming back.

"I was looking for Adrian." She crosses her arms over her chest. "Wrong door, apparently."

I tick my head to the side. "He's probably with the crew further down the hall."

"Thanks."

"You're welcome." My eyes drop to the lanyard around her neck, and I read her name, "Mercedes Lopez."

"It's Merry, actually."

I don't miss that she's gritting her teeth.

"Whatever you say, *Mercedes*," I tease, loving the slightest shade her skin warms at my comment. It might be in irritation, but I'd still love to see a little more of it.

"What do you need with Adrian?" I ask her, curious why she's looking for our band manager.

I've never been jealous of Adrian, but if he's fucking her, then damn, I will be.

Merry uncrosses her arms and dips her thumbs into her jean pockets, which tugs them the slightest bit lower on her hips and shows off the warm skin of her stomach.

Her gaze moves down my body, taking in my bare chest, and pausing at the bulge in my pants. I could blame my erection on the coke, but the truth is, the sight of her standing in front of me is the most tempting thing I've ever seen, and I can't help it.

When Merry looks back up at me, her expression is passive, and I love how nothing seems to phase her.

"He offered me a job." She leans her back against the door frame and kicks a foot behind her to prop against it. Like she's totally unaffected by the fact that she's alone in a dressing room with the drummer for the biggest rock band in the world. She couldn't seem to care less. I might as well be any other guy on the planet to her, and it's fucking fascinating.

"You going to take it?"

"Maybe." She shrugs one shoulder.

I reach my arms up along the back of the couch and stretch out, appreciating how her eyes trail over my chest once more. She might play coy about who I am, but there's no doubt she likes what she sees.

"Are you always so smiley?" she asks with a scowl, and I realize I'm grinning.

"Maybe." I cock an eyebrow. "You always so unimpressed?"

That brings the slightest tick of amusement to her face, and she wears it well.

It's easy to see she doesn't let people in. Everything from her stance to her expression is guarded. And while I'm sure her defenses put most people off, and that's probably how she prefers it, all it makes me want to do is crack this chick wide open.

I want to dig inside her pretty little head until I figure out what it is that made her like this—what makes her tick, what makes her feel, what makes her happy.

Not that I know what *happy* is anymore, regardless of the impression I give people. These smiles and grins I wear are all for show now. And just because I play the role of the carefree drummer well, doesn't mean deep down I'm not suffocating.

But it's easier this way. Smile through the emptiness and no one asks questions.

There was a time when my happiness wasn't total bullshit. A time when I actually still wanted everything that was coming to me. There was a time when the idea of being famous sounded like a dream come true. After all, people would call me fucking crazy to think otherwise. Who doesn't want the fame, the drugs, and the pussy?

Me.

At least, in the beginning I didn't. All I wanted was the music.

And I wanted *her*.

I found the girl, fell in love, thought it was forever. And like the dumbass I was, I honestly believed it. It didn't matter to me that I was headed out on tour and not going to see her for months on end.

Call me crazy.

Call me blinded by love.

I was ready to wait and make it happen with her when the time was right. Only, she wasn't.

While I was busy writing music that was going to change the world, she was busy resenting me for the fame, the stage, and the groupies. And when I noticed her drifting and I asked if she was okay, she lied to me. Secretly, she was growing bitter that I wasn't giving her the house in the suburbs and church on Sundays.

It didn't matter if I was faithful and committed. Or if I was wearing my stupid fucking promise ring and saving my dick for her alone. To the world, I was a rock god. But to her, I was becoming the devil incarnate.

Fine.

Leave my ass.

Or better yet, tell me.

Anything would have hurt less than her carving my heart from my fucking chest with a butter knife and playing with it until it was bloody and broken. But that's life, giving me the shit end of the stick. So here I am, enjoying what's left of it.

"You just gonna stand there or are you gonna join me?" I dip my gaze to the empty couch cushion beside me and then back up at Merry.

A dare.

A challenge.

She's too smart to go for it—I know that—but I can't help myself.

"Actually—" a knock on the door interrupts her as a woman starts to enter.

I recognize her as the redhead I met backstage. She looked delicious in her tight green dress that complimented her emerald eyes. I wanted her on her knees the moment she offered because she was beautiful, and her plump lips were made for sucking dick. But with Merry standing like a dark goddess beside her, the redhead seems suddenly average and unappealing.

Not that it will stop me with this raging erection in my pants.

"Candace." The redhead reaches out for Merry's hand and Merry shakes it, skimming her eyes over the girl once and then looking back to me with the closest thing to a smile I've seen on her face since she walked in my dressing room unannounced.

"Merry," she says to Candace.

"You joining us?" Candace asks, and my dick gets harder at the thought alone.

"For you, I'm tempted." Merry steps closer to Candace and runs her fingers along the length of her arm.

For a second, I think she might actually be considering it, but then Merry's narrowed brown eyes meet mine, so dark they're almost black, and she shoots me a wickedly amused grin.

"But…" Merry steps back. "I don't fuck people I work for."

And there it is, a line she's slowly drawing on the ground between us. Telling me she's accepting the job with Adrian and making it perfectly clear where I stand. Not that I didn't already know. Merry's so far out of my league that even the coke and bourbon can't convince me otherwise.

She probably thinks she needs to make that clear for me. She doesn't. After all, I'm not Sebastian, fucking every chick who comes into his line of sight like he's pissed the fuck off. Or Rome, impulsive and impossible to please. I'm the gentleman of the band, mostly.

If she wants to play this little game of chicken, then fine. I'll wait.

"Guess you better go find Adrian then." I reach down to strip my jeans off again, leaving myself naked once more on the couch, just like she met me.

Some people are shy about being naked, but I'm not one of them. In this profession, there isn't much room for modesty. When I'm not changing in front of people backstage, I'm getting naked at photo shoots. Privacy is something I haven't had in years. So if Merry doesn't want to see something, she can look away.

Except, she doesn't.

Merry stares at my dick for a long moment. The dent in her cheek makes me think she must be chewing the inside of it with whatever she's thinking. And when she looks up at me, there's an almost playful look in her eyes.

Instead of turning to leave, she walks straight up to me. She stands between my open legs but is careful not to touch. It's for the best, because the drugs are starting to get to my head at this point, and with her this close, I'm buzzing with electricity.

Merry leans down, and she smells like cherries. Ripe, like her perfect pouty red lips.

Her fingers dip under the ridge of a lacy black bra and pull out a small, square foil wrapper, that she hands to me. Our fingers touch as I pluck it from her fingers, and she doesn't miss that it makes my dick twitch.

Did this chick actually just hand me a condom? Who the fuck is this woman, and why am I only just now meeting her?

"Have a good night, Mr. Hayes," she says with a wink. "And wish me luck with Adrian. Maybe I'll see you on your next tour."

Then she turns and walks away, closing the dressing room door behind her. Leaving nothing but the smell of fucking cherries in my nose and in my head. She might as well have carved it into my skin. Because the scent is like her, unforgettable.

Candace walks over, unaffected by the whole scene that just played out in front of her.

Got to love that about groupies, they don't really give a fuck about where you screw them, or what's going on, or who's joining in. As long as you give them a piece then they're happy. Candace isn't here to fall in love. She just wants to play with my dick long enough to go home and tell her friends about it.

And that's fine—for now.

Candace reaches behind her back and unzips her dress, letting it pool on the floor by her feet. She kneels between my legs and grabs my dick, but my eyes are on the closed door behind her.

There was a time this used to make me feel less empty. A time when playing for tens of thousands of people was a dream come true. There was a time when all this was a blessing. But now, it's my curse. Because fame has given me everything I've ever wanted, while also taking away everything that meant anything to me.

Not that it should matter much right now with a naked woman between my legs and a pile of coke on the table next to me.

I take a deep breath and feel the white powder starting to coat my thoughts like snow in my brain. A blanket that hides my secrets. I let it settle over the spots that hurt and float in the white space of emptiness.

My dick disappears into the groupie's mouth, but it's not her lips I'm picturing as I hit the back of her throat and stare off at nothingness.

I'm seeing darkness, mystery. It smells like cherries. And it's almost good enough to bring me back to life inside. That is, if I wasn't already halfway dead.

October

1

Merry

The last time I was face to face with Noah Hayes, he was naked and five seconds away from getting his dick sucked by a groupie. It's only fitting that time number two is no more glamorous.

I wish I could say he looks worse than I remember, but that would be a lie. He's a mix of surfer casual and rock star glam with his shoulder-length blond hair, ripped jeans, necklaces, and bracelets. He pulls off looking like the boy you sit beside at church, while also being a rock star playboy who wears a dirty smirk like a damn statement.

Noah Hayes is a bad decision, wrapped in a deceptive pretty boy package.

"Five-star rehab, how very rock star of you," I say, as he stops in front of me, smelling like fresh laundry and mint.

"What can I say." Noah shrugs, the biggest smile climbing up his cheeks. "I like what I like."

The sparkle in his eyes makes the comment feel more like an innuendo than a statement about his accommodations, so I avoid it.

The last time I saw Noah, he wasn't exactly subtle about his interest in me. He might have been high as a kite and horny, but I recognized the look in his eyes.

Genuine curiosity.

But whether he's interested in me or not is irrelevant. I'm not dumb enough to fall for his pretty-boy drummer routine. I work for the band now. Those guys are officially in the *no-fucking-way* column.

Besides, the last thing I need is any man thinking I'm a good idea. Rock stars might come with a lot of baggage, but I come with more.

Noah shifts in front of me, raking his hair off his face. I realize he's taller than I remember. Even in my lifted boots, he still towers over me by at least half a foot.

"So, Mercedes Lopez, you got the job, I see."

I'm surprised he remembers who I am, considering the amount of powder he stuck up his nose when we met. But standing here now, his pale blue eyes are clearer, and I actually believe he might be sober.

We'll see if he stays that way.

"Lucky me, got the job and now I'm picking your sober ass up." I narrow my eyes at him, but he smirks in return. "And the name's still just Merry."

I turn and head for the rental car.

Adrian didn't want to draw attention to Noah's rehab stay, so he sent me to pick him up. He figured correctly that no one knows who I am or that I work for the band, so I could easily slip in and out of a world-class rehab facility with one of the world's biggest celebrities unnoticed.

Not that it should matter. Rehab and fame go hand in hand, especially for rock stars.

"Merry is an awfully cheery name for a girl who rarely smiles," Noah says, walking so close our arms brush.

"What can I say, I'm ironic." I slip on my sunglasses and walk around the car to climb in. But as Noah gets in the passenger seat, I can't help myself. "Or maybe I'm full of smiles. And you just bring this sour mood out of me."

"Doubtful." He grins.

Fuck, that shit is blinding, no wonder the man is constantly surrounded by groupies. Luckily, I've learned a thing or two about keeping my wits around smiles like that. Charming or not, I know better than to fall for the glitz and glamour that is Noah Hayes.

"Buckle up," I tell him, throwing the car in reverse and ignoring the fact that Noah won't stop with his ridiculous cheeriness. "God forbid something happens to that priceless face of yours. I'd be out of a job before I even got started."

He buckles his seat belt, and we head out into traffic. LA is a shit show this time of day, but I don't mind because I'm finally doing what I want with my life. Pursuing a career in music. Or, at least working in the music industry in some capacity.

Being an errand girl for Enemy Muse might not be exactly what I envisioned when I decided to drop out of college, but it will do for now. We all start somewhere. And if I need to make industry connections by fetching things for spoiled rock stars for a few years, then so be it. I'll do anything to make my dreams come true.

It also doesn't hurt that I'll be touring the country and partying with the biggest names in the industry. Goodbye, boring co-ed life, and hello world.

My mom might be pissed, and my dad might be temporarily not speaking to me for dropping out a year before graduation, but it's my life, and I'm tired of not living it.

"We need to make a stop," Noah says, flicking through his phone.

I glance over and notice he's tapping his fingers against the back of the case and looks annoyed with whatever's on the screen.

"Adrian asked to see you, I'm supposed to—"

"I'll text him." Noah starts typing away. "We don't leave until tomorrow, right?"

I nod.

"Good." Noah looks up and scans the road. "Then make a right."

Wonderful. As if driving around LA isn't enough of a nightmare when I know where I'm going, Noah's sending me on a wild goose chase.

Turning right, I notice we're heading in the direction of downtown. He continues spouting off directions, looking between his phone and the road, and when we reach close to the center of the city, he finally directs me to park.

"And we are?"

"Here," Noah says, climbing out of the car.

He circles as I'm getting out and reaches for my door with a grin on his face. Noah really is Mr. Fucking Sunshine, apparently. Yes, in magazines and TV interviews, I've noticed he's always smiling. But in person, I expected him to be a little more like the rest of the band—guarded, reserved, pissy.

Not Noah, Mr. Perma Grin. And for some reason, that gets on my nerves.

"Are you seriously holding my door for me?" I ask him, as he holds it open.

Noah shrugs. "I'm a gentleman."

"Sure, you are." I roll my eyes.

But when he shrugs again and closes my door behind me, I wonder if he's for real. Because I get a strange feeling the thoughtful, caring energy Noah puts off isn't total bullshit. I'm not sure how the industry didn't chew him up and spit him out. Although he just got out of rehab, so who knows, maybe it did.

I follow Noah along a few storefronts before he stops outside Twisted Roses, a tattoo parlor I recognize from its reputation, even if I've never been. These are world-class artists, inking the biggest celebrities, and they're ridiculously expensive.

"You're getting a tattoo?" I look him up and down, remembering what he looks like totally naked, whether I want to or not. I know he only has one patch of ink on his surfer boy skin, a solid black band that wraps his forearm.

"Figured now is as good a time as ever." Noah holds the door open for me.

"Isn't there some kind of rule when you get out of rehab about not making any big, life-changing decisions?"

Noah dips his arm down on the door frame as I take a step forward, and it cages me right outside the shop. This close to him, I get another hit of mint from the gum he's chewing as he looks down at me.

"Says the girl covered in tattoos?"

"Exactly. Says the girl who knows a little something about permanence."

He narrows his eyes as he thinks my words over, dipping his stare to my lips, before meeting my eyes with that shimmer he wields like a weapon.

"Maybe some things are worth the risk of regret," he says, finally moving his arm and letting me pass.

His statement swirls around in my head as I walk past him, and I swear I feel his eyes watching me as he follows me into the shop. He's not being as obviously flirtatious as he was in his dressing room when I met him, but that feeling is still there like he's mulling me over, deciding what he's going to do with me.

Rock stars, thinking they can have whatever they want.

It's annoying.

"Noah Hayes." The woman behind the counter practically gasps, her eyes going wide as she takes him in. She hops off her stool and straightens her shirt, tugging the bottom so it shows off more of her cleavage, leaving little of her tits to the imagination.

He walks up like he has no effect on her and leans his elbows on the counter as he shoots her a Hollywood smile.

"Hey, doll." He beams, and I have to hold back the vomit in my throat. This man's charm is insufferable. "I don't have an appointment, but curious if Blaze or Rachel have any openings."

Noah knows exactly what he's doing, throwing his celebrity status around because he's well aware they aren't going to turn him away no matter how busy they are.

After all, he's Noah Hayes.

Barf.

I roll my eyes and walk away from them, heading over to a wall of artwork on the other side of the parlor. If I walked in here today asking for a tattoo—assuming I had the cash, of course—they'd tell me they're booked up for a year. I'd have to wait my turn like everyone else.

But looking over my shoulder and seeing half of the parlor staff gathering around, I know that's not going to be the case for Noah.

Let's all stop the universe from spinning to make sure he gets what he wants at any given moment.

It must be nice, to reach that point of fame where you have other people to worry about your bullshit, so you no longer have to. And so what if maybe I'm a little jealous seeing it in action now that I work for the band. But watching how they've reached a point so high that they're no longer affected reminds me, if I ever get my shot, I'm going to appreciate it. And I'll try to not be a total asshole.

"Find something you like?" Noah's voice coming up behind me makes me jump.

I've been zoned out, staring at a sketch of a woman with rose vines wrapped around her, pulling her under. It's highlighted with splashes of watercolor and it's gorgeous.

"Just looking." I spin around, shutting down Noah's question.

He seems like the type to offer up a joint tattoo session even though he barely knows me, and from the look in his eyes right now, the last thing I need is him thinking we're going to have some kind of ink-induced bonding moment. I don't want him getting any ideas.

"What are you getting done?" I ask, trying to ignore the fact that he's standing really close, and I'm boxed in between him and the wall.

Noah's eyes move from mine to the sketches behind me, skimming them over.

"Another ring around my arm," he says, looking back at me.

He holds his forearm out between us, and I notice his thin cotton shirt is rolled up to his elbow, showing off the thick veins in his forearm.

I'm not blind, everything about this man is downright sexy. He's tall and lean with solid muscle. A surfer body that matches his untamed shoulder-length blond hair and tanned skin. But luckily for me, his irritating charm is enough to remind me I'd never go there in a million years.

I reach out and wrap my hand around his arm, flipping it over to get a better look. I've seen the tattoo in pictures, and that day I met him naked in his dressing room, but never this close. It's a solid ring of ink that wraps in a full circle around his forearm. It's about as wide as a quarter, with no other details or intricacy.

"What do the rings mean?" I release his arm and dip my thumbs in my jeans pockets.

Noah's eyes do that thing where he watches everything I do, and it's a little unnerving. He rolls his thick forearm over a couple of times, rubbing where the new band will go.

"They represent big moments," he says, dropping his arm.

"And this is big?"

Going on another tour?

Leaving rehab?

Finishing an album?

Something more personal?

I don't ask him to elaborate.

"Let's hope so." Noah smiles, but unlike the ones I've been used to all morning, this one is darker, and it doesn't quite reach his eyes.

I'm not sure when he got so close, but I have to tilt my chin up to look him in the eyes.

I haven't worked for the band long, just the past week as we prepare to go out on tour. But from what I can tell, Noah isn't as guarded over his personal space as the rest of the members seem to be.

There's Sebastian, the lead singer, who is a total disaster. Rumor has it he wasn't always such a mess, but I'm not convinced. When he's not wasted, he's high. And he's pissed off one hundred percent of the time, so I avoid him.

Then there's Eloise, Sebastian's sister and the bass player. She's friendly enough, but she keeps to herself, so I don't have much of an opinion.

And finally, there's Rome, The Riff King, as the press likes to call him, covered in piercings and tattoos. His lap is never empty, and I steer clear. Because although he seems happy to be in every girl's personal space, I have no interest.

I take a step back and turn my body away to break Noah's stare, scanning the sketches on the wall once more. The look in Noah's eyes goes a lot further than what I'm used to getting from guys who just want to fuck me, and I need to shut that shit down.

The last thing I need is Noah forming some kind of attachment just because he thinks I'm pretty. That's all on the surface. If he dug deeper, he'd learn the truth. And he'd get too close to things I don't want him, or anyone else, near.

I didn't take this job to make friends or find a boyfriend. This is a stepping stone in my career. That's it. The line is drawn, and I'm not crossing it.

"We're ready for you." A man with tattoos from his scalp to knuckles slaps Noah on the back of the shoulder and gets his attention.

Noah nods at him, then looks at me. "Coming?"

I shake my head.

"I'm good, I've got some messages to catch up on." I grab my phone out of my back pocket and wave it between us.

A hint of disappointment crosses his face, but he doesn't argue as he turns to follow the man into the back.

It's better this way.

Just like Noah's at this tattoo parlor to mark a big moment in his life, I need to do the same. This tour, this job, this year—It's the start of something new for me. I'm going to embrace it. And I'm going to do it all by myself.

2

Noah

There might as well have been a whole lifetime before rehab because I feel resurrected walking onto the plane and facing the band again. It's only been two months since the tour ended and Adrian shipped me off to get my shit together, but it feels like a lot longer.

"Back from the fucking dead," Rome says, walking up to me and throwing a tattooed arm around my shoulder.

If only he knew how true that statement is. I might have a sixty-day chip in my pocket to prove I'm *well enough* for them to release me back into the world, but I can still feel the demons knocking around in my head.

"You know it." I plaster a time-perfected grin on my face.

I'm clean, it should be enough. One can only hope.

"We missed you," Eloise stands and pulls me into a warm hug. My arms wrap fully around her tiny frame, and even though I'm not sure if I'm ready to be back in my life quite yet, there's something comforting about reconnecting with the band that feels like home. After all, they're the only family that means anything to me anymore.

"Missed you too," I tell her, as she pulls away and gives my arms a final squeeze. "Even those pieces of shit."

I look over at where Rome has taken a seat by Sebastian again, and they both just flip me off.

Eloise shakes her head, and it swishes her sandy brown ponytail around. She's unaffected by us at this point—basically a little sister to us all, even if she's only blood related to Sebastian, her twin.

I drop into a seat across from Rome and Sebastian, while Eloise sits down beside me. The four of us back together. Part of me expects Hell to open its mouth in this moment and decide we've already done enough damage, and our time is up. But that's wishful thinking.

"Hey, man," Sebastian says, tipping his chin up at me. "You good?"

"You know it."

He nods, but I'm not sure either of us believe it as he rests his head back in the oversized seat and closes his eyes.

On every tour the private planes and buses seem to get more extravagant. And this one is no different. As if we can't find enough ways to blow the money we're making, the label is intent on helping us spend it.

This plane is proof. We won't even be using it much this tour since we'll be mostly on buses. But it's decked out like we might as well be moving in.

There's a bedroom in the back and a full sitting area up front, with plenty of room for the band and our personal crew. There's a full staff on hand already making drinks, which Rome seems well aware of as his gaze trails a busty beauty around the plane. It's all a little ridiculous. Such is life when you get rich and famous enough.

I've been out of rehab for five seconds, and I already know this next tour is going to be a shit show. As if the alcohol and drugs aren't enough to tempt a person, there's sex everywhere.

Speaking of temptation—just when I think we're ready to take off, a certain dark goddess trails Adrian onto the plane.

Mercedes Lopez, a woman I can't seem to figure out yet.

She gives off a constant *fuck-you* vibe, especially to me. But there's something about those narrowed dark brown eyes that might as well be a magnetic force pulling me in. Because the more she tries to push me away, the more I'm compelled to orbit around her.

And that's after only meeting her twice. We've got an entire tour ahead of us.

Merry's eyes meet mine as she walks onto the plane, and I wonder if she feels what I do—the universe playing some kind of sick joke placing her in front of me when it knows I'm just kicking one addiction and itching for another. But as quickly as she looks my way, she breaks gazes, and the hollow void in the pit of my stomach widens.

What is it about that woman?

It could be that I met her right before my entire life spiraled into a black hole. Or that for the first time in years I feel like someone is actually seeing through all the bullshit I put out there. But really it just feels like her.

I'm used to being surrounded by fake company. Plastic bodies and brainwashed minds. Besides the band, and a select few on the crew, everyone else is around simply to please us. A never-ending parade of bullshit, and it's exhausting.

But Merry seems one hundred percent real, which is rare in this business. Like a black diamond in a sea of transparency.

Today is no different, as she's wearing a skintight long sleeve black top that hides every inch of tattooed skin on her arms. The neckline meets her throat, and she's paired it with dark gray leggings. I'm struck by the fact that every inch of her skin can be covered, and she's still so damn tempting.

Her eyes drift my way once more as she tightens her dark wavy hair in her ponytail, and I'm tempted to walk over and say something. But before I can, she drops onto a seat as far away from me as possible and faces the opposite direction.

For someone who has the power to knock the air from my chest on sight, she doesn't seem to share the feeling.

Smart fucking girl.

"Noah," Adrian says, walking up to me and taking a seat with the band as the door to the plane closes.

I nod at Adrian, as he looks me over. He's trying to figure out if I'm already fucked up again or if this rehab stay is going to stick. Not that I blame him.

"I'm clean," I say, trying to get him to stop looking at me like that. I know I'm a piece of shit without everyone always seeking confirmation.

Adrian nods. "Good."

A man of few words, which I appreciate in this moment. The last thing I need is for him to ask questions when I'm currently in a wrestling match with the demons in my head. There's nothing to numb them or keep them at bay—their fingers are clawing.

I pop a stick of gum in my mouth and try to forget the fact that I'm crawling out of my skin as the plane starts to move. Rome's eyes drift down to my hands, and he smirks. I'm tapping my fingers against the arms of my chair. Maybe it's because I'm a drummer, or maybe it's that I'm sober, but I can't sit still.

Sebastian is across from me with his eyes closed and his head tipped back, but he's twisting his thumbs around each other, so I know he's not sleeping. From the look of him, he's probably fucked up out of his mind.

Is it wrong that I'm jealous?

While I've been in rehab, Eloise has kept me updated on the band, and apparently Sebastian's still in a bad place.

Six months ago, his best friend, and our crew manager, died from an overdose. And even though I wasn't much help, being along for the ride as he drowned his grief in booze, then drugs, then women, it's clear he's not over it.

I might be sober now, but while I was getting my shit together, Sebastian seems to have gotten worse.

That's how this business works. Living in the eye of the fucking storm.

I'm honestly not sure if any of us are in a good spot to prep for this next tour, especially after how the last one went down, but as the label says: *you've got this.*

Translation: *make us some fucking money or be washed up like all those who came before you.*

I thought I was bad, but looking at Sebastian across from me, twitching and clearly on edge, maybe I'm the least of their problems. His shaggy blond hair is longer than usual, falling to his eyebrows, and he looks like he hasn't shaved in a week.

Mr. Clean Cut looks fucked up in more ways than physically.

"Who do I need to fuck to get a drink around here?" Rome says, looking over his shoulder.

"Rome." Eloise glares at him, before darting her eyes in my direction.

"It's fine," I tell her.

I'm not under any delusions that this tour isn't going to be the ultimate test of my sobriety. If I wanted to take the easy road, I wouldn't be here at all. But my music is all I have left at this point. That, and the band.

So unless I want to lose the last things keeping me from snapping, this is where I need to be—booze and all.

"I'm a big boy, I can handle it." I nudge Eloise's arm and try to play it off.

She buys it and relaxes. They always do. I'm good at pretending nothing gets to me. Which is clear from the way Rome grins in my direction and then starts looking around again for a flight attendant.

I rub my forearm, where the fresh tattoo is hidden by my long sleeve shirt, and take a deep breath.

I can do this. I have to.

Once more, my stare moves to Merry, who's talking to Quinn, our social media manager. She's clearly making herself comfortable with the people around her, and I shouldn't be surprised. She strikes me as a girl who will be able to hold her own on this tour—and in our world.

My world.

Not that I belong here much anymore.

"So, what's the plan?" I ask Adrian, trying to distract myself as the plane starts to lift off.

No matter how much I've traveled, I never get used to that feeling. My insides going into a state of suspension. As if they don't already feel uneasy on a daily basis, wind catching under the airplane's wings sends me floating.

"We're stopping in Denver first so you guys can have a week off at home to chill." He says 'you guys' but they're all staring like it's me they're really worried about. They want to give me time to settle in, so I don't immediately fall off the wagon.

"Got it." I'm not thrilled that I'll be getting these questioning looks on a regular basis. "And after that?"

"We're heading to Vegas," Adrian says, a little less sure about that statement, even though it makes Rome whoop loudly.

Eloise kicks Rome in the shin, and he flips her off just in time for Sebastian to open his eyes and catch him. So Sebastian elbows him in the arm.

"Fuck you both," Rome says, rubbing his shin with one hand and elbow with the other.

Adrian watches them like they're children. We might as well be. Rock stars aren't the most well-adjusted people given we get handed everything we want and don't have to apologize for anything.

"We're not going to Vegas for you to get your dick serviced," Adrian says to Rome, who just shrugs back at him. "We're meeting with the production team for the tour. The label wants your sets nailed down for their approval by the end of November."

"When does the tour start?"

"December."

Fuck, the label really isn't giving us any time to breathe anymore. In the beginning, we would have at least six months between tours. Now it's a rehab stint and two months max before they ship us out again.

"Merry," Adrian yells across the plane, and she turns to look at him.

For once she doesn't have that scowl on her face, and I realize she's reserved that demeanor for me alone. Not that I've given her the best first impression.

"Did you confirm the flights to Vegas?"

She nods. "October Seventeenth."

"Good." Adrian leans back in his seat, and Merry turns back to Quinn without so much as looking at me.

Either she's purposely avoiding me, or she really doesn't give a shit. And I'm not sure why I care so much. It's been years since I've paid this much attention to one particular woman, seeing as I can have as many as I want. But there's something about her.

"What's her deal?" I ask Adrian.

"Merry?"

I nod.

"She's fucking hot," Rome says, and I can't help but glare at him.

"She's a good employee," Adrian says, pinning me with his stare when I look back at him. "So, try to keep your dick in your fucking pants, because I'd like her to stick around for more than five seconds."

That makes me smirk.

"Seriously, Noah," Adrian warns, and I'm surprised at how stern he sounds. "I see something in her. She wants to do a lot more in this industry than clean up after your sorry asses, and I think she's got a chance if she can survive all this shit."

"What does she want to do?" I ask, genuinely curious.

"Sing."

Interesting, the girl is full of surprises.

"Just try to keep it professional."

I rest my hands behind my head and plaster that fake smile on my face. "Will do, boss. Will do."

But my gaze drifts her direction as I say it, and I know *professional* is the last thing Merry makes me want to be.

3

Merry

If the shows on tour end up being anything like the band's practice sessions, this might officially be the end of Enemy Muse's reign.

Sebastian looks like he's going to fall over or pass out, Eloise is stressed as fuck, Rome is distracted by every pair of legs that walks by, and Noah looks miserable, even if he is smiling through it.

I've seen them live a few times over the past couple of years, and this is nothing like what I remember.

"What the fuck was that?" Adrian might as well have smoke coming out of his ears because his face is flushed red in frustration.

"Lady Sunshine," Sebastian says with a look in his eyes that tells me he wants to see how far he can push Adrian over the edge.

We've been in Vegas for two weeks, and it's been a shit show. While the production team works on designing their tour, the band has been trying to find their rhythm again. But it's a fractured mess, to say the least. It's almost as if the band's never played with each other before, and since I'm new to the crew I'm not sure if this is normal after every break or if they've officially lost their spark.

"I'm aware of what song it was *supposed* to be." Adrian steps onto the stage. "It sounded like shit. Do I need to pull the plug on this whole thing?"

Sebastian shakes his head like he's not taking Adrian's threats seriously.

"Do whatever the fuck you want, man." Sebastian sets his microphone down and laughs as he walks off the stage. "I'll be in my hotel room. I'm over this shit."

He disappears, and I'm surprised they all let him. No one says anything, even though Eloise's heated gaze has a whole silent conversation with the back of Sebastian's head as she watches him walk away.

"Take a break," Adrian tells the rest of them, walking off the stage and making his way over to me. "We'll try again tomorrow."

He's shaking his head, and for a man of few words and even fewer expressions, I'm not sure I've ever seen him so pissed.

"You can head out too, Merry." He gathers a stack of papers from the seat next to me. "We'll resume this shit show when they've gotten some rest."

"You think that's what they're actually going to do right now?" I raise an eyebrow. "Rest?"

He lets out a deep sigh. "Who fucking knows anymore."

"Rock stars," I say, under my breath, watching them all walking off the stage laughing at something Rome said like this is any other day.

"You get used to it." Adrian takes a seat next to me and stretches out.

In the few weeks I've worked for the band, I've started to learn their dynamic, and I'm not sure how Adrian puts up with it. He seems to be the sole reason they're still together, the glue that keeps them in place. And what pisses me off is that none of them seem to appreciate it.

"They're lucky to have you," I say to Adrian, grabbing my bag and standing up.

"Tell them that."

I dip my chin down and look up at him. "Oh, I do. Repeatedly. I'd be happy to rough them up a little if you think that would help."

"Tempting." Adrian grins. "But knowing the guys, they'd enjoy it too damn much."

I can't help but laugh because he's probably right.

Adrian stands up and grabs his things as the rest of the crew starts to empty the stage. "Go enjoy a long night off, it's Vegas after all. We'll pick back up tomorrow. And with any luck, they won't make our ears bleed."

"And what about you?"

"Tonight, I'm over it. Fuck them. I'd rather not know whatever shit they're about to get into, so I'm going to bed."

"Understood, boss," I say. "Enjoy ignorance."

Adrian nods and walks away, looking like he could use a month of rest and it still wouldn't be enough. His job is no joke, with the band continually forcing him to clean up their shit. And it doesn't help that Adrian doesn't seem to know how to blow off steam like the rest of them. For the manager of the biggest rock band in the country, he doesn't party much.

Unlike me.

Even if the band can be insufferable, and babysitting rock stars is a massive headache, I reap the benefits by joining them when I need to let loose. If I have to put up with their bullshit, you better believe I'll be enjoying the perks as well.

I'm not sure what I was thinking bringing heels to Vegas because there's too much walking involved to wear them. Instead, I swap them for boots and decide that at least they add a little edge to my skintight black minidress.

The nice thing about Vegas is you can wear next to nothing and still appear fully covered depending on the scene you're hanging out in.

Hitting the lobby button on the elevator, I lean back and start swiping through my texts. Still nothing from my parents. Apparently, they're intent on not speaking to me until I decide I've made a huge mistake and head back to college.

Too bad that's not going to happen. I'm twenty-three and going to live my life. Staying in Seattle and chasing a career I don't care about would be torture.

The doors are about to close when a hand slides between them. Slowly, they peel open to reveal Noah standing there with a smirk on his face. He steps inside, but not before scanning me from head to toe.

"Mercedes," he says with a smile, propping himself way too close to me.

"Noah." I groan, trying to avoid his gaze.

He might look all right in his simple gray T-shirt and black jeans, but I'm not going to let him catch me staring.

Noah strikes me as the kind of guy who enjoys the chase, because that's all he's done for the past three weeks, no matter how often I shut him down. But I know what happens when the thrill fades and he realizes I'm not the girl he thinks I am.

Noah is better off sticking to the sweet, pretty-girl type—blonde hair, blue eyes, looks like she'd make a nice Stepford wife. A cookie-cutter copy of one of the many groupies he attracts.

And he attracts a lot of them.

"Looking beautiful as always." He leans closer, and I get an inhale of the wintergreen gum he's chewing.

"Do those cheesy pick-up lines actually work on women?" I swipe closed the apps on my phone and turn to face him.

"You tell me." He grins.

His hair is tucked behind his ears, showing off his chiseled jaw and those piercing blue eyes he uses to try and spear straight through me.

"No." I narrow my gaze, which only seems to amuse him.

"Good thing in my profession pickup lines aren't really a necessity then," he says with a shrug, looking straight ahead.

I roll my eyes and tuck my phone back into my purse, crossing my arms over my chest.

"Where are you headed?" Noah turns his head to the side and once more scans me over. My stomach defies me by twisting, which I don't appreciate.

There's this energy Noah puts off that I wish I was better at ignoring. Something about the sunshine that radiates out of him makes you feel like you're orbiting whether you want to or not. And I'm not blind to it.

"Out."

Noah chuckles. "Funny, that's where I was headed."

"You aren't following me."

"Maybe I was already headed wherever you're going." He gives me a one-shoulder shrug.

"You weren't."

"Wasn't I?"

We're in the same standoff I've found myself in with him almost every time we've come face to face. Him pushing to get closer. Me kicking him away. The guy is intent on breaching whatever he has identified as a wall within me.

Good luck. Not happening.

Just because I'm different from the girls he's used to surrounding himself with, doesn't mean I'm dumb enough to fall for him being temporarily interested.

I get it. I was the strange girl in school, always wearing dark clothes and drawing on myself with Sharpies. I never quite fit into the same mold as everyone else, which my classmates were happy to remind me of.

Half the time, I was being made fun of. The other half, I was being chased by guys who wanted to work out their strange fetishes. Either way, it always resulted in them leaving when they were done and had their fill.

But that was then, and this is now. I'm smarter—stronger—and I know better than to think it's a good idea to let anyone in.

"I get what you're doing, Noah." I stand up taller, even if there's no way I'll match his height, especially in my boots.

Noah turns to face me in the elevator, leaning against the back of it and crossing one ankle over the other with an amused look on his face.

"Oh, you do?" He quirks an eyebrow. "Well then, enlighten me."

"You're trying to throw me off balance." I cut my eyes in his direction. "And I'm sure that works for you with most women—swinging your dick around and smiling at them with that stupid grin on your face. But I've dealt with pretty boys chasing me before. Guys only interested because I appear dangerous or forbidden. And I know better. There will be no panties melting, so you can drop the act."

He's grinning wider now, looking me over like he's trying to break my resolve with his eyes.

"Interesting," he says, his expression growing more devious by the second.

"What is?"

He shifts, and somehow the space in the elevator seems to be shrinking because he's so close I feel like I'm breathing him in.

"I think I do tilt you off balance, Mercedes Lopez." His gaze drops to my mouth for the briefest second. "And I think you don't know what to do with that."

"I'm not going to have sex with you if that's what you're after."

"It's not," Noah says, looking me over once more. "Not that we both wouldn't enjoy it."

I let out an unamused chuckle. "Cocky much?"

"Very." He shoots me a look that snaps something deep inside, just as the elevator pings and the doors peel open. Noah stands tall and takes a step back, waving his hand out. "After you, beautiful."

"Such a gentleman." I roll my eyes to prove I'm not affected. Because I'm not—I can't be. So I do what I do best and glare at him before walking away.

Noah Hayes is infuriating. Delusional. Stubborn.

He might think I'll break someday. But not a chance in hell.

4

Noah

When you're sober, there are only so many ways to dull the pain. Only so many ways to quiet the demons. Being balls deep in someone is one of them, which used to be a great solution. But Merry has me so fucked in the head it's not as enjoyable as it used to be.

Across the club, she's grinding on some guy. She's clearly well versed in all sorts of tricks she can deliver with that tight little body of hers. The girl is physical and doesn't hold back when she wants to have a good time. It's one of the many fun facts I've learned about her since I got out of rehab a month ago. And Vegas seems to be the perfect playground to bring that out in her.

Physical is good, a language I understand.

What I don't like is watching it play out in front of me with some other guy. My bed might not be cold and empty, but fuck, Merry is tempting enough to drive a man insane.

"What's your deal with her?" Sebastian asks, leaning over and almost spilling his drink on me when he does.

"Who?"

"Don't play fucking dumb with me, man." Sebastian knocks me on the arm. "Merry. You do realize you're staring, right?"

I am one hundred percent staring because when she's in a room, there's really nowhere else worth looking, even when she's grinding on this guy's dick and sending my blood pressure skyrocketing.

"I don't know what you're talking about." I look at him.

His eyes are glazed over, and it's clear he's fucked out of his mind, so even if I told him the truth, there's no way he'd remember it tomorrow.

"Whatever man." He waves me off, his eyes moving to the crowd of women slowly forming near our table.

It doesn't take long for word to spread when the band walks into a club. Eventually, the hordes gravitate in our direction. Kind of takes the fun out of it after a while.

No chase.

No thrill.

Which is why Merry thinks I want her. And maybe at first, she was right. I liked the fact that a woman wasn't falling all over me for once. She was flat-out denying me, and I couldn't remember the last time that happened. But that's not what has kept me captivated by her.

She's real—raw… in a way I've never seen a person. I want to drown in that reality and feel for once what it's like to strip away all the bullshit.

I want to know everything about her, and I want her to know everything about me. Not that she seems to have any interest in doing the same. As evidenced by her grabbing this random guy's hand and pulling him off the dance floor behind her.

"Let's get you a distraction," Sebastian says, noticing whatever look must have crossed my face.

Sebastian waves at the chicks standing on the periphery of the VIP section and points out a couple of them to the security guards standing watch. They let the ladies in, who are all too eager to make their way over to us. Some cute blonde chick sits down on the other side of Sebastian, and a sexy brunette in a tiny red dress slides up next to me.

Why is it every woman lately just seems *fine enough*? I miss the days when I could snort a pile of coke and not have to deal with all these empty feelings.

"Lisette," the girl introduces herself, leaning close enough that I could get drunk on the smell of vodka in her drink.

"Nice to meet you." I sit back and stretch my arm out along the couch behind her, which she seems to appreciate.

Merry's right, I don't even have to try anymore. I could ignore Lisette all night and she would still come back to my room with me.

"Want a drink?" she says, looking down at the water sitting in front of me on the table.

I shake my head. "Don't drink."

"Okay." She laughs like she doesn't believe me, but I don't try to explain myself or convince her. I don't really give a fuck if she knows that I'm sober. It's not why she's here.

Lisette slides her hand onto my lap and her fingers rest right at the edge of where my dick sits, slowly moving her hand up and down my thigh like an invitation.

"Did you want to dance?" I ask her, but she shakes her head.

Leaning in, her mouth gets really close to my ear. "I'd rather go somewhere a little quieter."

Sebastian nudges my arm, and when I look at him, he's grinning with the blonde latched onto his neck. He shoots me a wink and then tips his chin to the chick beside me. The only good thing about him being a fucking disaster right now is he's helpful with the distractions. But sooner or later, the guy is going to need to deal with his shit.

"All right." I stand up and hold out my hand, which Lisette happily takes.

At least if my mind insists on living inside a black hole tonight, I won't have to go there alone. And she seems more than willing to help me out.

Help out, she does. On her knees, from behind, the girl is very helpful, apparently.

But once she's dressed again, and I'm in sweats with her perfume coating my body, I don't feel the relaxation I was looking for. I just feel dirty.

"I had fun." She lifts onto her toes to kiss me goodbye in the doorway to my room.

I'd rather not, but if it'll make her leave faster, then so be it.

It's not her fault I'm basically a shell at this point. Or that once she disappears down the hallway and I shut the door to my room behind her, I feel another piece of myself break off and wither away.

The same feeling I get every time lately. My soul going through a cheese grater, the pieces slicing off one at a time, until pretty soon I don't think there'll be anything left.

Even a hot shower doesn't rid me of it. But at least it washes off her perfume. The last thing I need is a reminder of how the random groupie's scent is just one more thing that doesn't smell like the one person's scent I'd rather be inhaling.

I'm about to climb into bed when a knock comes at the door.

I swear if Rome locked himself out of his room again, I'm going to let him sleep in the hallway just to prove a point. But when I open the door, it's not him who comes toppling inside, it's Merry.

She falls into my arms, like the door was holding her upright, and without it, she's lost all balance.

"Noah." Her eyes widen.

I steady her until she's finally balanced on her legs again, before pulling away.

"I didn't know you and Eloise were fucking," she says, and I feel like maybe I'm dreaming because I have no idea what she's talking about.

"How drunk are you right now?" I tip her chin up and look into her dilated eyes. "We're not fucking."

"Then why are you in her room?" Merry crosses her arms over her chest, looking a little irritated.

"I'm not." I widen the door further, so she can see the empty space. "This is my room."

She steps back and looks at the number on the door again. "Crap, I thought she said this was her room number." Merry slaps her hand over her forehead and lets out a frustrated sigh.

"Everything okay?"

"I was going to crash in her room tonight. But…" She shakes her head, her eyes drifting down the hall, and I realize she has no idea where she is.

"Come on." I move aside and wave her in, but she just stands there. "Merry, get in the fucking room. You're too drunk to wander the halls knocking on every door until you find her."

"Fine." She pouts as she walks inside.

When Merry is drunk, she actually lets her guard down a bit. Even if she is still prickly and difficult, there's a softer, more vulnerable side that shines through.

"But don't get any ideas," she says, walking past me with her finger pointed in my direction.

"Wouldn't dare." I smile, and that breaks the slightest smirk on her face.

She stops just inside and peels her jacket off. Her eyes scan the room, and if I didn't know her better, I'd think she looks almost a little nervous as I close the door.

"Make yourself at home." I walk past her and try hard not to think about the fact that this is the first time Merry's been in my room alone with me, even if it's not for the reasons that I would like.

"Mind if I use your shower?" she asks, setting her things on one of the couches.

I wave my arm toward the bathroom, but just before she disappears into it, I call out, "Here."

She pauses and the soft expression on her face makes me want to wrap my arms around her.

I pull a T-shirt from my suitcase and walk over to hand it to her. "Something to sleep in."

She looks down at the shirt in my hands and her eyebrows pull together, like somehow the shirt is confusing to her, and I wonder just how drunk she really is. Reaching for it, her eyes dart back at me, and even though her eyeliner's a little smudged and her eyes are drunk and distant, she is still the most beautiful girl in the world.

"Thanks." She nods.

I leave her to shower, dropping onto my bed. Even if I'm tired, closing my eyes doesn't do any good, because my nerves might as well be vibrating beneath my skin. I bury myself under the blanket and try to think about anything besides her being in my room.

But it's impossible.

And when she walks out in only my T-shirt, with wet hair that's already curling at the ends, and a makeup-free face, I can't help the feeling that comes to life somewhere deep inside me.

I expect her to go for the couch, and for me to have to tell her she can just share my bed. But she surprises me by walking over and climbing in the other side unprompted.

She curls up under the covers, facing me. Even in this dark room, I can still make out her eyes clearly with the moon shining through the break in the curtains, and they're focused on me.

"Did you have a good night?" I ask, propping my head up under one of my hands and facing her.

Merry nods. "Yeah, you?"

"It was all right."

The corner of her mouth ticks up and her eyes roll.

"What?"

"You don't have to pretend you didn't enjoy yourself for my sake," she says, propping her head up to match me. "I'm sure some groupie made you very happy."

"They always do."

She chews the corner of her bottom lip, and I wish I knew if that makes her jealous or if she really doesn't give a shit.

"Not that you looked lonely tonight, yourself," I say to her.

Merry shrugs one shoulder. "He was all right."

"That's because you're fucking the wrong guys."

I expect her to give me some snappy remark in return, but she doesn't. She nods her head as her eyes skim me over. My chest is bare outside of the covers, and I wonder if her cheeks are flushed and it's just too dark in the room for me to see it.

"Why do you like me, Noah?"

I almost think she's making a joke, but the somber look on her face surprises me.

"Why do I like you?" I rake my hands through my hair.

It's a bold question, but that's Merry.

"You're beautiful," I say, and she rolls her eyes. "But, that's not all."

She holds up her hand and waves it in a circle, egging me on.

"You're tough as nails, borderline terrifying." I fake a grimace, and it makes her laugh. "You're thoughtful, even though you don't want people to know it, so I promise to keep that to myself. But mostly, you're just real. You don't pretend to be someone you're not, and that's rare these days."

An unreadable expression crosses Merry's face but fades as quickly as it came.

"There's still a lot you don't know about me," she says. "I'm not the girl you bring home to meet your parents."

"Good thing I'm not speaking to my parents then."

"I mean it." Her tone is harsher this time. "I can't be anything more than a friend to you, Noah. It's better this way."

She rolls onto her back and stares at the ceiling. The inches between us in the bed suddenly feel like miles I wish I could cross.

Usually, when Merry shuts me down, it's initiated by my flirting. But this—what she said—feels different. Like a warning. Like maybe there *is* more, and she does feel it, but whatever is on the other side of her walls is too scary for her to face.

I roll onto my back to match her, staring at the shadows making faces on the ceiling. They fade out and in with what must be clouds passing in the night sky. Merry's breathing evens out, and I think she's already asleep until something warm brushes my hand beneath the covers. Without saying anything, she takes my hand in hers and holds it. Our fingers are laced together, and she warms me somewhere deep.

"You could give me a shot, you know," I whisper, even if I should be dropping the subject.

"I can't." She shakes her head. "For more reasons than I can tell you."

"Fair enough."

I'm tempted to spend all night arguing with her, but she's not the kind of girl you corner, so I'm smart enough to drop it.

"Thank you for tonight, Noah," she whispers, sounding almost asleep, as her grip softens in mine.

I squeeze her hand. "Anything for you, beautiful."

July

5

Merry

Sweat beads on my skin as Noah's hand grips my hip and holds it down. His fingertips trace the edge of my stomach and all my muscles tense. My entire body might as well be vibrating under his touch.

"Fuck, Noah." I tip my head back and close my eyes.

Pain might walk that fine line with pleasure for me, but the sensation right now reverberates all the way down my spine and if I'm not careful, I'm going to break a molar.

"Hanging in there, gorgeous?" Noah smirks, looking up at me through the thick blond hair that curtains over one of his eyes.

"I hate you," I tell him, but he just shakes his head and laughs like he always does when I tell him how much he drives me absolutely insane.

"This was all you, beautiful." He drags upward and the tattoo needle scrapes over one of my ribs, sending a shock wave up to my jaw.

There's no better way to figure out what nerves connect through your skin than for a tattoo needle to draw a path of discovery across your body.

What the fuck was I thinking when I agreed to this? He might have a light touch, but it doesn't stop the pain from radiating through me.

For a guy with barely any tattoos himself, Noah loves to tattoo others. It's a hobby he picked up in high school, and he's been doing it ever since. Occasionally he'll tattoo roadies, sometimes fans. And today, after him bugging me about it the entire tour, I finally gave in and let him mark my skin.

But only after threatening his balls if he dared to put his name on me. Not that I think he would do that. Noah is actually a gentleman, as annoying as that can be sometimes. But it didn't hurt to instill a little fear before we got started, given his never-ending flirtation.

"You good?" The buzzing stops and Noah gazes up at me with a genuine look of concern on his face.

I must look as rough as I feel, because he's seen me get tattooed enough times in parlors to know my reactions by now, and his eyes pinch in worry. Not that it's his fault. I'm the dumbass who chose to place the tattoo on my rib cage. A decision I'm regretting more and more by the minute.

This is what happens when you start running out of empty skin on your limbs and start itching for more ink.

Pain.

"Can we take five?" I ask him, propping up on my elbows.

"Sure thing, babe." Noah squirts some antiseptic on the tattoo and wipes it clean.

Looking down, I see Noah has moved onto the shading. The line work was bad enough, but the needles grinding over already tender skin is torture. At least the tattoo itself is beautiful so far. Wings that stretch across the upper part of my abdomen, right beneath my breasts. They fan out from where an Egyptian goddess already sits between them. It's a big tattoo, but flawless.

"When you get tired of all this rock star shit, you can come work in my shop," Blaze says.

Blaze owns the Twisted Roses tattoo parlor, where Noah had me take him after picking him up from rehab. He's in town from LA to see the band, and from what I gather, he and Noah go way back. Every time we're in the area, Noah makes it a point to stop in and see him. And he's even let Blaze add a few tattoos to his arm recently.

"You've got natural talent," Blaze says as Noah sets the needle aside and reaches for my hand to help me up.

"Thanks, man." Noah nods, his pale blue eyes flicking up to meet mine. For a cocky guy, he looks nervous about this.

"It's beautiful, Noah." I nudge his arm and he smiles brightly.

"Anything for you, love."

Noah and I have become really good at playing this game with each other. He's flirty, while I push him away. He chases, I run. From the outside, people probably think he's obsessed, but at this point, I'm pretty sure he continues only for his amusement.

He's in a rock band, after all. He doesn't need to wait around for me when he gets plenty of pussy. Words are just words, even if the looks he gives me travel a little deeper than tattoo ink.

Besides, I made it clear to Noah from the start. What he wanted, I wouldn't give him, so friends is all he's going to get.

Noah squeezes my hand before turning away, so I can slip on a loose T-shirt. Not that it matters, Noah and Blaze have both been staring at me with my breasts out for the last few hours while Noah has worked.

"Bathroom," I say, snatching my purse off a chair and excusing myself.

I'm almost to the door when Noah shouts my name over my shoulder and grabs my attention.

Turning, he holds up a water bottle and shakes it.

"Thanks." I catch it when he tosses it my way.

He's so thoughtful that I can't help but feel a little bad. Because no matter how chaotic touring is, or how pissy I get with him sometimes, Noah is always there looking out for me.

I bring the water into the bathroom and dig into the bottom of my purse for my meds, pulling out the handful for today. As I swallow them down, I stare at myself in the mirror and let the morning sink in. The buzzing from the tattoo needle still vibrates through my skin. Eyes heavy from lack of sleep.

If I'm going to make it through tonight's show, I'm going to need to start chugging some caffeine.

Cassie, one of my best girlfriends, is flying in, so skipping it is not an option. Sebastian is surprising her with

FOREVER AND EVER 59

a song he wrote about her, so it's my job to keep her distracted. I need to be on my game.

Who would have thought when I started working with the band that Sebastian would be the first of them to settle down. Apparently, all it took was one pink-haired friend of mine.

When I leave the bathroom to rejoin Noah and Blaze, they're sitting on the couches in the hotel room with the new Enemy Muse album blaring.

"Aww, listening to your own music. Cute." I sit on the couch beside Noah. "Your ego knows no bounds."

Noah tips his head back and laughs. "It was all Blaze, I swear."

"I'm sure it was." I pat him on the thigh.

"Here." He reaches over and grabs a baggie from the coffee table and hands it to me. "Eat something so you don't pass out from low blood sugar."

"Yes, dad," I tell him with a salute, taking the baggie from his hand. "How much longer do you think we've got? Don't you have to head to sound check soon?"

"I'll be done in the next hour," Noah says. "Sound check isn't until four."

I grab a handful of Froot Loops and sort them in my palm by color, eating them in the order of the rainbow just like I did when I was a kid.

"Is that dry cereal?" Blaze asks, lighting up a cigarette and bringing it to his lips.

Noah pokes me in the side. "Yes, she's insane. She doesn't drink milk."

It catches me off guard how Noah remembers that. How he seems to pick up everything about me, even at times when I don't realize he's paying attention.

"Because it's gross," I frown.

"Whatever you say." Blaze shakes his head, letting the smoke curl out from his lips with a laugh. "So Merry, when are you gonna let me take you out?"

"Out? As in, a date?"

"Can't turn me down forever."

I don't miss that Noah laughs under his breath at the comment, taking another big drink of water.

"We're out right now." I pop a Froot Loop into my mouth and try to avoid the question.

"This is far from me wining and dining you, honey," Blaze says, leaning his elbows on his knees. "I want a real date."

Blaze smiles as I shake my head. He's an objectively attractive guy. Wavy, thick hair and killer emerald eyes. He's tall, built, and his dark skin is covered in ink. If he weren't so close with Noah, I wouldn't mind working out some of my sexual tension with him. But even if I'm horny as fuck and haven't screwed anyone in a couple of weeks, Blaze is really close with Noah, and I don't like messing around with friends of friends.

It gets messy. And I don't do messy.

"Sorry babe, I don't date." I pop another Froot Loop in my mouth.

Blaze's eyes skim me up and down, and I almost think he's going to proposition for a lot less, but his gaze moves to Noah, and whatever expression he gets in response makes him shut his mouth.

"Got it." Blaze leans back and takes a long drag of his cigarette.

Noah stands up and his eyes slide in my direction. "You ready to get back to it, or do you need a few more minutes?"

Blaze's gaze moves between us with a look I know too well because I see it all the time. People wondering what's going on with Noah and me. Not believing when I say it's just friends being friends. Heaven forbid a man and woman hang out and not fuck each other.

"Ready." I hop up.

Blaze stands. "I've gotta make a call. I'll see you after the show, all right?"

"Yeah, man." Noah and Blaze give each other a half hug with a pat on the back before Blaze disappears out the door.

"So, what do you want to listen to?" I ask, trying to ignore the sudden awkwardness.

I pull out my phone when the Enemy Muse song ends and start skimming my playlists. Noah pats the table for me to hop up as he takes his seat.

"You can pick," he says.

I set my phone on my lap and look at him. "You're the one working here."

"And you're the one who needs to be distracted." He sets his hands on the table on either side of my hips.

I'd argue, but the expression on his face tells me not to, so I press play on Nothing But Thieves and set my phone to the side.

Noah's eyes watch as I reach for the bottom hem of my T-shirt and peel it up and overhead before tossing it on the chair next to him. I might not want him to be interested in me as far as a relationship is concerned, but I don't mind the appreciation he clearly has with my tits in his face.

"Enjoying the view?" I smile, lying down and grabbing my boobs to hold them up and away from where he's working. They're not big by any means, barely filling my small hands, but it keeps them out of the way while he works.

"Not minding it, that's for sure." Noah grins at me with that blinding Hollywood smile he's mastered.

He slips on fresh gloves and grabs the bottle of antiseptic, splashing it on my skin and rubbing the tattoo clean.

"Almost done," he says.

A tendril of his blond hair has come out from his bun, and I reach up to tuck it behind his ear without thinking, which makes him pause. His eyes lock on mine and they're so pale blue they're almost gray, like an overcast sky just before it rains.

Sometimes I consider that I might be crazy for turning Noah down over and over again. Any sane girl wouldn't. He isn't your average rock star. Although he has no problem fucking his way through groupies, he isn't doing it for the same reasons as the other guys in the band. Deep down, I know he wants more. And sometimes I do wish that things were different, and it could be me who gives it to him.

But that would require me telling him everything—and that's not something I'm prepared to do. So I drop my hand.

"You know," Noah says, turning to the ink and adding some to the needle. "After this, you can't deny that I've been inside you."

His attempt to lighten the mood makes me laugh. "Your needle, Noah. Not *you*."

"Just saying." He gives me a one-shoulder shrug that compliments his devious grin. "Inside is inside, I'm counting it. Besides, doesn't really matter how deep, considering no one's really getting in there anyway."

The buzzing starts and he leans in for that first deliciously painful drag over my skin. It takes everything inside me not to flinch.

"What's that supposed to mean?"

Noah's eyes follow the needle. "You don't let people in," he says, turning to add more ink.

"I'm no virgin," I point out.

"No shit." He laughs. "But that's physical, and I know you well enough to know that doesn't mean crap to you. Letting people past the bullshit, that's a whole other world, gorgeous."

I swallow hard when his pale blue gaze briefly flicks up to mine.

"Who says there's anything in there worth getting to?"

Part of me wants to sound nonchalant, like I don't give a fuck if there is or isn't. But the other part of me is terrified to find that there really is nothing but darkness left. Spaces where dreams used to fit. Broken shards even Noah knows nothing about.

"There is." Two words so certain coming from his lips. "Inside you are places a man can only dream of."

The needle strikes my skin again and the vibrations travel so deep I almost think they find the places in me Noah might be talking about.

Almost.

6

Noah

They say when you're dying, you'll see a light at the end of the tunnel.

Maybe that's true. At least, some version of it.

I saw stars. Millions of them. Flickering like streetlamps going out. Struggling against the blackness of the universe, until one by one, they were swallowed in darkness.

I saw my reflection rotting away in front of me. Some parts I recognized and other parts I didn't. I assumed at the end I'd see memories because that's what people make you think. That you'll relive the good things that made life worth living.

Only, none of what I saw was comforting.

And then the switch flicked off and there was nothing. No hope, no light, no salvation. Just emptiness.

I'm reminded of that moment right now, as I'm watching the audience. Lighters, phones, and glow sticks sparkle out in the vast darkness of the stadium. But instead of feeling myself fading, I'm coming to life with every beat of the drums.

My arms are dead, and sweat is pouring down my face. My whole body is going to be sore tomorrow. And it's worth every ounce of pain as I strike my drums and the entire stadium screams.

Beyond the edge of the stage, I see the bodies jumping up and down to the beat. Moving with the music as it spills from my bones.

This is why I fell in love with music. To feel something bigger than myself. To be consumed.

Writing the soundtrack to other people's lives is a strange feeling, knowing that what we create marks moments of love, lust, and heartbreak for them. I feel it in every uninhibited scream and every bated breath of silence.

It permeates this stadium.

They treat us like gods writing their fate, and there's really no getting enough of that.

The song ends and my limbs might as well be liquid, ready to puddle on the floor. But I manage to stand up and hold my drumsticks overhead to grin out at the audience. Tens of thousands of faces staring back. Most of them are blurry and dark but I know they're there. Worshiping us, when deep down I know they shouldn't.

If they knew the truth, they probably wouldn't.

I'm a fraud, a fake, a phony—just like the smile always painted on my face. I might appreciate the perks of fame, but unlike Rome and Sebastian, who embraced it like true gods of rock, I never felt like anything more than a human slowly being eaten up by the world of music.

I walk to the edge of the stage to join Sebastian, Eloise, and Rome, as I toss my drumsticks out to a sea of hands. Fans pile on each other in a game of conquest until one becomes the victor and some chick surfaces with one in each hand. Her hair is sticking up in all directions, and she's got a nasty bruise already forming on her face.

Proof she fought for them.

It's strange to think people will strangle each other over something as simple as drumsticks. In the beginning, before the world tours and albums, when we were just nameless faces that could have been any other band, they wanted nothing from us. It wasn't until someone told someone else who told someone else that we were special that anything changed.

Next thing I knew, the world dislodged its jaw in an effort to devour us whole. They couldn't get enough. Taking, taking, taking. It never mattered that we were still people underneath the surface, and we only had so much to give.

They always want more.

As the years wore on, I started to see it in each of us. Sebastian and his sanity, Rome and his scars, Eloise and her distance. And then there's me. I gave it all until it stopped my heart and I was finally done. Only something bigger said the torture wasn't over just yet.

My eyes fall to the crowd at the front of the stage, where Sebastian's girl Cassie is beaming up at him after hearing the new song that he wrote for her. Merry and Quinn are on either side of her with arms linked, and when Merry catches my gaze, she shoots me a triumphant wink for pulling this off.

After all, Sebastian kind of royally fucked it up with Cassie for a minute there. But that scruffy ass face of his managed to win her back, and I'm kind of glad. Because dealing with wasted Sebastian was bad enough. But dealing with heartbroken Sebastian... Someone was going to need to put a bullet in our heads.

Who would have guessed Sebastian would be the first band member off the market? Honestly, I never pictured Sebastian as the settle-down kind of guy. He's fucked his way around the world more than once and seemed perfectly content doing so. But then he met Cassie, and everything changed. The rain clouds parted over his head, and he saw a clear sky. The sun, the angels—

Blah, blah, blah.

I'm fucking jealous.

But at least I'm getting better at hiding it.

Walking off the stage, I pat Sebastian on the back and grin at him. "Good job getting the girl, buddy."

"She showed up," he says with a big smile.

He drops his chin and shakes his head, wagging around that floppy dark blond hair as he practically laughs in surprise. This dude is done for. Cassie is it for him, and that look on his face proves it.

I'd know because I've felt it twice in my life, even if it didn't work out the way I wanted either time.

The first time I felt what they call *love at first sight*, was when I met Kali at fourteen. Her family had just moved to town and her parents sat next to my parents in church.

My leg brushed hers as she walked past, and I knew she was the girl I was going to marry. We shared candy, hung out by the tire swing, swam in the lake at sunset. All that stupid crap you see in movies. I was in love with her bright blonde hair and sugary sweet smile.

She was everything to me.

Only, I was young and an idiot, so I hadn't quite figured out it wasn't love. It was hormones. And I hadn't quite learned that she wasn't an angel at all, she was a fucking demon in a pretty sundress waiting to destroy my soul.

Fun times.

The second time I fell in love was the first time I laid eyes on the tattooed goddess who is currently walking toward me. Merry stepped into my dressing room without knocking and gave me that same unimpressed expression I've become all too familiar with. She shut me down on the spot, and that was only the first of many times that followed.

She's dark, pessimistic, angry. The polar opposite of all things Kali, while being just as intent on never loving me back.

I'm a dumb fuck when it comes to my heart.

It's been proven, not once, but twice.

So here I sit.

In purgatory.

"Good show," Merry says, slugging me on the arm like I'm her big brother.

It pisses me off. Almost as much as it did earlier when I was digging a needle into her skin and still couldn't seem to get through the thick ass barrier of hers.

She'll sit naked in front of me, let me ink her beautiful skin, pass out in my bed. But that's it—friends.

A year ago, I would have solved this problem with a pile of cocaine, maybe even a little heroin if the coke didn't do the trick. Being clean blows when all I want to do is forget.

"Thanks," I say, pulling my hair off my face and tying it in a knot at the base of my skull.

I'm sweating and gross but buzzing with energy.

"So, tour's over," Merry says, looking strangely nervous.

"Yep."

Her face pinches and her eyes move to where I feel my jaw clenching. "What's wrong?"

"Nothing."

"Bullshit." The faintest smirk that ticks up on the corner of her mouth only aggravates me more.

"It's nothing," I say again, getting annoyed.

The last thing I need right now is to get into it with Merry after I've been drowning in Sebastian's love-struck mood all night. I'd like to say I'm not affected but seeing the way Cassie looks at him has brought out all my dumb ass feelings.

Besides, no good will come of this conversation with Merry. It's the same drain we've spent the entire tour spinning around. Me, trying to convince her to give me a shot. Her, intent on shutting me down.

She doesn't want to hear it, and I'm tired of repeating it to her in this moment.

Merry narrows those dark brown eyes, and they almost disappear with her thick lashes and eyeliner. Her teeth drag over her cherry-red bottom lip as she tries to read me, but all it does is get under my skin.

I'm not sure what's worse, being around her and not being able to have her or knowing she's disappearing for the next four months while we record this next album.

And I can't help but take it out on her because the other option would be to slam her against the wall and fuck her until she realizes that we're meant to be together, and that's not something she'd appreciate at the moment.

"Noah." A pretty little blonde with big fake tits slides up next to me.

One look and I know two things: I've never met the girl before in my life, but she's down to fuck right here if I asked her to.

Merry gets that amused look on her face as she eyes the girl's Enemy Muse T-shirt, like *here we go again*. As if she can talk with her own personal revolving door of men and women. This game of sexual warfare we've got going is exhausting. Not that she seems to share the same feeling.

Maybe it's that Merry is only twenty-three and I've got a few years on her. Or maybe it's because I've actually spent time in a long-term relationship. But her stamina for putting me off is draining.

The blonde with the hourglass body slides her hand around my arm and grips my bicep. Personal space isn't really a thing when you're a rock star. They grab and take and consume. I might as well be a commodity, not a person.

"Want some company at the after party?" the blonde asks, and I don't miss how Merry crosses her arms over her chest. Putting up those walls like the pro she is.

"You good company?" I ask the pixie blonde, appreciating that Merry gets really pissed when I flat-out hit on chicks right in front of her. She could do something about it, but she never does.

The blonde lifts up on her toes and presses her pretty tits against my arm. "You know it."

Her eyelashes flutter, and she wets her lips. The girl is ready.

"Give me a second." I pat the blonde's hand and she unwinds herself to step back.

She makes her way over to her friend, who already has Rome's attention, along with a few other chicks. But her eyes don't leave me, even when Rome tries to pull her in.

The way Rome works his way through women makes me look tame, and I have no problem getting around. But unlike me, who is in it for the distraction and the fun, he does it like he's pissed at the world or trying to prove something.

"She's friendly." Merry forces a smile.

Her teeth grind the slightest, and although she tries to act nonchalant, she's a shit liar about some things.

"Just say the word and I'm all yours."

Merry laughs so hard it shakes her dark curls, but I'm not joking. "You can't say shit like that, Noah."

"Why not?"

I might have understood her not wanting to get involved back when she first got hired because she had to prove herself and all that shit. But now? No one cares.

Half the band and crew expect it even.

She's it for me.

"Because," she says, dipping her hands in her pockets. "You know why."

I really don't, but there's no point arguing, so I nod my head in silence instead, watching her shift from one foot to the other.

To most people, Merry is intimidating. I don't think she's worn a drop of color in her life unless you count the streaks she puts in her hair, her tattoos, or her piercings. She's standoffish, cold, and has mastered the art of tearing people down with just one look. But I've watched her closer than most people, and I know there's a lot more under the surface.

Like the fact that she chews the inside of her cheek when she's nervous. Or that she tucks her hands in her pockets when she'd rather fidget. Her eyes avoid contact when she's questioning herself. And even though she's spectacular at making people think she doesn't give a shit, she's fiercely loyal to the few people she does care about.

"Whatever you say, gorgeous." I take a step closer, loving that it forces her to tip her head back to look up at me. "I can wait."

I brush her hair out of her face and tuck it behind her ear before turning. If I don't walk away now, I'll make a bigger fool of myself than I already have these past few months, and I'm really not in the mood to be shut down by Merry for the thousandth time on the last day of a tour.

Instead, I'll celebrate with this willing blonde chick who smells like strawberries and cheap perfume. Not overly pleasant, but she'll do. I don't need it to mean something for her to get my dick hard.

Anything is better than waiting on Merry, who is already walking away with one of the guys on the crew who I know wants to get in her pants.

Thank God this tour is over. Four months without her. Four months to screw my head back on straight. Four months of silence.

I'd hate her if I didn't love her so damn much.

7

Merry

Noah walks into the post-tour party alone, but I can tell he's already been laid by his demeanor. The vibrating energy he carried after the show is gone, and now, he's just chill.

He sits beside me on the couch, smelling like that blonde chick's awful perfume. I hate smelling other women on his skin, even if I don't say anything to stop it. I hate knowing he's relaxed after they've worked the tension out of him.

Worst of all, I *hate* that I hate it.

It would be easier if I genuinely didn't care who or what Noah did. But I care about him—as a friend—or something resembling it. And I don't like watching him bury himself in other women to get out of his own feelings.

He rests an arm behind me on the couch, but I stand up and walk away. This is the point where I'd usually grab onto the nearest willing person and let them fuck me in the bathroom just to prove to Noah and myself that his actions don't faze me. But tonight, I can't bring myself to do it.

As a matter of fact, it's been a couple of weeks since I've even let someone touch me. Ever since I started feeling off. Physically, mentally. I can't place what's wrong, but I don't feel like myself.

Avoiding a group of roadies trying to capture my attention, I head over to Cassie, who's standing next to Sebastian and Adrian. The pink tips on her blonde hair look freshly touched up, and they brush her shoulders as she laughs at something Sebastian says.

The smile hasn't left her face since she watched him perform that song for her on stage, and I give myself a pat on the back for introducing them. Or, at least getting them in the same room together, even if I only ever expected them to fuck, not fall in love.

My matchmaking skills are a little too on point.

"Merry, good, I was going to find you," Adrian says when I come to a stop.

He scratches the shaved stubble on his head and nods at Eloise as she walks up to us. She has an unreadable expression on her face.

Eloise is the picture of elegance. She's tall and stoic in a way that makes her sharp facial features seem statuesque. She knows how to hold her own in a band surrounded by men, and because of it, most people find her intimidating. But I've seen glimpses of her other side. Even if she comes across as cold and emotionless at times, there's a softness to her underneath. She just has to trust you enough before she shows it.

"What's up?" I say to Adrian.

"We mapped out studio time for the next album, and between writing and recording, it's going to take about four months."

"Okay." I nod, not sure why he's telling me this. I'm well aware of the timeline, and I'm not sure if he's trying to rub it in that I'll be out of work for that long between tours or if he needs me to help out with something in the process.

"Anyway," Adrian says. "Only half of the next Enemy Muse album is currently written, which frees up the studio more than anticipated while they finish writing it."

I nod again, still not sure what he's getting at.

"I'm saying it's yours if you want it." He crosses his arms and stands taller, lifting an eyebrow at me.

"Mine?"

My gaze moves from Adrian to Cassie. She's bouncing with excitement as she stands next to Sebastian.

"Mine," I say again, letting that sink in.

"Let's record that demo." A smile breaks across Adrian's face. "If you're up for it, that is."

"You're fucking serious?" My heart starts to race.

Adrian nods, and even Eloise is smiling at me now.

I've been waiting for this. The past nine months—my whole fucking life.

I've been working my ass off for the band. I've done the grunt work, and slowly worked my way up to prove myself. I knew nothing was going to be handed to me, but I was starting to think it was never going to happen.

I was worried that by accepting a job behind the scenes for Enemy Muse, I had pigeonholed myself, and no one would take me seriously as a singer. It's easy to fall into the role and never look back. I've seen it happen to several roadies who once had dreams of their own.

I worried that Adrian would see me as nothing more than an assistant and never give me a chance.

Clearly, I was wrong.

Adrian grins at me with the kind of smile that's rarely ever spotted on him, and I appreciate the genuine gesture. He's been a mentor to me, giving me insight into the industry, teaching me all the tricks in his spare time. He's like a big brother, protective, always looking out for the people around him. Myself included.

"Oh shit." I let out a breath that takes the weight of my chest with it.

"You've earned it," Adrian says.

Eloise wraps a willowy arm around my shoulders and pulls me in for a half hug. For her, it's unusually warm, and I'm a little taken aback by it.

"You have," she says, letting me go.

"Yes." Cassie throws herself at me, and I almost stumble backward. If it weren't for Sebastian catching her at the waist, we probably would have.

"You're going to be a rock star," Cassie squeals in my ear, pulling away to squeeze my shoulders before letting me go.

A *rock star*.

My head feels suddenly fuzzy. Breaking out in this industry is a one-in-a-million kind of thing. You can work the hardest, be the best, and still never make it. It takes a mix of talent and luck, and all of a sudden, I'm worried I might not have it.

"We're gonna take off," Sebastian says to the group.

His eyes land on Cassie and it's no secret what he's planning for their dirty little reunion, so I roll my eyes at them.

Sebastian holds his palm out and Adrian slaps his own palm against it as they clasp hands and pull in for one-armed hugs.

The two of them are physical opposites. While Sebastian is lean, Adrian is a solid hunk of muscle. Even their hair plays like a yin and yang with Sebastian's dirty blond locks and Adrian's almost black stubble. And even though Sebastian's rocking a golden tan from the summer touring schedule, it pales to Adrian's dark skin. But when they pull apart from the hug and smile at each other, the friendship you feel from both of them is the same. And that's why I love working for Enemy Muse, even if they cause me massive migraines.

It's a family.

"Call me tomorrow," Cassie says, as Sebastian pulls her away.

I'm nodding, but words are no longer coming out as I stand there in shock.

"So, I take it you're onboard?" Adrian says as I turn back to him and Eloise.

"Yes, of course." I croak like a frog I'm so excited.

"Good," Adrian nods, "because it's going to be long hours and hard work. Plus, you have to be willing to work around whatever time the band needs the studio, so it might mean late nights or early mornings."

"Done."

There's no way I'm passing up my chance at my big break just because the hours are a little inconvenient. I've been touring with a rock band on and off for almost a year. I've learned how to not need sleep to survive.

"And you'll be able to be in Denver?"

Shit, I told my mom and sister I'd head to Seattle for a few months, but I'm sure they'll understand. After all, my dad is still barely speaking to me, so what will it hurt to put off his disappointment for another couple of months?

"I'll make it work," I say, knowing there's no other option.

The band members all have homes right outside of Denver, Adrian included. And since his house has a studio built in, that's where they do most of their recording.

"I'd offer for you to stay with me," Eloise says with a frown. "But my home renovations got moved up, so I'm crashing at Adrian's."

She looks over at him and I notice him swallow hard.

Interesting.

"That's fine, I'll sort it out."

"You could stay with my brother maybe?" she offers.

"And interrupt the Sebastian and Cassie love fest?" I laugh. "No thanks. I'm sure I can find a temporary rental in the city."

"A rental for what?" Noah slides up beside me with a confused look on his face.

Crud, another thing I didn't think about. Four months in Denver also means there's no avoiding Noah for the time being, something I think both of us were looking forward to.

We might be friends, but things have gotten awkward more than once on this tour. And avoiding the conversation he wants to have with me is becoming more and more difficult.

"Merry's coming to Denver," Eloise says. "Adrian's going to help her record her demo when the studio is free, so she's looking for a place to stay. Sebastian and I still have so much writing to do on the album, the studio will be empty a lot."

Noah looks at me with a raised eyebrow. He's the one I'd expect to show some kind of excitement, but he's the exact opposite. Cold, closed off, stoic.

"Congratulations," he says, but it's forced.

I try not to be hurt by the fact that Noah doesn't seem to give a crap that I'm finally going to pursue my dreams and turn back to Adrian. "Don't worry about me, I'll be there. I'll get a car—drive out at whatever hours you need me to. I'll make it happen."

Adrian gives me a cool nod.

"I'm out of here," I say, feeling Noah's icy chill beside me. I avoid his gaze and slip away before he can say anything else to crush my mood, weaving through the crowd to the door.

This is what I've been waiting for—my opportunity. So why did it feel instantly less the second Noah got that look on his face?

Dipping out of the hotel room, I'm relieved the hallway is quiet. I feel like I can finally breathe again from the jolt of excitement that just rushed through my body. I'm not generally comfortable baring my feelings, but I couldn't help the rush of energy that shot through me when Adrian handed me this opportunity.

I pull out my phone and shoot off a quick text to my sister, Monica, letting her know we need to chat about my post-tour plans, before taking a deep breath.

In my head, I'm already sorting through my notebooks trying to decide which songs will be the best fit. What order they need to go in to tell the story I want them to. I'm rearranging the lyrics to fit my mood and decide what will best reflect me.

The words I've written will finally be making their way off the page.

"Merry."

I jump, realizing I was zoned out with my eyes closed. Noah's standing right in front of me with his arms crossed over his chest and his hands tucked in his armpits. That cold blue gaze of his burrowing straight into me.

"Noah," I say, still annoyed that he couldn't even muster a half-hearted congratulations at my news.

"So, you're coming to Denver?"

I nod. "Guess so."

He really doesn't look thrilled at that statement, so I'm probably right that he was looking forward to four months away from me.

"And you need a place to stay?"

My gut suddenly gets that sinking feeling. I know what he's about to say. And I know him well enough to tell by the look in his eyes that it's going to pain him to say it.

"I'll find something quick. Denver's a big place." I try to brush off where this is going.

"It's an hour's drive to Adrian's place from the city."

He's not wrong. The band lives well outside of the city center. They wanted land, space, privacy. And that means the commute won't be the most convenient.

"And fall will be here before you know it," he says. "Then snow."

"I'll make it work. What wouldn't you do for your dreams?"

Noah's face softens and he tips his head back, like my statement took him somewhere in his mind. Noah doesn't talk to me about the band's rise to fame and what came with it. He doesn't like to discuss how I met him. How he was fucked out of his head, and then a couple months later walking out of a rehab facility. But I've picked up enough to know he gave a lot to get to where he is. And he has to understand I'd do the same.

When he dips his chin to look back at me, his arms fall to his sides and the rigid posture dissipates.

"Just stay with me," he says, like it took a heck of a lot for him to say it.

"With you?"

He nods.

I take a deep breath and try to hold it, searching for clarity that is definitely escaping me right now. "Is that a good idea?"

Noah's nod says a lot. It's quick, uncertain, and feels like there's a giant weight behind it.

"It's a big house." He rakes his hair away from his face. "And it's two minutes down the road from Adrian's. Friends do favors for friends, right?"

There are a lot of reasons for me to say no. Like how I know I've spent the majority of this tour unintentionally leading Noah on, and how lately it's become clear he's been barely hanging on a string. Or how, out of nowhere, these past couple of months my resolve has been slipping with him, and I'm not sure what that means.

But most of all, I'm worried that with him that close, he might finally see through me. And what if once he does, once he truly gets to the heart of me, I finally hear what I've been anticipating all along?

It's not worth it.

"I see you trying to be stubborn," Noah says, facing off with me.

I shake my head, but he keeps going.

"What wouldn't you do for your dreams, right?"

He gets me with my own words. "Right."

"Then that's it, you're moving in," Noah says, but neither of us seem that excited about the prospect.

"For a few months," I say and he just nods. "Thanks, Noah."

"Anything for you, gorgeous." But instead of shooting me the smile I'm used to following that comment, he turns and walks away.

8

NOAH

EMPTY KITCHEN SHELVES STARE at me where the bottles of booze once lived. It used to be easier to drown out the demons, and part of me wishes I would have just let them take me years ago instead of insisting on playing this sober game of chicken.

If it wasn't for my family, I might have let it happen. But even if my mom prays for my soul every Sunday and refuses to speak to me, the memory of her tear-streaked face in the hospital is enough to make me close the cabinet and walk away without considering filling it with whiskey.

It's enough to stop me from reaching for something worse.

My house feels cold every time I return to it, reminding me just how fucking lonely this lifestyle is. I'm traveling two-thirds of the year with no real roots besides this empty pile of timber. I have no dog greeting me at the door or kids running around waiting for me to get home. There's no woman in my bed at night. At least, not one there for more than my dick.

The freedom used to have less weight to it. Now it's just empty space.

Dropping my suitcase in my bedroom, I head to the sink and splash water on my face. If only I could wash away the nightmares with it. But when my eyes meet the reflection in the mirror, they're there like always, staring back at me. Begging me to quiet them.

Hell catches up with all of us eventually.

As if on cue, the doorbell rings and shocks me out of my thoughts.

I was supposed to have four months away to clear my head. Four months with a couple of states distance between Merry and me, and maybe, just maybe, I'd finally get the fuck over it. But I'd do anything for that girl, even if it means inviting her to stay with me and shaving away the parts of my soul that are left.

It's been a week since the tour ended, and when I open the front door, I'm hit once more with that feeling from the first time we met. An overwhelming tug in the pit of my gut that screams out for me to listen. Except, as the months have gone on, it hurts a little more each time. Because Merry never returns it.

"Hey," she says, looking unusually nervous.

Merry's in a black cropped T-shirt and cut-off jean shorts that show off the sexy flower tattoos on the front of her thighs. She's changed out her belly button ring for a spiked stud that the sun hits just right, bringing a little shimmer to the warm skin on her stomach.

There's that tightening in my chest I've become all too familiar with. No matter how much I wish it would dull, it just won't.

"Hey," I manage to say, when I realize I've probably been staring at her for way too long.

Stepping aside, I wave an arm out to invite her in, and she drags her suitcase behind her.

I close the door and she stops to spin, looking up at me through her overdone eyes, thick with eyeliner. She's prettier without makeup, but I don't tell her that because she seems more comfortable in it.

"Thanks again for letting me stay," she says, pushing her dark curls off her shoulders and nervously wrapping them with her hands like she's about to put her hair in a ponytail, even though she isn't.

"Of course." I walk past her, trying to ignore the tension that fogged the air the second she stepped inside.

There are a lot of things I want right now.

To fuck her.

To love her.

To keep her.

But that's not what this is, and it's something I've been sure to remind myself.

Merry is staying with me as a friend so she can record a demo, that's it. She'll be writing music and recording, while I'll be working on the next Enemy Muse album. We'll get our work done, keep our distance, and stay focused.

After all, this is her dream, and I want her to have it.

I might have been a bit of a dick to her when I found out Adrian had offered her time in his studio, but that's only because she was talking about renting someplace in the city when I have this whole giant house she could stay in. It didn't even occur to her to ask me. She'd rather have driven an hour each way.

Every time I think I'm making progress or getting close; she shuts me back down.

Merry follows me into the kitchen, and I grab water from the fridge, draining it down my throat and gaining my composure. I reach down inside myself and pull out the character I know the world wants to see, especially Merry. The guy who's carefree and doesn't give a shit. It's what makes them comfortable.

You can do this.

Spinning to face her, I lean against the fridge and force a smile that seems to relax her posture.

She rests her hands on the marble island and looks around. It's not like she's never been here before, but it's almost as if she's seeing it for the first time when not much has changed. Her eyes take everything in like the sight of it's brand new.

I'm honestly not sure I've ever seen her this nervous.

"How's the tattoo healing?" I ask, spotting the very bottom edge of it peeking out beneath her cropped T-shirt.

"Good," she lifts the shirt up a little so I can see it.

That and the bottom of her lacy bra, covering her perfect tits. I don't think she knows what the sight of her does to me, the way she nonchalantly stands there with her dark nipples peeking through. My self-control is making me question why I asked about the tattoo in the first place.

Because you're her friend, you care...
Fuck you, brain.

She drops her T-shirt and smiles. "I love it. You did a really great job."

"Maybe you'll let me stick you again, then?" I grin.

Merry shakes her head and holds back a laugh. "Maybe."

Next time I tattoo her, it will just be the two of us. I don't like how Blaze spent four hours staring at her tits while I worked. Or that he had the balls to ask her out on a date right in front of me. She might not be mine, but there's no way in hell I want her to be Blaze's. She thinks she's a bad girl? Well, he's a bad guy. Even if he's a good friend, the dude has legally questionable connections.

"I should unpack," Merry says, looking at her things sitting by the door. "I need to work on a couple of songs tonight and figure out what I want to start recording first."

"Let's get you settled." I head to the entryway.

"If you try to stick me in your bed, God help you Noah Hayes," she says with a smirk, and I can't help but laugh.

"Wouldn't dare, sweetheart. The day you climb into my bed, it will be your decision and well worth the wait." I wink at her and don't miss that she swallows hard at the comment.

Grabbing the handle of her suitcase, I roll it down the hall, noticing she keeps a safe distance between us.

It's not like we haven't been alone together before. We've shared the bed in my hotel room on more than a few occasions, albeit fully clothed. But ever since Merry walked into my house, she's maintained a safe amount of space, and I can't help but wonder if she doesn't trust herself not to close it.

Although, that's probably wishful thinking.

"Here we are." I stop outside one of the guest rooms and roll her bag inside.

Merry's eyes look from the guest room to the end of the hall, where my room is only one door away.

"I figured you'd put me on the other end of the house," she says, looking back at me and tucking her hands in her pockets.

"This is the only guest room with a bed. Bachelor, remember. So, unless you'd like to stay in the poker room or movie theater, this is what you get."

She scans the room, her eyes landing on the far wall. "Good thing I brought my headphones." She looks back at me with a tentative smile. "Wouldn't want to lose sleep over all the moaning."

She moves to take a step inside the room, but I throw my hand against the doorframe, stopping her, and caging her outside as her big brown eyes look up at me.

"Let's get something straight." I promised myself I'd keep my composure, but clearly that was a pipe dream. "I'm not going to be fucking other people under this roof as long as you're here."

Merry's breathing is quick, but she tips her chin up and faces me with the strong determination I'm used to seeing in her.

"Okay," she says.

I lift my finger under her chin and rub my thumb just below her puffy cherry-red lips, wishing I could sink my teeth right into them. "And you won't be either."

Dropping my hand, I walk away before she can respond because I'm not willing to hear it. I don't care if it pisses her off. I don't care if she's a free-spirited single woman who can do whatever the fuck she wants. She'll have to go elsewhere. No one is going anywhere near her under my roof.

Because fuck that.

She can call me controlling, jealous, or whatever else she wants.

Or she can leave.

I close my bedroom door behind me and lean against it, tipping my head back and knowing this is probably the worst idea I've ever had. Unrequited love is fucked up enough when I can't escape her on tour. But to live with her, even temporarily, is a whole other mess.

I hear her close her bedroom door and finally peel myself off my own, stripping my shirt up and off in one swipe. Walking over to the mirror, I stare at the dark rings tattooed around my right forearm. Twenty-six years old and I've still only got two of them.

One for my record deal.

One for my sobriety.

And I can't help but wonder if anything else will matter enough to add a third. By this point in my life, I figured there would be a lot more worth celebrating than managing to get myself out of bed every day.

Guess I was wrong.

My phone pings, and I pull it out to see a text lighting up the screen.

Rome: Strip club tonight
Noah: When did you get home?
Rome: Just walked in the door
Noah: Shouldn't you be unpacking
Rome: Don't bitch about it, just show up.

He attaches a GIF of two shirtless women making out.
Fucking Rome, the guy is out of control lately. Not like Sebastian was when he went on his yearlong bender, but almost. He's never not surrounded by people, and I can't help but think there's more to that than him just being bored.

Noah: Where?
Rome: Vixen City @ 11
Noah: I'll be there

I turn on the shower as hot as I can handle it and strip out of the rest of my clothes. My dick is half hard from Merry's lace-covered tits, and if I don't do something about it, I'll be busting a nut in my jeans at the strip club, embarrassing myself.

Although, when I think about it, a strip club has never sounded so unappealing. If I didn't think Rome needed a babysitter to make sure he shows up to our band meeting tomorrow, I probably wouldn't have even agreed.

I'm exhausted from touring and still haven't processed the pessimistic brunette that is causing chaos in my brain and in my house. The last thing I need right now is a night out when I'm already on edge.

But I need to find a way to keep myself busy if Merry's going to be staying under my roof. And a room full of tits might be the only way to do it.

9

Noah

Five minutes in and I'm already covered in glitter. At least it's worth it for the distraction of the perfect pair of DDs in my face.

The nice thing about being a rock star is you don't have to fight for attention. The second Rome, Adrian, and I walked inside Vixen City we were taken to a room with a private stage and the finest girls in the place. They know we'll spend money and have no problem helping us do it.

Living the dream, as Rome would say.

A girl in nothing but a G-string twirls around a pole in a way that will make any man's dick stand at attention. Then there's the girl in my lap twisting her hips against my cock like her life depends on it.

But I'm just not feeling the scene tonight, because it's the same thing playing on repeat again and again since the day the band made it big.

I really sound like a dick for complaining. But I've seen it all before—which, in and of itself, is a douche thing to say. After all, most guys can only dream of getting this much pussy without having to work for it. But after a while, a tit is a tit, and a chick is a chick. They all run together, and it gets old.

Rome's working on the sexy little redhead who's grinding against him, and Adrian's sitting stripper-free beside us. If I seem somewhat uninterested, Adrian looks entirely checked out. He's probably only here for the same reason I am—to keep a leash on Rome.

Adrian is so fucking uptight lately. Back when we first made it big, he used to party with us. He had no problem popping a few pills and joining in on whoever was down to fuck. But as time went on, things changed, and I'm not quite sure what caused it. He grew colder, more focused. And now when he goes out, he usually limits himself to a couple of drinks while playing babysitter.

"So, what's this shit I hear about Merry staying with you?" Rome says, staring at the ass of the girl who's bent over between his legs.

"What about it?"

"Really dude?" He looks over at me and cocks an eyebrow before taking a long drag of his joint.

"Really."

Rome chuckles and smacks the stripper on the ass. If he was anyone else, she'd probably be pissed. But he's Rome Moreno, and the way she looks back at him makes it clear she doesn't mind. Probably even wants a little more.

"Give us some space, sweetheart," Rome says to the stripper. She pouts at him, so he wraps his hands around her waist. "Don't worry, we've got all night. And next time you're in my lap, I want these off."

He snaps the band of her G-string, and she gives him a wicked smile before walking to the stage with the girl who was riding me a second ago. They join the girl already up there. Twirling. Grinding. It should be doing something to bring life to my dick, but it isn't.

"Talk." Rome lifts his drink at me.

I look at Adrian, but he just shakes his head. "Don't look at me, I just offered to record her album, you're the one shacking up with her."

"We aren't shacking up. She's a friend." I take a long drink of water, even though I could really go for a shot right now.

Or five.

Or ten.

Or maybe something heavier.

And that's your problem.

Rome clasps his fingers behind his head, leaning back and looking at me. He's covered neck to knuckles in tattoos, and he's showing them all off tonight in a sleeveless tank. Scarring on his arms peeks through some of them, but I make sure not to stare at it.

Rome's like a brother to me, and one hundred percent loyal to the band. But he doesn't like to talk about the skeletons in his closet, so I know better than to broach those subjects with him.

"You know you've got to get over her," Rome says.

"I am over her."

"Bro." Adrian shakes his head, and they both laugh.

"All right, how about, I'm working on it," I say. "Besides, what do you care? It's not like it stops me from being your wingman. I'm here, aren't I?"

"Physically, yeah." Rome's eyes follow the girls on the stage, before flicking back to me as he drains his drink. "But not up here."

He taps his finger on his temple, and Adrian nods in agreement.

"You know I love Merry," Rome says. "But she's not the settle down and pop out babies kinda girl, Noah. And I see that look on your face, even when you're fucking around and acting like you don't give a shit. You'd drop it all in a heartbeat for her. But she's never going to give that to you."

My throat tightens because I know everything he's saying is true. If only my twisted fucking heart would listen to my head.

"Plus, she's been off lately," Adrian says, leaning forward in his seat and propping his chin up on his knuckles. "I think there's more going on there."

"What?" And how have I not noticed?

Adrian shrugs a shoulder. "Hard to say. She's been disconnected. Still gets her job done fine, but Merry's usually a firecracker. And lately..." Adrian sighs, leaning back. "She's just been acting different."

My mind goes to the last night on tour when she left the party early. And not just early, but alone. And how nervous she was when she arrived at my house earlier. How didn't I see that something else might be going on?

"Maybe she's just nervous about recording?" I'm not sure if I believe it or just want it to be the case.

"Maybe." Adrian's eyebrows furrow. "Who knows, maybe El is getting in my head with all her conspiracy theories. This is why I live alone, less drama. But even if it's nothing, that doesn't change who Merry is. Rome is right. Merry isn't that chick you settle down with. And after we record this demo, the world's gonna eat her up, and she'll be gone. The girl's got talent."

Merry doesn't sing around me often, but I've heard her once or twice. And even if I spent the entire time teasing her, poking her, or being anything but serious, I can't disagree that her voice is next-level amazing.

Pretty soon, the whole world is going to know it. She'll record this demo, get swept up by a studio, go on tour, record her own albums.

She'll be theirs, just like I am.

"Speaking of bitches crashing on couches, what's up with you and El?" Rome nudges Adrian on the shoulder.

Adrian shoots him a hard glare. "First of all, not a bitch. Second, nothing is going on."

"Fucking shit." Rome throws his head back and laughs. "You guys are such pussies, I miss Sebastian."

Rome reaches for another bottle of whiskey and skips the glass altogether, drinking straight from the bottle. Adrian looks over at me as we watch Rome chugging it with that look on his face that tells me Rome's the next mess on his list.

Good luck with that.

Rome isn't like the rest of us. Adrian got lucky with Sebastian because he met Cassie, and she settled his lovesick ass down. I'm sober now, so even if I stick my dick in every chick who walks past me, I'm otherwise boring. And Eloise is practically re-virginizing herself the way she's sworn off dating.

But Rome—I'm not sure what's going on with him, except that every tour it gets worse.

"Ladies." Rome stands up and walks toward the stage. "Who wants to suck my dick?"

Fuck.

Adrian rolls his eyes and stands up to remind Rome this isn't a whorehouse. But as soon as the words are out of Adrian's mouth, one of the girls tells him she'll be off in ten minutes, and they should hang out.

Here I thought this break in our tour would bring a little reality back to all of us. But, besides Sebastian, the rest of the band seems as fucked as ever. Adrian and Eloise are probably at his house arguing non-stop and torturing each other. Rome's going to get kicked out of every strip club in Denver.

And I've got Merry.

If the next four months don't destroy me, I might be tempted to finish what I started before rehab.

My house is quiet when I get home at almost three in the morning. Adrian finally managed to drag Rome's drunk ass out of the club, but not until after he disappeared into a private room for about an hour.

Merry's door is closed as I walk by, and I wonder when she went to sleep. She was still in there when I left for the club, and I'm not sure if she's tired, busy, or just straight avoiding me.

Maybe it's for the best.

I hop in the shower, so I don't go to bed smelling like strippers, but I'm not tired. I'm hungry and buzzing with energy. Once I'm clean, I look at the clock and realize I need to be at Adrian's house for a band meeting at nine, and at this rate I'm not sure I'm going to get much sleep.

Walking into the kitchen, I see a faint glow coming from the fridge, with bare legs peeking out the bottom of the door.

I could get used to this, Merry in my house, barefoot. Looking for food in the middle of the night before crawling back into bed.

Thoughts like that are dangerous.

Merry closes the fridge and jumps when she sees me. "Fuck, Noah." She holds her palm flat on her chest. "You scared me."

"Sorry, just got home." I circle the island and stand opposite her.

"I heard you come in," Merry says, rolling her eyes. "Figured you went to bed."

"Not tired."

Her big brown eyes do a once over, and I can't tell what she's thinking. Without makeup, her eyes are wider, and she looks younger. Softer, even. Her hair's in a messy ponytail with a few waves tumbling on the sides of her face.

Her hands move to the hem of the oversized T-shirt she's wearing, and she tugs it slightly, not that it does anything to cover her bare legs.

"Foo Fighters," I read her T-shirt. "You break my heart."

I slap my hand on my bare chest and feign a heartache.

"You know Dave Grohl is my one true love." She winks.

I do, it's something she's told me many times just to piss me off.

"So, how are the guys?" Merry grabs her glass of water and takes a drink.

"Adrian's good. Eloise hasn't killed him yet. And Rome fell in love with a stripper." I shrug with a laugh. "So, nothing new."

"And you?" she says, walking up to me and getting really close. She smells like berry body wash, and I'd love to drown in that smell. "Have fun spending time *not under your roof?*"

I should have known she wouldn't let the conversation go from earlier. But instead of seeming irritated about it, there's something else in her narrowed gaze.

A challenge maybe?

"Jealous?" I take a step in because damn this woman is a magnet, and I couldn't stop if I wanted to.

"It's your life," she says, her eyes dipping down and tracing over my bare chest. "And your body. You're free to do what you want with it."

I don't like that answer one bit.

"You know what I'd rather do with it," I say, getting really close to that line she likes to keep me on the other side of.

"Noah—"

"Why them and not me?" I know I shouldn't. Maybe it's the conversation with Rome at the club, or Merry being half-dressed in my kitchen at three in the morning, but I'm tired of dancing around the same shit we've spent months circling. "And don't give me the '*I work for the band*' bullshit, because I know you're more than capable of detaching when it comes to sex."

"You're right, I am," she says with a cold expression.

She's close, so close.

Is it her who stepped in or me? Because I feel her body heat in the inches of space between us and she's looking up at me.

"I'm perfectly capable of treating sex just like it is—physical," she says. "But you're not."

She looks like she's trying to catch her breath, or maybe I am.

"I do it all the time," I remind her, not missing the flash of pain that crosses her face at my statement. She tries to look away, but I step closer and force her chin up with my hand, holding it between my thumb and finger. "Not that I want to."

This close, her chest brushes mine, and I can feel her breath on my mouth.

"With groupies, sure." Merry lets out a sigh. "But you can't with me. And what you *need* from me, Noah, what you *want*, I can't give you."

"Who says I need more than sex?"

I don't even believe those words myself, but I don't take them back because damn it, I wish they were true. Maybe if I say them enough times, they will be.

"Just because you say that doesn't mean it's how you *feel*," Merry calls me out. "You want this? Only this?"

She tips her chin up further and faces off with me.

"Then fine, you can have it. I'm not going to lie and say that it wouldn't feel good to let you fuck me. But it would just be sex. Can you honestly look me in the eyes and tell me you can handle that?"

Our lips are an inch apart, and her breath is as frantic as mine. I should be shouting *'yes'* and dragging her onto this couch to fuck some sense into her right now. I should be ripping her clothes from her beautiful body and burying my face between her tattooed thighs. I should be the rock star the world thinks I am and fuck her without looking back.

But I'm frozen.

My grip on her chin loosens.

"That's what I thought," Merry says, backing up. "Goodnight, Noah."

And I can't say a damn thing to stop her as she walks away. Because anything she wants to hear right now would be a lie.

10

MERRY

NOAH HAS ALREADY LEFT for his meeting with the band when I wake up, and it's probably for the best. I'm not sure why I tested him the way I did last night. The fresh Denver air must be getting to my head.

I told him he could fuck me, no strings attached if he wanted. And even if I knew he wouldn't do it, what was I thinking? Because once the gauntlet was thrown, the stable ground I'm used to standing on shook, and I still can't find my footing.

I spent months perfecting how to respond to Noah. Acting like he has no effect on me is second nature now. But something about being under his roof is making every feeling I've ever buried about him seem closer to the surface. And I can't let that happen.

Offering him anything would be leading him on, and that's not fair.

Noah might pretend to be a playboy rock star, but at the core of him, he's not. He's caring and cautious. Like how he holds doors open and only gets the rare tattoo when it's really going to mean something. He has the kind of energy that makes people comfortable when he walks into a room. Noah is a beam of sunshine, so bright sometimes that it's downright irritating.

He's got a heart so big it blinds me when he smiles. While I'm the darkness, inside and out.

Then there's the fact that he comes from the kind of family he wants to create someday. Churches, barbeques, bake sales. He wants a wife who can give him lots of kids and fill his house with laughter. And whether I wanted that at one point in my life or not, I gave up on that kind of thinking years ago.

I've been reminded by one boyfriend after another that I'm not a girl capable of those kinds of relationships. That the broken parts are a little too shattered to think they can be put back together. That what's under the surface isn't worth it.

I might look pretty from far away, but I know the result of letting people into my dark places.

What Noah wants; I can't give to him.

End of story.

Pulling my phone off the nightstand, I read his text again.

Noah: Band practice, see u later

I'm not sure how I feel about him checking in with me, because it's not something anyone has ever done before. I don't do relationships where the other person cares to tell me where they are.

But there Noah's text sits on the screen, offering me some kind of odd comfort.

I shouldn't dig too far into it. It's probably just a cordial roommate thing, letting me know when he's coming or going. But at the same time, nothing with Noah feels like it's a cordial roommate thing. And although this text from any other person might irritate me because I don't need anyone keeping tabs, for some reason, it doesn't.

His words make me feel like a fifteen-year-old girl sitting here waiting for her boyfriend to get back from banging on the drums with his friends.

It makes me feel like I want to know where he is and when he'll be back.

It makes this house feel empty without him.

Bad thoughts that I can't let crawl in.

I roll over in bed and grip my stomach as a sharp pain runs through me. I was hoping the cramping would have subsided by this morning. But even if it's better than last night, the dull ache is still there.

Pulsing.

A reminder of all the ways I'll never be the woman a man like Noah wants.

Fuck.

I clutch harder and hope it fades.

This is not the time. Cassie and Quinn will be over for our girls' day soon, which is going to take all my energy. Plus, I still need to work on one of my songs to prepare for my early morning recording session at Adrian's tomorrow.

Climbing out of bed, I head into the bathroom and unscrew the lid on my ibuprofen. First, downing it, followed by my daily meds. I climb in the shower and sit on the floor as the warm water runs over my naked body and I wait for the ache to subside.

It will.

It has to.

If the pills don't work then I'm back to surgery, and that can't happen when I'm finally getting the chance to record this demo.

I close my eyes and tip my head back, still seeing Noah's face on the other side of my eyelids. I'm not sure when that started happening, but the man is in my head. His face from last night is clear as day, with the kind of hurt in his eyes that's impossible to forget because I've seen it more times than I can count.

It's not that I want to hurt Noah, I don't. If it were up to me, he would have stopped chasing me months ago and saved himself a shit load of heartache. But like moths to a flame, we keep circling back to each other, whether it's what's good for us or not.

Last night I almost caved for the first time since I met him. I could practically taste the mint on his lips. I could feel myself reacting to that rock-hard body of his and I wanted to say fuck it and just close the distance.

Up until now, I've managed to stay strong. I'm around gorgeous rock stars almost twenty-four-seven. Pretty faces don't bring me to my knees. But Noah is edging his way in bit by bit, and everything he's ever done for me is building up and starting to slowly spill over.

How he takes care of me, even when I'm a total bitch and tell him not to. How he gets me water and food when he notices I've been running around all day and not eating. How he lets me crash in his bed on tour with no expectation of sex. How he offered to let me stay in his house to record this demo, even though it seemed to hurt him to do so.

I'm going to destroy him, and he seems intent on letting me do it.

It takes a good fifteen minutes, but the ibuprofen kicks in. I'm able to shower and finish getting ready before the girls arrive.

Cassie decided we should have a girls' day before Quinn heads back to her hometown for a few weeks. And since Cassie herself will be going back and forth between Seattle and Denver for the next few months, she's decided we need to catch up any moment we can.

But I'm not dumb, I know why they're coming over. They want the dirt on me staying at Noah's house, and this is their not-so-subtle way of dragging the details out of me.

Once I'm ready, I make my way back into the kitchen, wearing way more makeup than necessary for an afternoon with friends. But fuck it, just because I'm in the middle of nowhere doesn't mean I need to leave the badass chick I am at the door. And that's definitely where I am: the middle of nowhere. Standing at the slider and looking at the thick forest that surrounds Noah's house.

Painful silence all around.

Whether I get grilled by the girls today or not, I'm glad they're coming over, because I don't like how quiet it is here—how far away from civilization it is.

I've never been good at sitting still, and I'm already feeling antsy.

The doorbell rings and I can't get there fast enough, pulling it open to see the girls on the other side.

"Is your hair getting pinker by the day or something?" I ask Cassie, noticing how the pink that used to just coat the tips of her long blonde hair, now goes up a good five inches of it.

Cassie gives a shy shrug. "I like it."

"Mhmm," I grin at her and notice her cheeks flushing. "You and a certain lead singer."

Her cheeks brighten in embarrassment, but she doesn't deny it, ignoring me instead and walking past me toward Noah's kitchen.

"Speaking of pink, I'm surrounded," I say as Quinn steps into the house next in a tiny blue sundress that shows off her almost fully tatted-up skin. Her hair is pulled in a tight bun on her head.

"I'm considering going blue, but you'll just have to wait and see." Quinn winks, before giving me a big hug.

When I joined Enemy Muse, Quinn was the first friend I made. She handles the band's PR and social media accounts and is as sweet as her cotton candy hair.

"Don't forget me," a voice comes from behind Quinn.

I look around Quinn and see Stacy filling the doorway with her tall frame. As per usual, the woman doesn't know how to relax and has shown up in dress slacks and a perfectly pleated red shirt that matches her lipstick. The color stands out against her dark skin and from the way she carries herself, she knows it.

"What the hell, I thought you left town already?"

Stacy props a hand on her hip. "I should have last night, but I booked a flight for tomorrow instead. Cassie said we were having a girls' day, and after this last tour, I need it."

"Touché."

Between the drama with Megan releasing a sex tape of Sebastian and Cassie, and the issues with a few of the roadies, the last tour was even more eventful than I like. Everyone involved is no doubt ready for this break.

Stacy walks past me without a hug, which doesn't offend me because I know she's not a physically affectionate person, and I follow them all into the kitchen.

"So, what's the plan?" I ask.

We all take stools around the large marble island and Cassie starts pulling things from a brown paper bag.

"Margaritas," Cassie says, pulling out the mix and some limes.

"Uh—"

"Virgin." Cassie smiles.

"Thank you."

It's no secret that all of us girls drink, but this is Noah's house, and even if he doesn't care how much I drink or if I smoke weed when we're out partying, I know better than to bring that shit here.

Whether he opens up to me about his struggles with drugs and alcohol or not, I sense sobriety is hard on him. It's something he tries to hide from the band and pretends he doesn't live with. But I see it. And I'm not about to be the person who makes things more difficult.

I'm proud of Noah for getting sober, and for staying that way in the environments he's always in.

I get up and walk across the kitchen to get four glasses out of the cabinet.

"Look at you, knowing where the glasses are." Cassie smirks.

"They're glasses." I roll my eyes, already knowing where this is going.

"Noah's glasses."

"Still just glasses."

"Sure, they are." She winks.

I set them down on the island and level my gaze at her. "Just get this over with already. What do you want to know?"

Cassie gives me a fake questioning expression, but Quinn doesn't hold her tongue. "You fucking Noah yet?"

"There it is." I pick up the virgin margarita mix and start pouring. "No, we aren't fucking. Never have, never will."

"Never is a long time," Cassie says. "Especially under one roof."

"I'm not fucking Noah Hayes," I repeat, as she starts slicing up the limes.

"Why not?" Stacy asks, and it catches me off guard. Not because I didn't expect the inquisition. I did. But because Stacy was the one to say it.

Of all the band's staff, she is by far the most professional. She's never caught out partying and doesn't believe in mixing work with pleasure. But here she is, joining the rest of them.

"I'm just saying," Stacy continues, with a shrug. "It's Noah, and it's you. Under one roof."

"We're friends." The word almost sours at the thought of our almost kiss last night. "And we're very different. Total opposites. That would be a bad idea on so many levels."

All three of them are looking at me like the words coming out of my mouth are total bullshit, but I'm not going to justify whatever romantic comedy they want to write for my relationship with Noah in their heads.

"How's Sebastian?" I veer the conversation, which gets me a giant eye roll from Cassie.

Luckily, she might be annoyed, but she allows it.

"Good. Busy." She squeezes a lime into each of our drinks and passes them out. "Him and Eloise have been spending a lot of time writing the new album. He seems excited about it."

"I can't wait to hear it."

Stacy and Quinn nod their heads in agreement.

It's been almost two years since Enemy Muse has put out new music. Sebastian and Eloise are the primary songwriters for the band, and after Sebastian's best friend, who is also Cassie's brother, died, Sebastian went into a drunken spiral I wasn't sure he would ever come out of.

Between meeting Cassie and seeing a therapist, Sebastian is finally breaking out of his long-lasting slump, and it's good to hear he's writing music again.

"What about you?" Quinn asks. "When do you start recording?"

"Tomorrow." The nerves in my stomach kick up again.

I'm confident about my singing and songwriting ability, but it doesn't stop that faint whisper of doubt from creeping in.

"You better share it with us once it's done." Cassie nudges my arm.

"Of course." I take a drink, grinning at her over the rim of my glass as it leaves my lips. "As soon as you stop bothering me about Noah."

That earns me a big laugh and a slap on the shoulder.

"Tell you what." She holds up her glass between us. "You make it through the next four months without fucking him or falling in love, and I'll let it go."

"Deal." I clink my glass against hers confidently. "Not. Going. To. Happen."

And I take a long, thirst-quenching drink, wishing it was tequila with the power to wash my thoughts away.

11

MERRY

THE BAND HASN'T RECORDED an album in the time I've worked for them, so I've never actually been inside the recording studio at Adrian's house. Until today. And to say it feels spectacular would be the biggest understatement.

After spending almost a year around the band, it's hard to get impressed by things anymore. I've seen it all, partied around the globe, met some of the most famous faces on the planet. I've probably become one of those people I used to hate who never appreciates the small things. But in this moment, I don't care. Every feeling pales in comparison to walking into Adrian's state-of-the-art studio knowing I'll be the one recording in it.

Warmth wells in my chest.

Appreciation.

Awe.

Years I've dreamed of being in this exact position—imagined this moment. Since I was a child standing on the porch singing at the top of my lungs like it was my stage.

I'm finally here.

"Feel free to set your stuff down and get comfortable," Adrian says as we settle into the control room.

He takes a seat at the mixing board and starts adjusting settings on a few of the computers. Adrian is a big guy who takes up space in just about every room but seated in front of the vast panel of buttons, even he's dwarfed in comparison.

It's a big production and I'm humbled by it.

I'm sure when Enemy Muse is in here recording, it's a much bigger event. They probably have sound mixers, producers, and audio engineers piled into this room making sure everything is perfect. But today, it's just Adrian and me, recording the demo I can only hope will be the catalyst of my career.

I settle on the couch and pull out my notebook, scribbling out a few lines and making final adjustments while Adrian cues up the beat. We're working on my song Thought It Was, and after emailing back and forth for the past week discussing what type of beat to put behind the lyrics, we finally got it nailed down.

The door to the control room opens and Eloise slips in with a messy knot of hair on her head. I've spent a lot of time with the band, but I've never seen Eloise Kane look quite like this. Practically... human?

She's wearing an oversized T-shirt with baggy pajama bottoms that hang loose on her thin frame. There's not a dash of makeup on her freckled face, and it easily takes five years off her. In each hand is a steaming mug.

"Coffee?"

Adrian's eyes slide in her direction, discreetly doing a once over before returning to what he's doing.

"I'll take some," he says, and she hands him a mug.

Now I get why Cassie and the girls practically crucified me over staying with Noah. Because if the questions swirling in their heads are anything like what I'm thinking watching Adrian and Eloise pretend they don't give a shit about each other, they're justified in thinking it.

But that's hypocritical. Adrian and Eloise could easily just be friends. Staying under one roof doesn't mean you have to be sleeping with a man, so who am I to judge?

"Merry?" Eloise holds a mug out to me. "Yours is tea with some honey to help warm up your throat."

"Thanks," I say as she sits on the couch beside me and curls her legs up.

For the hard exterior she shows the press, she's anything but. Eloise is secretly the caretaker of the band, and even this small gesture of bringing me tea before my first recording session is a reminder of that.

"You're up early." It's barely five in the morning, but like Adrian said, I have to work around the band's schedule, so I'll take what I can get.

Eloise shrugs. "Haven't gone to bed yet. It's hard to break the sleep schedule I pick up on tour. My brain doesn't know what to do right now. And on that note, don't be offended if I pass out on this couch listening to you. It's nothing personal."

"No offense taken."

Adrian stands up and walks out of the room without saying anything, which Eloise notices as her eyes follow him.

I've worked with him long enough, and close enough, that I know not to be offended by his silent treatment. He's not a bullshitter. He'll talk when he has something important to say, but that's it. He isn't going to fill silence just to make people feel comfortable. Small talk is not his thing.

"How's it going at Noah's?" Eloise asks. But unlike when the girls were grilling me about it yesterday, it doesn't feel like I need to immediately go on the defense.

"Good." I sigh. "We're making it work. But it's only been a few days so ask me again in a week, and I'll let you know if we're plotting to kill each other in our sleep."

"Understood." She smiles.

"How is it going here?" I eye the closed door that heads upstairs.

Eloise bites her bottom lip, and I realize it's the first time I've seen her look anywhere near this close to vulnerable.

"Fine, I guess. I appreciate him doing me the favor, so I don't have to stay at Sebastian's and listen to my brother having sex with his girlfriend every five minutes." Eloise rolls her eyes. "And at least he doesn't bring his girlfriend over, they go to her place if he's planning to stay the night."

"Adrian has a girlfriend?" The guy might not talk much, but the fact that I have no idea about this shocks me a little. I wonder if he's even told Noah and the rest of the band.

"Yes." Eloise sighs so deep her shoulders deflate with it. The look on her face is the closest confirmation I've seen that she has feelings for Adrian because she looks far from happy that he's dating.

I nudge her arm and try to change the subject. "What about you, rock princess? I never see you with a man—or a woman, if that's your thing?"

She shakes her head.

"All right then, what gives? You do realize you could literally have any guy on the planet, right?"

"Guys aren't worth my energy right now," she says, but there's definitely a lot more behind it than that. "Besides I've got a best-selling album to write."

"Damn right." I nod my head in agreement and her wide smile returns. "Four albums, you guys are pros by now. Please tell me all your secrets."

Eloise tips her chin up and taps her finger on it like she's thinking, but the big smile crossing her cheeks is playful.

"Well..." She looks at me with a sweet smile. "Honestly, try not to think too much about it. Write from the heart. Sing from the heart. Don't try to be someone you aren't. Not that that's ever been a problem for you."

She nudges my shoulder and I laugh, but deep inside I feel the cracks widen. If only she knew how little of myself I actually let out. What people see as an authentic tough exterior is simply armor for me. It protected me from getting my feelings hurt as a kid when I was made fun of

FOREVER AND EVER 119

for being different, and I've used it to guard myself ever since.

But all I say is, "You know it."

Not even Eloise is prepared for my truths.

The door to the studio opens and Adrian walks back in with his phone in his hand, like he just got off a call. Tucked under his arm is a blanket that he walks over and hands to Eloise.

"In case you get tired," he says, turning before she can respond.

It's an awfully thoughtful move for a guy with a girlfriend. Not that I say anything about it.

"You ready, Merry?" Adrian adjusts the sound panel once more.

"As I'll ever be."

It's eerily silent walking into the recording booth. The door closes behind me and every sound is stamped out. It's just me and my heavy breathing as I try and calm my nerves until Adrian's voice comes through a speaker.

"You've got this," he says, and I look through the glass to see him sitting there looking at me. He nods, and it feels like enough to give me some confidence. "I have the beat uploaded, and we're going to start with the chorus. Once that's nailed down, we can duplicate it as needed and then focus on variations near the end of the song. That's probably all we'll get to today, but we'll focus on the verses in your next session, so have those ready by then."

"Will do, boss." I nod, hoping my nerves aren't showing on my face.

Adrian adjusts something in front of him, and over his shoulder I see Eloise sitting watching me. The realization makes me feel a little like a caged animal. As if being in the desolate forest outside of Denver isn't enough to make a girl stir crazy, the tightening in my chest intensifies from their stares.

"Go ahead and put the headphones on." Adrian points to the headphones dangling from the microphone stand. "The beat will feed through there. You'll see me doing a countdown, and once you hear it, wait for your mark and then sing."

"Simple enough," I say, putting the headphones over my ears and being once more drowned in silence.

Adrian holds up three fingers as he slides a lever in front of him and starts to slowly count down.

Three.

Two.

One.

The beat trickles into my ears, quiet at first, slowly building, just like the song will as it prepares to hit the chorus. I stare at my notebook on the stand in front of me and the words might as well be paint swirling on the page because my head feels suddenly fuzzy. I hear my cue come, and on that mark, I try to forget my nerves and just sing.

Every line comes out exactly as I wrote it. My throat is warm from the tea, and I'm thankful Eloise thought of it. I sing as hard as I can into the microphone and spill myself out, but when the chorus ends and the music fades, I see in Adrian's face what I already felt.

Stiff.

He taps his ear, and I know to move the headset off my own.

"That was good," he says, although I kind of think it's for my benefit. "Take one is always a little rough. We need to warm up your vocal cords and get you in the right mindset. This time, try not to think so much. Just sing."

I nod and give him a smile I hope isn't as forced as it feels.

Just sing.

If only it were that easy.

The next take isn't any better. If anything, it might be worse. I remember feeling this chorus when I wrote it, but right now, everything that comes out feels like it might as well be someone else's song.

Adrian starts from the top and we go again.

And again.

Eloise is leaning forward now, not falling asleep like she said she might, even if she's tucked in Adrian's blanket. She's listening to every take and absorbing it. Her head nods along, and I can tell when my voice is sharp or flat from reading her expression.

I scribble out a couple of lines in my notebook and rearrange them. It feels a little like a battle alone in this room. But I'm not sure if I'm fighting the lyrics or myself.

The back of my neck is sweaty, and I feel my hair matting to it, so I pull the hair tie off my wrist and wrangle my curls into a ponytail.

We do another take, and although I feel myself warming up, I'm not getting there.

I'm just thankful whatever frustration I'm feeling isn't being reflected back at me from Adrian's face. Because I feel like he should be kicking me out of the studio by now, but he doesn't.

"Merry," Eloise's voice is the one that comes through the speaker this time, and I realize she's standing at the control panel next to Adrian. The expression on her face has morphed into something stern, and I realize this is Eloise Kane, badass bass player for Enemy Muse, giving me the full force of her attention and energy. "You're in your head."

"I know."

"You can do this. The first time is the hardest, try to remember that. You just have to let go." Eloise nods like it's the punctuation mark on her sentence. "Remember what I said. Sing from the heart. Show them *you*."

I swallow at the lump in my throat and nod my head as I slip the headset back on and try not to feel the pressure of it closing in.

Me.

The girl incapable of opening up.

The girl with scars much deeper than the ink on her skin.

The girl with nothing more to give.

I take a deep breath and close my eyes. My heart hammers between my temples. Inside, I feel like I'm shaking, but I can't let it out. Won't let it out.

I exhale once more and will my breath to steady in my chest.

In. Out. In. Out.

You can do this.

You've fought harder battles.

I'm not sure how long I stand silent, with eyes shut, but it feels like a lifetime passes before the music starts in my headphones and slowly starts to build. This time, I hear more than just the chords. I hear the tension that stirs inside them, I hear the echoes of all I've held back trying to get out. I hear my heart in the drumbeat.

I hear myself.

And without thinking, or analyzing, or striving for perfection, I take a breath that releases the world with it. And I just sing.

"Even if I try, every single time, dangle on the wire of this thinning thread.

All you hear's goodbye, even if I might not want it just yet.

And we could hold on.

We could make it happen now.

We could hold on.

We could try to break us down.

But I won't change, and you won't budge, and we won't be the thing I thought it was.

I won't change, and you won't budge, and we won't be the thing you thought it was.

What we thought it was.

What we thought it was.

We can't be the thing we thought this was."

The words that come out might as well be my soul spilling open because I feel empty by the time the chorus ends. Out of breath and energy. I feel like I left myself in those lyrics. And when I open my eyes, there are three faces staring back.

Noah must have shown up while I was spilling my all into that chorus because he's standing next to Eloise in the control room with his arms crossed over his chest. The look on his face says more than I wish it did because one expression and I see it all.

The take was perfect.

Raw.

Real.

And in his eyes, I see the words I just sang staring me in the face.

12

Noah

The house smells like peppers and onions when I finally get home. Music hums from the living room. There's energy radiating, and it stirs something in me walking into a house that isn't permeating in stale silence.

I turn the corner to the kitchen and spot Merry standing at the stove with a spatula in hand as she swishes her hips to the music she has playing. The hem of her T-shirt rides dangerously close to the top of her thighs as she swings her body around.

Fuck.

This woman is going to be the end of me.

I haven't gone back to the studio since dropping in a few days ago. If I thought her living in my house was torture enough, seeing her sing is much worse. The tough chick she likes to pretend to be slips away when she's standing in front of a microphone. And all I see is the girl I wish would fall for me, singing songs that sound too close to confessions I know they aren't.

Hoping for more with Merry is the kind of crap that gets a guy in trouble. So I'm cutting that shit out.

"You're cooking?"

Merry spins in surprise at the question, and it's cute that she looks irritated that I've caught her with her guard down. God forbid I actually see that she's human.

She tightens her dark ponytail and tips her chin up ever so slightly. But it's too late, I've already seen it, so I just shake my head and take a seat at the island to watch her.

"It smells good. What are you making?"

"Fajitas." Merry smiles proudly, turning around to stir the peppers and onions around in the pan. "But don't tell my dad I baked the chicken. He considers meat without grill lines sacrilegious."

"If you introduce me to your dad, you better believe that me bringing up chicken will be the least of your worries."

She shoots me a glare over her shoulder, but I don't miss the smile she's trying to hide as she turns back to the stove.

I could get used to her in my kitchen. Her in my house when I get home. Her in my life.

It hurts to even think it.

"Hopefully you're hungry," Merry says. "I made way too much. Downside of coming from my family, I suppose. Like my mom says, better to make too much than not enough. Wouldn't want anyone to leave hungry."

She's waving the spatula in the air as she says it, almost like she's imitating her mom, and I'm curious if she's anything like her.

"Starved," I say, appreciating that she seems extra chatty today.

"How was practice?" She tips the pan to empty the peppers and onions into a bowl.

Her eyes dip to where my hands rest on the island, and I realize I'm tapping my fingers against it.

"Fine. Mostly uneventful." I shrug, burying my hands in my pockets. "Sebastian and Eloise got into it about one of the songs. El's been kind of grumpy lately."

Merry spins around and braces her hands on the counter. "Speaking of grumpy Eloise, I've been meaning to ask you, did you know Adrian has a girlfriend?"

"Adrian?" I cock an eyebrow. "No fucking way."

"That's what Eloise said." Merry shrugs one shoulder and purses her lips.

"It would explain why he's been too busy to go out with me and Rome."

Merry rolls her eyes. "Or maybe he's just tired of the seedy strip clubs you two frequent."

"He's a dude. No guy is ever tired of seeing tits."

That gets me an even bigger eye roll, but it's better than telling her that I'd gladly give up strip clubs, and anything else she wanted if it would make her happy.

Fuck, I'm lame.

"You're back in the studio tomorrow, right?" I change the subject.

"Yes." Her face winces and she grabs her side for a second.

"You okay?"

Merry's face pales the slightest, but she spins around and avoids my gaze.

"Fine," she says, but she seems flustered all of a sudden. "Just period cramps."

The look in her eyes seemed like it was a little more, but what would I know.

She busies herself serving all the food, making two big plates of fajitas, and setting out an array of toppings on the counter. On tour, we've shared hundreds of meals together, but there's rarely any cooking happening. Food is always either being made for the band or delivered.

But this meal is something else. Another peek inside the woman who tries to remain a locked fortress. I had no idea she could cook, much less something that looks so delicious.

"This is incredible," I say, filling my mouth with food, which makes her shake her head and laugh.

"Glad you like it."

"Like it?" I swallow. "I love it."

I love you.

It's a good thing she can't read my mind.

"Your mom taught you how to cook?" I ask between bites.

She shakes her head, and her lips turn down in the slightest frown. "More like my dad. Yes, my mom can cook, but he's the one who does the majority of it."

"How are things with him?"

It's no secret that Merry's parents weren't thrilled with her going on tour with us. And I don't really blame them. Tour isn't the tamest place. But what they don't seem to realize is that their daughter is wilder than half the shit they fear. They might not want to accept it, but Merry is who she is. There's no taming her, and fuck anyone who would try because she's perfect as is.

"I think my dad is waiting for me to *get it out of my system*." She throws up air quotes with her fingers. "They think it's a phase I'll outgrow. I don't really blame them; I just wish they would at least try to understand."

"Give 'em time." I shrug, trying to be supportive. Although, if my family is any indication of how long parents can hold a grudge, then I don't have much hope to give.

"I love my parents," Merry says. "But I was never close with them like my sister. They keep wanting me to turn into someone I'm not. I'm not sure they ever really understood me."

I nod, pushing away my empty plate. "I definitely get it." More than she knows.

Merry sits back in her chair and folds her arms over her chest giving me that calculating look I love and fear so much.

"You don't talk about your family," she points out.

"Nope." I raise my eyebrows and pull my hair back.

"Why is that?"

This conversation isn't territory I like treading into. And not because my parents are cruel like Rome's dad was, or mostly absent like Sebastian and Eloise's parents. But because they're the opposite, and yet, they still rejected me.

"My family is complicated," I say, knowing Merry was bound to broach this subject at some point, and I should be thankful that she even gives a shit to ask.

In the time Merry's worked for the band, she's been careful to maintain a safe amount of distance between us physically and emotionally. She tries to keep the conversation light and doesn't dig into tougher subjects. But sitting in my kitchen, here she is...asking.

Merry's interest is what I've wanted since the day we met, but I'm surprised to feel my defenses fortifying at the thought of talking to her about my parents. Certain subjects dig into deep wounds where only infection festers, and this is one of them.

"All families are complicated." Merry hitches her eyebrow because she no doubt knows I'm avoiding the question.

"Yeah." I wipe my palm over my face and lean forward, placing my elbows on the island. "My mom and dad are good people, you know? Religious, involved in the community, all that bullshit. The church band is where I first fell in love with music. My sisters and my brother all got involved once we were old enough."

"How Hallmark of you." She smiles.

"You'd think," I say, taking a deep breath. "That kind of perfection is exhausting, and it wasn't real. Because even if they walked around touting acceptance, they didn't live by it. My parents had certain expectations for all of us, and they weren't too happy when I went against them."

Merry sits there quietly now, watching me closely. I'm not sure how it is that she always sees between my lines, but she does.

"When I told my parents I was joining the band, they basically threatened to disown me. I kind of figured they were joking and would get over it. I mean, they were the ones who got me into music, and God wouldn't want them to turn their backs on their own son, right?" I shake my head. "It all started to fall apart when we were recording the first album, and then, after what happened with Kali..."

Her name catches in my throat.

There's a lot of shit I'm willing to tell Merry if she really wants to know, but for some reason, I can't bring myself to go down this particular dark tunnel quite yet.

"My parents said the devil had his hooks in me." I lean back and rub my palms together. "Easier to sleep at night when you give yourself the right excuses. Haven't talked to them much since. But who cares. Now I'm a rock star, so fuck them."

Merry nods, but it doesn't feel the least bit comforting. Because in her eyes, I might as well be transparent.

"Fuck them," I repeat, but it's almost a whisper this time.

Standing up, I grab our plates and carry them over to the sink, and Merry lets the subject drop. It's one of the things I appreciate about her. She knows when to push, and when to let it go.

She joins me, standing at my side, and helps me with the dishes. Washing, while I dry them. And we do it in silence, cleaning the kitchen and just existing in each other's presence. It's comforting, like being around her always is to me. We don't have to fill the void with empty words. We can simply be, and it's enough.

"Missed a spot." I hand a plate back to her and point at an almost microscopic spec.

Merry rolls her eyes, but smiles. "Think you can do better? We can always switch sides."

"I'd rather you be the one getting wet," I grin at her, and her eyes drop to her hands in the water.

"You're ridiculous, Noah Hayes," she splashes me with a little bit of water.

I lean in real close, and she's so focused on my eyes, she doesn't notice my hands slipping into the sink.

"You love it," I scoop a pile of bubbles out of the water and plant them on top of her head, making her shriek and jump back with a murderous look on her face.

"You're going to pay for that," she says, reaching in the water.

I take a step back and grin. "Bring it on, beautiful."

Merry swipes a mountain of bubbles off the top of the water and hurls them at me with all her might. They land square on my chest and soak through my shirt. A smile widens on her face, and I can tell she's proud of herself for the hit.

I toss the dish rag at her, and she barely dodges it, as she reaches into the sink to splash me some more.

Her laugh fills the room and it's infectious—raw, free. It's unlike anything I've heard from her. It's unfiltered, no holding back. Completely unguarded and defenseless. The sound cracks me wide open.

She swats bubbles at me again, and I spin away this time before they hit me. But when I rear back ready to return fire, Merry is hunched over grabbing her stomach.

"Hey." I reach for her shoulders and realize she's shaking. "What happened? Are you okay?"

Her hands are clenched, wrapped around her sides. And even though she said she was having period cramps earlier, this seems more intense than that.

"No." Her body heaves forward, and I pull her closer to steady her.

The laughter that filled the room moments ago is replaced by the kind of silence that can cut through everything. Her bones shaking, her knuckles white. I might be holding her, but she's never felt so far away, and I'm not sure what to do.

"Sorry, I just need to lay down," she says on a sigh.

Her posture relaxes the slightest, and I think some of the pain might be fading.

I push her curls out of her face and her complexion is paler than I've ever seen it.

"Can you walk?"

She nods, even if her face tells me she isn't so sure. But I don't push it, because I know how much she hates accepting anyone's help, especially mine. She's so damn stubborn that she could probably be bleeding out and would still insist on doing things herself, which leaves me frustrated and helpless.

She slowly makes it all the way across the house, not letting go of her stomach. I stay by her side the entire way, even if I don't reach out. When we get to her room, her shoulders are still slightly hunched, so I prop up a few pillows on her bed to try and help her.

"Can I get you something?" I ask as she climbs up carefully.

"Tylenol?"

I nod and leave her to grab it. When I return with the pills and water, she's still sitting but has managed to get herself fully onto the bed.

Merry downs the Tylenol and drains the water from the glass before handing it back to me. "I just... I'm not feeling great. It's no big deal."

"Period cramps," I say, not believing it.

Merry is a professional gatekeeper with her secrets, and even if it's something worse, she's not going to tell me. I've seen the pill bottles in the bathroom. There's clearly something more going on. But whenever I've asked her about it, she shuts down the conversation almost immediately and now is not the time to push her.

"Thank you for the Tylenol." She gives me a faint smile.

"Anything for you, beautiful."

Merry tries to adjust the pillow but winces, so I set down the water glass and help her get comfortable.

"Thanks." She settles, closing her eyes.

I brush the back of my knuckles along her arm. She's so soft, and warm, and smells like the sweetest berries. "Let me know if I can get you anything, okay?"

She nods, but her eyes remain closed, so I turn to leave, hoping sleep will fix whatever is wrong. But her fingers tangle through mine and stop me before I can take a step.

"Noah?"

There's a lot I want to read in the expression on her face when I turn back around. Her guard is down. Her eyes show defeat. I'm seeing past the persona she's constantly wearing and it's just Mercedes Lopez staring back at me.

There's a lot I want to think about the fact that she's showing this side to me, that she's holding my hand how she is, that her voice sounds desperate.

But I shouldn't.

"Stay with me for a bit?" Merry presses her lips together and I feel the anxiety building inside her with that question.

On any other day, I might make a joke about climbing into her bed. But tonight, I just nod and lay down beside her, trying not to think too much about it. I tell myself it's because she isn't feeling well, and this doesn't mean anything.

But as she rolls onto her side and rests her head in the nook of my arm, I can't help it. Because as her fingers trace the tattoo rings on my forearm, I feel myself soaking her in all the way through to my bones.

I'd hold her forever if she asked me to, no matter the damage.

13

NOAH

It takes me a minute to figure out where I am when my eyes open. My room is usually dark from the blackout curtains, but the sun blinds me as I blink the bed into focus. And that's when I remember last night.

Holding Merry in my arms all night as she winced in pain. Pretending not to notice that something worse is going on than she's willing to tell me.

I roll over and see she's no longer laying down. She's sitting on the edge of the bed and tying her wild hair into a bun on the top of her head.

"Hey." I reach out and brush her arm with my hand.

She looks over her shoulder just barely. "Hey."

"How are you feeling?"

"I'm fine."

Her posture tells me otherwise. Besides seeming tired, she's still slightly hunched and her muscles are tensed.

"Do you need me to get you anything?" I sit up and try to shake off whatever energy she's giving off right now.

"No," she says, and I feel those familiar walls coming up.

"Merry—"

"I'm fine." she turns sideways and forces a smile. "Everything's fine. Can we move on?"

"That would make you happy, right?" I clench the bedsheet. Because right now I'd really like to scream. I'm so tired of her finding every way imaginable to shut me out, even after I've been there for her.

Last night, she was real with me. I had her in my arms and it felt like maybe I was making some kind of progress. There was a wall down, but I should have known better. One barrier breached just means there are twenty more standing ready to take its place.

Merry crosses her arms over her chest and narrows her already dark eyes. "What's that supposed to mean?"

I climb off the bed and circle around it to stand facing her. Just because she's more comfortable avoiding me, doesn't mean I'm going to let that happen right now. I'm not even sure what's driving me. Lust, anger, irritation, all three—knowing that no matter what I do, this is always where I end up. In front of her, trying to get through something impenetrable.

"I'm saying it's okay to ask for help sometimes." I move closer and she has to look up at me. "It's okay to not be okay. But you're *you*. And we both know I'm shouting into a fucking void right now trying to get you to see that. So, have it your way. You don't want help, I'll stop offering."

"I told you I'm okay, Noah."

"Good," I say, even if we both know she's lying. "I'll give you some space then."

I leave her room and head down the hall.

Sometimes I'm honestly not sure why I even try anymore. Any inch gained inevitably forces me a step backward. Maybe I've officially gone insane, and this is some loop I'm living in. Being rejected by her over and over again.

Pulling out my phone, I shoot off a text to Rome.

Noah: You up?
Rome: Which part of me?
Noah: I'll take that as a yes… and gross
Rome: Not my fault these chicks can go all night long.
Noah: Put some fucking pants on. I'm coming over.
Rome: Buzz kill
Noah: See u in 10

I need to get out of my house. Merry is everywhere, same room or not. And if I'm looking for a distraction, Rome's place is guaranteed to make that happen.

By the time I'm pulling up to Rome's house, there are three women piling into a car. One stumbles over another and it's clear they're still drunk, so I'm glad to see Rome at least has his driver chauffeuring them back to wherever they came from.

Rome, for his part, stands in the doorway with a shit-eating grin on his face.

"Fun night?"

"Always," he says, stepping aside. "The redhead was limber."

I follow him into his kitchen and help myself to his coffee pot, turning it on and filling it with water. Somehow, I feel like I got the best sleep I've ever had, while still being exhausted.

"What's got you in such a shit mood?" Rome quirks an eyebrow. "You're not fucking Merry yet?"

I look up at him and narrow my eyes.

"Come the fuck on, Noah." Rome sits on a stool at the island. "Get in or get the fuck over it already."

"Please tell me how you really feel."

"My house," Rome says. "So, you're either going to listen to me tell you how it is, or you can pout in your own home."

I ignore him and dig the coffee grounds out of the fridge. It doesn't matter that I don't want to hear whatever fucked up shit Rome is about to say, he's going to speak his mind. And maybe that's exactly what I need to hear. Because whatever it is I'm currently doing is not working.

"Let's just set the whole Merry mess aside for a second," Rome says, taking a sip, and I realize he's drinking whiskey at seven thirty in the morning. "A relationship is the last thing you need right now, man. We're about to go back on tour. Not worth it."

"Not sure you're the one I should be taking relationship advice from."

"You showed up on my doorstep, not Sebastian's. If you wanted advice from a pussy-whipped motherfucker, I'm sure that dickhead would be happy to help."

Rome's eyebrows lift in a challenge as he takes another drink, and he's right. I thought about texting Sebastian, but he's too lovestruck by his relationship with Cassie at the moment. I don't need unrealistic bullshit to give me false hope. I need someone who's going to kick me in the nuts and wake me the fuck up.

Which, at the moment, leaves me with Rome. I love the guy and respect the crap out of him as a member of the band, but he's not the guy you go to if you want someone to hold your hand and tell you everything will be okay in the end, especially when it comes to relationships. I don't know if he's ever even been in one that lasted longer than one night.

Which makes him the person I need insight from right now. My head can't be trusted when it's continually circling back to Merry. Rome's lashing is what I deserve.

"Point taken." I sigh.

"Good, because I'm not going to tell you what you want to hear. And it's not because I don't like Merry or don't think you two could be good together. But she's not there with you." Rome narrows his eyes. "I know you don't want to give her up, but you need to ask yourself if this is worth all the fucking pain? Because if it is, then have at it, my brother. More power to you. But you can't bitch every five seconds when it hurts. Either be in the shit or get out."

Somehow through his drunken haze, Rome is making a lot of sense. Merry has never been the easy choice. If I wanted a girl who would happily settle down, I could have started chasing someone else months ago. Anyone else.

Merry is a constant knife to the fucking chest.

Painful. Draining.

Worth it.

Fuck.

That right there is the thought I need to kick. Maybe I'm a masochist and I'm only just now realizing it.

"Is that why you don't do relationships?" I ask. "Not worth the pain?"

"Fuck no," Rome says with a dark chuckle. He spins his drink on the counter and watches the whiskey swish around. "Pain doesn't scare me. That's the easy part. It's the other side of it that's not worth it."

"Which is what?"

Rome doesn't look up at me. He swirls the whiskey in his glass, and I think maybe he's drifted into his own world. His fingers flex on the glass, drawing out the muscles in his hands, buried in ink.

When he finally looks back up at me, there's a dark look in his eyes.

"Realizing you might be going through it all for nothing," he says. "The pain you can suffer through, maybe it'll even make you numb to it after a while. Fuck, you might even be stronger because of that shit. But getting on the other side of it and finding nothing there looking you in the face—realizing it was all for nothing—not worth it."

"Who says it would be all for nothing?"

Maybe I want him to convince me that there's a chance with Merry. That even if I know she doesn't want more, and everyone around us thinks I'm wasting my time, he might see something in there to help me understand why I keep beating my head against a wall trying.

Rome shrugs. "You don't know 'till you get there I guess."

An empty feeling creeps up inside. "Guess so."

Rome finishes his drink and sets it down with a thud as I slide a mug of coffee across the counter to him.

It makes me wonder what Rome found on the other side of his own pain. Because I know it's there, hidden beneath the demons that paint his skin. Secrets, a past, hurt, trailing so deep it's made it impossible for him to see anything beyond it.

Was it whatever his dad did to him? Was it his mom he never mentions? Was it a girl who broke his heart before we ever met him?

"I want you to be happy, man," Rome says, with the glimpse of genuine care.

"Appreciated. But maybe you're right. What if it's never worth it?"

"In that case," Rome gestures his coffee toward his living room. "You fill your time with groupies and strippers."

I shake my head and laugh. "Perks of the business."

"Damn right it is," Rome says. "I might be a drunken idiot half the time, but I know you haven't taken any of the chicks up on their offers lately. You just need to get laid. Work this shit out of your system."

"Maybe."

I haven't fucked anyone since the night the tour ended, and it's been even longer than that since sex meant anything. But even though I've had opportunities when I've gone out with Rome and Adrian, Merry being in my house fucks with my head. I can't seem to get there, no matter how much I know I probably should.

"I'm having a party this weekend." Rome circles the island and slaps a hand on my shoulder. "Come, enjoy, let loose."

"Aren't you having a party every day of the week?"

Rome shakes his head. "Not like this. Promise, it'll be worth it. You just need to get balls deep in some chick and all these problems will go away."

"Whatever you say, man."

Maybe for him, it really is that easy. Letting someone ride your dick to forget. But this is Merry we're talking about. She's not just in my home, she's managed to reach places that didn't exist inside me before I met her.

She's taken up residence, and I don't want her to leave, even if it rots me to the core.

14

Merry

I'm such a bitch.

The worst.

The closer Noah gets, the more I push him away. As proven by the fact that I'm letting this random guy stick his tongue further down my throat in an attempt to forget my problems.

"You're fucking hot," random guy says, as his hand slides up my sides and under the hem of my cropped black T-shirt.

He told me his name—something that sounded like Tim or Jim or who cares. I don't give a fuck. It's not like I ever plan on calling this guy or seeing him again.

I'm not even sure where Rome found all these people.

His house is packed, and the music is blaring. We're an hour outside the city, but even that didn't thin the crowd. Not that I should be surprised.

While every member of Enemy Muse has a home outside of Denver, Rome's house isn't like the rest of them. It's one hundred percent a bachelor pad and built specifically for parties like this. He has two stripper poles permanently fixed in the middle of his living room and there's a full bar in his kitchen. If I took a trip down the hallway, I'm pretty sure I'd find more than a few occupied bedrooms.

It's chaos.

It's crazy.

It's Rome's life.

"Let's find a quiet room," the guy says to me, leaning in a little closer so I can feel his breath on my ear.

I should be tempted. After all, he's not a bad kisser so I'm sure he'd be all right in bed. But for some reason, he's just not doing it for me. Him or anyone else lately, it seems.

"Maybe in a little bit," I say, pushing off the wall and turning to walk away from him.

He grabs my wrist and tugs me against his chest. "Come on, don't be a tease."

I roll my shoulders back and tip my chin up to face him, clenching my hands in an attempt to stop myself from breaking this guy's nose.

"Let. Go. Of. My. Fucking. Hand," I say, narrowing my eyes, daring him to try anything.

He lets go and backs away slowly, scoffing as he turns. Fuck him, and guys like him. I'm allowed to change my mind at any given second and not have it held against me.

I walk over to where Rome and Noah are talking with a group of people. More than a few women are laughing at something they probably don't even find funny. They're simply hoping if they show the right kind of interest, they'll nail a member of Enemy Muse.

"Making friends?" Noah asks when I slide up beside him.

I look up at him, but he's not facing me. Instead, his eyes scan the room.

"Friends? No," I say with a shrug. "Why, jealous?"

His jaw clenches, and I know it's a bitch thing for me to say, but, like I tell him... I'm a mess.

"Jealous?" He laughs under his breath, even if I know he's not amused.

Shifting his body closer, he leans down so he's right inside my bubble where no one else can hear us.

"Jealousy is for guys playing the short game, Merry." His eyes lock on mine. "Do whatever the fuck helps you sleep at night. But make no mistake, once you do finally get over your shit and let down that fortress you've been building, I'll still be here, waiting for you to open your eyes and see me."

Noah turns and walks away, leaving me standing there feeling like he lit me on fire, and I'm stuck in the flames.

Meeting Rome's gaze across the circle of people, he cocks an eyebrow at me, looking kind of pissed at whatever he must assume just happened between me and Noah. As if he has any room to judge. But I guess I can't blame him. They're friends. And I'm the woman who has somehow managed to transform Noah's playful flirting into something that feels like an all-out war between us.

Rome takes a step toward me, but I turn away before he gets close. I know that by me staying at Noah's house, it's fucking with him. And I know right now I'm the worst person on the planet. I don't need Rome to remind me.

Winding through the crowd, I seek out the nearest booze.

The nice thing about partying with rock stars is that it's really easy to forget your problems when you want to. Whether it's through alcohol, drugs, or other people, you can basically take your pick. Tonight, my weapon of choice is vodka, and I'm going to drink until I drown in it.

Between the tension with Noah ever since he slept in my bed the other night, and my conversation with my doctor the next morning, I'm maxed out. No matter what my dreams are, my body has other plans, and I'll be lucky if I get through this demo before needing surgery.

Music blares through the house and people are getting wild. The dancing spills outside onto the grass, and the pool is filled. Some people are still wearing their clothes, while others have stripped down to nothing. I weave through the crowd, searching out Eloise, Adrian, Sebastian, or Cassie, but it doesn't look like any of them are here.

"Dance with me," someone says, tugging on my arm.

I look over my shoulder to see a chick with half black and half bleach-blonde hair grinning at me. Maybe that's what I need right now—especially after handsy guys have been pissing me off all night—a woman to make me feel good.

"All right."

Following her to the dance floor, she starts spinning circles around me, rubbing her hands all over. I move my hips, but that's about it. The vodka's hitting hard and if I'm not careful, I might fall on my face.

"What's your name?" she asks as her fingers run the length of my spine.

"Merry," I try to yell over the noise, but I'm not sure if she hears me.

She presses her chest against my back and wraps her hand up into my hair to pull it off my neck.

"I'm Celeste," she says, as our bodies grind to the music.

She feels good against me—soft and sweet. Like all the things that the random guy from earlier didn't.

I tip my head back and it rests next to hers against her shoulder. Our bodies sway and I try to lose myself in that feeling. The swishing, the spinning. Her hands moving up and down my body. Up my stomach and over my breasts.

But as much as I want it to feel good, it's like everything else lately—unsettling.

Like I'm reaching out but can't quite get there. My life moving farther away by the minute. My dreams might be coming true, but I'm facing a pit with its mouth wide open, and it's ready to swallow me whole.

The crowd parts, and although I still feel Celeste behind me, my attention moves to Noah sitting across the room. He's looking down so he doesn't notice me staring, and there's a dark, distant look in his eyes. Something working deep inside him as his jaw clenches.

He's seated at a table with a number of other people, and there's a woman happily propped behind him with her arms around his shoulders, not that he seems to notice.

But that's not what bothers me. It's something about his energy and his posture. The music slows and he swallows hard, his Adam's apple bobbing in his throat. And a chill runs from my neck to my toes.

Something is off.

Turning to Celeste, I give her a smile. "Thanks for the dance, but I've got to go check on something."

She nods and dances in a circle until she's latched onto someone else.

Spinning back around, the gap of people has closed, but I start pushing through in the direction I saw Noah only moments ago. The mass of bodies feels endless, a few grabbing at me as I walk past. But the sinking feeling in my gut urges me to continue, and when I finally get through them, I see him.

There are three other people seated at the table around Noah, not including the girl dangling on him like a desperate ornament. But he isn't looking at any of them, his eyes are fixed downward, where one of the guys is slowly working a razorblade through a pile of coke.

The razor slides through the white powder, pushing it into perfect lines. Noah's eyes focus on every drag and there's something dark playing in them I haven't seen since the night I met him.

As I take a step closer, he finally looks up, and his stare locks on mine.

I read everything I need to know in that look. Because as much as I like to lie and say he's like anyone else to me, the truth is, I know him better than anyone. There's the smile he wears as a shield, the laughs he uses to cover up how he really feels. And then there's this expression right here. Where he's physically present but inside he might as well be sinking.

Noah's pale blue eyes are darker than I've ever seen them, and even if I know Noah's sobriety is tested almost daily, this moment feels different.

He looks like he wants to give in.

"Noah," I say, and it earns me a glare from the redhead who's hanging on him.

He nods at me but doesn't say anything. His eyes dip as another line gets drawn on the table.

I reach my hand out to him. "Let's go home."

The woman who is trying to claim him now seems thoroughly annoyed, but she can fuck off and find another dick to ride tonight. I don't care about pissing her off if Noah is on some kind of ledge and there's a threat of him tipping.

"We were just getting the party started," some guy seated at the table says, grabbing onto my hand, which from the look in Noah's eyes, he doesn't appreciate.

At least the movement snaps Noah out of whatever was going on because he stands up and starts moving in my direction. Except, I'm already on it.

"Touch my hand again, and I'll make you regret it." I narrow my eyes at the guy.

He grins wide but drops my hand. "Feisty, I like it."

Leaning down slightly, I get in his face because it's been a long night, and I'm tired of dealing with men like him.

"I didn't ask if you liked it, asshole."

Noah reaches me, and I feel his fingers lace between mine. I take his hand before I'm tempted to hurt someone. It's another reminder of how Noah really is different from the rest of them. He's thoughtful, sweet, protective. He cares.

The guy grins and goes back to the coke.

"Let's go," Noah says, and I move to follow him.

Noah leads the way, weaving us through the crowd of people. We pass the guy who tried to get handsy with me earlier and I flip him off as we go by. More people are arriving as we make it outside, and only then does Noah let go of me.

He rakes his hands through his hair and pulls it back, stopping in front of me and tipping his face up to the sky.

"You okay?"

He shakes his head and laughs, but there's pain buried in the chuckle.

"No." The word nearly chokes in his throat. "It shouldn't be so fucking difficult."

He could be talking about resisting the drugs, or he could be talking about a whole mess of other things, but I don't ask him to clarify, because I can feel the energy radiating off him like the start of a nuclear explosion.

And all I can say is, "I'm sorry."

I'm sorry this is hard.

I'm sorry I'm not a better friend.

I'm sorry I can't give you what you want.

I'm sorry you're being swallowed whole, and I don't have it in me to save you.

Noah dips his chin and looks down at me, the darkness in his gaze replaced with something emptier, and much more terrifying.

"I know," he says, reaching out and taking my hand in his own.

If only my heart didn't skip when he did it.

15

MERRY

I EXPECTED NOAH'S CONSTANT tapping to annoy me after a while. His fingers and hands make a drumbeat on every surface, every minute of the day. It's like muscle memory from him playing the drums for so many years that his hands just can't help it.

Somehow, it's strangely calming.

His tapping fills the silence of the house, and I almost forget that we're in the middle of nowhere surrounded by nothing but trees.

Almost.

Noah sits on the couch opposite me playing a video game, tapping the back of the controller with his pinkies as he focuses. When he dies for what feels like the hundredth time in the last hour, he tips his head back and lets out an annoyed grunt.

"I don't get it," I say, setting my notebook in my lap.

Noah turns his head to face me wearing that blinding smile on his face. "Don't get what?"

"If the game makes you so frustrated, why do you play it?" I wave my hand at the television screen he's spent the last hour yelling at.

"Because." He shrugs. "I like it."

"Doesn't sound like it."

"That's because I'm losing." Noah lifts an eyebrow at me.

I level my gaze at him. "Yet you keep playing."

Noah sits up and swings his legs off the couch to sit facing me. "Like I've told you before, beautiful, the hardest-fought things are usually worth the wait."

Then he winks. He fucking winks. Of course, he has to go and make this about us.

I roll my eyes and hope it masks the cracks I feel in my armor every time he says something like that. I might be immune to Noah's rock star charms, but that doesn't make me entirely impenetrable by him, the man.

The man who won't give up. The man who makes me feel like the center of his universe. The man who wants me, whether he should or not.

"Funny." I brush him off.

But he just smirks and leans back against the couch cushions, reading me like a book he's looked over hundreds of times.

"You going to sing some of it for me?" His eyes drop to the notebook in my lap.

"Figured you didn't want to hear it. You haven't been back to the studio."

I'm not sure if Noah's been busy or avoiding it, but since he caught the tail end of my first recording session, he hasn't been back. Not that I should be complaining.

It's easier to focus when I'm not staring him in the face. Something about him hearing my lyrics stirs feelings I'm not ready to put a name to.

"The timing hasn't worked out," Noah says, but his expression doesn't sell what he's saying. "Come on, let's hear it."

I nod and stand up, walking over to the couch he's sitting on and dropping down onto the cushion near him. I lean against the arm and tuck my feet up to face him.

This man has the strangest effect on me, a draw that pulls me in. I could just as easily sing from across the room, but something about the distance feels even more exposed than if I can quietly mumble beside him.

"All right." I flip through the pages, trying to decide what song has the least amount of exposure. Something about Noah being in the room makes all of them seem vulnerable, but I aim for one that feels safe.

Noah stretches an arm along the couch, and it puts his hand dangerously close to my knee as he flexes his elbow.

I take a deep breath, realizing Noah is hyper-focused on me. "Why are you staring?"

"Nervous?" Noah grins, knowing I'd never admit to something so revealing, which means he's purposely challenging me.

"Never." I swat him with my notebook. "Your stupid grin is just distracting."

"I'm sure it is." He wiggles his eyebrows, and I let out an annoyed sigh.

"Just..." I stammer. "Don't stare."

"Fine."

Noah throws his hands up, palms out, in defeat. He tips his head back against the couch and closes his eyes to listen.

It's not that I have stage fright. But his eyes do something unfamiliar since I started staying in his house, and I'm not exploring that right now.

"This one is called Fairytale," I say.

I set my notebook on top of my crossed legs and smooth my fingers over the pages, sitting up tall and taking a deep breath.

"Take it all
They said they'd take it all away
Breathe it out
Even if your life starts to fade
Swim away with you
I'd love to... swim away
But in the breath that fades
I empty you
you... empty me
I empty you
you... empty me

I'd love to see what we can be
Search your heart for the piece of me
I'd love to bring us back to life
what's dead inside, what's dead inside
But
Rainbows don't reach pots of gold
And darkness is where stories are told

I'll sing for you, a lullaby
But you won't find your peace tonight

Take it all
They said they'd take it all away
Breathe it out
Even if your life starts to fade
Swim away with you
I'd love to... swim away
But in the breath that fades
I bury you
you... bury me
I bury you
you... bury me"

I breathe the final note out and realize my chest has been fluttering the entire time.

"I'm still ironing out the rest," I say, slapping my notebook shut and pulling my hair off my face. "But that's where I'm at."

Noah opens his eyes but doesn't lift his head as he tips his face to look at me. There's that same unreadable expression in his eyes from the morning at Adrian's recording studio, and it slices straight through my skin. For a man who's usually so easy to read, I can't figure out what he's hiding in that look.

"That was beautiful," Noah says.

He sits up and leans his elbows forward on his thighs, dipping his chin. When he turns to look at me again, he's smiling.

"That was…" He tucks his hair behind his ears and sits back again. "I loved it."

"Thanks, Noah." I feel my cheeks heating.

Why am I so nervous all of a sudden?

And what is this warm feeling?

I've spent almost a year around Noah, and up until now, I've felt nothing but calm and collected. But a few weeks of living in his house and he's turning everything inside me upside down.

"What's this?" Noah reaches for the clear crystal hanging from a string around my neck. His fingertips graze the exposed skin on my chest just slightly, and a gesture that wouldn't have affected me a few months ago now sends a trail of fire along my skin.

"Q-Quartz," I stammer, trying to gain my composure. I'm never flustered so I'm not sure what's happening.

It must be the close quarters getting to me. That's it.

"It's pretty." Noah examines the stone.

"It's supposed to be for growth and healing."

He hums, spinning the crystal between his fingers. But he doesn't ask me what I might be trying to heal, he just thinks it over.

"Have you always been into stuff like this?"

"I guess." I shrug. "My mom rubbing off on me."

Noah drops the crystal and my hand wraps around it. My mom gave me this necklace before my first surgery, and over the years I've always subconsciously worn it when I start not feeling well.

"She was always collecting stones and crystals and leaving them around the house or making jewelry with them," I say, and it hurts a little to remember with the distance between us lately. "Like the black tourmaline in the windowsill by the front door for a safe home. And her agate bracelet she'd wear anytime she was weighing some heavy decision. Then there's the jewelry she made for my sister and I, like this necklace."

"That's cool." Noah stares at my necklace. "Do you think it works?"

I spin the crystal in my palm once more. "Maybe. I'd like to think it does."

Just because I've had my fair share of health struggles growing up, doesn't mean I don't have any faith left. After all, the universe isn't there to fix your problems. You have to do that on your own, clinging to what you need to in order to make it happen. For me, it's this necklace.

"What about you?" I ask. "What do you believe in?"

Noah mentioned how religious his family is, and from the way he made it sound, they're pretty strict in their beliefs. But I've never heard Noah talk about it himself, and I'm honestly not sure if he believes in anything.

Noah stretches his arm along the back of the couch and turns to face me, bringing us much closer to each other. His free hand reaches out and traces the infinity knot I have tattooed on my shoulder.

"I don't know what to believe anymore," he admits.

"Because of your family?"

"Not exactly." He shakes his head. His eyes lift to mine and there's a familiar darkness in the pits of them. "I didn't go to rehab because of an OD."

Noah's statement is the first time he's brought up his rehab stay with me voluntarily, and now that he is, I have a bad feeling about it.

"Okay." I nod.

His eyes move back to my shoulder where he traces his finger from the tattoo along the vines on my collarbone and then back again.

"I mean, I guess technically, I did OD, but that's not really the point." His hand stops on my shoulder, and he squeezes it.

This is usually the moment where I'd push Noah's hand away and we'd share some playful banter about how it's never going to happen. But two things stop me. First, I sense something a lot like a storm brewing inside him. Second, I'm starting to doubt the way I feel under his touch because it feels good.

Too good.

"I wasn't supposed to wake up." Noah swallows hard, and I feel my insides tighten. "I didn't *want* to wake up. So, yes, although I did overdose, it wasn't exactly accidental."

"You..." I can't even get the words out because it hurts too much to think it, much less say it. Cotton fills my throat, and I feel my heart racing in my chest as I realize what he's confessing.

Noah tried to kill himself.

When I picked him up from rehab, I assumed he was just another rich, spoiled rock star snorting too much coke or smoking too much weed. I had no idea that what led him there was... *this.*

I think back to standing inside the tattoo parlor when he said the second ring on his forearm was to mark a big moment. At the time, I thought it was for his sobriety, which made sense, even if it was also a little hasty. But there was more to it, and it aches in my chest.

Reaching out for Noah's arm, I trace the tattooed ring on his forearm with my fingertips.

"A second life." He watches my fingers draw the line over his skin. "That's what the bands mean. Getting my record deal, getting sober. Both times, it was like one version of me died and a new one was born. And not in a bad way, but like a shedding of skin."

"I had no idea." I feel like the biggest bitch in the world for how I was toward him that day.

Noah shakes his head. "You wouldn't have. No one does, actually. Everyone in the band just thinks I OD'd, and that's how I left it. They were worried enough about me not being able to perform, I didn't need them thinking I'd off myself one day and they'd need another drummer."

"You're not just a drummer to them," I say, but it makes him flinch—in realization, in pain? "They're your friends. Your family."

"I already lost one family," Noah says with a cold look on his face. "Couldn't risk losing another."

My heart tightens in my chest thinking about how Noah has carried this around silently for almost a year now. He let everyone think all he was struggling with was a drug addiction when really, it was so much more.

And he trusted me enough to share this.

Me.

Merry.

Girl who shuts him out every chance she gets.

Girl who refuses to reveal her own secrets.

I open my mouth, and I think maybe this is it, I can tell him everything. If he's going to cut open his chest, then the least I can do is the same. But the doorbell ringing cuts me short.

Noah flinches at the sounds, and it shakes me out of my head.

"It's all right, I'll get it," I say, standing. But before I walk away, I pause in front of him and hold out my hand, which he takes.

"Thank you for sharing that with me." I squeeze his hand. "Just know I'm here for you. Always."

He nods tightly and forces the faintest smile. "Always."

The knot in my chest hasn't loosened as I make my way to the door. Instead, it's settled deeper. It's growing roots. It's planting itself inside me and spreading. And I know for certain, I won't be able to escape it.

Swinging open the front door, I find a woman standing on the doorstep. She's young, maybe a few years older than me, and pretty. She has shiny blonde hair and bright blue eyes that draw out the sweetness in her heart-shaped face. A schoolgirl Barbie with her buttoned-up blouse and pleated skirt. She looks a little like she might be selling bibles or something.

"Can I help you?"

She skims me from head to toe.

Maybe it's that I'm in all black. Maybe it's the excessive tattoos and piercings. But when her gaze lifts once more to meet mine, her doe eyes look a little terrified all of a sudden.

"I—" she starts but stops when her eyes fall on movement behind me. "Noah."

"Noah?" I'm not sure why I'm saying his name like a question. It's his house, why else did I think she was at the door.

But when I look over my shoulder and see Noah standing behind me, the look on his face catches me off guard. The pale expression, the wide eyes. The slack jaw as he takes in a sharp breath.

He's in shock, but that's not what's drawing my attention. It's a sparkle in his eyes. Something familiar as he stares at the prissy blonde chick. And I realize I've only ever seen him look at one other woman that way.

Me.

16

NOAH

When you purge your sins, you're supposed to feel some kind of relief. Not that it's promised. I guess I just assumed.

I spent enough time in confession as a kid to know that no matter what dumb shit came out, you'd feel better once the truth was set free. What was done, was confessed.

As an adult, I thought it would work the same.

I sat on the couch across from Merry and told her all the shit I've been holding back from her and everyone else for the past year. There should have been church bells ringing, a choir singing. I had been cleansed. I had been purged.

The truth was out.

The worst was over.

Instead, the devil had other plans. Because not even five minutes after baring my blackened soul to Merry, there she was, standing on my fucking doorstep with a fake halo hanging over her bright blonde head of hair.

"Kali," I say, not sure how I don't choke on her name.

It's been a long time since I've said it. Even longer since I've seen her. And her showing up can mean only one thing—the past is catching the fuck up and it wants to take my present with it.

I'm not even sure how Kali knows where I live. It's been four years since I've spoken to her. And in the few trips I've made back home to Fairfield, California, I've made sure to avoid her entirely.

My parents have my address, but they've never visited. That would require them to admit they haven't disowned me, and I don't see that happening.

Merry looks confused, and I don't blame her. If only she knew what the sight of the two of them standing side by side does to me.

Kali looks like an angel on the outside. Her hair is so white blonde it almost glows. The apples of her cheeks are rosy, and her bright blue eyes are bursting with energy. Merry, on the other hand, might as well be the darkness. Wild wavy hair, nearly black eyes, skin slowly being eaten up by black and gray tattoos. To anyone looking in, they'd see a yin and yang. A good and evil. Only, their assumptions about who is what would be wrong.

Maybe an alternate universe just opened its mouth and swallowed me down.

"Kali?" Merry repeats her name like a question, with a furrow of her eyebrows, before her eyes widen as realization hits. "Oh, Kali."

As if I'm not lost enough in this moment, Merry looks like she was just hit by a bus. And it isn't necessarily shock that stains her face. It's hurt... maybe.

Merry isn't the kind of girl who lets people see that she's been affected, so I'm still learning those expressions on her. All I know is that her cheeks flush and her fingernails are digging into her palms. I feel her clenching in and closing off, and I'm desperate to stop it.

She was finally opening up. We were sitting in my living room, and she sang her beautiful song that shot straight to the darkest pits of my bones. We were talking, confessing, getting closer.

For as long as Merry has held back, her guard was finally down. She was right on the edge of sharing parts of her I've been waiting for. I could feel it.

And then the doorbell rang.

The fucking doorbell.

Fucking Kali.

If it weren't for Merry's eyes holding in my last bit of sanity, I'd go swallow a bottle of pills right now and pray for oblivion.

"What do you want?" I turn to Kali. Harsh, but I don't really care. I might be the most carefree motherfucker on the planet, but Kali Matkowski brings out my absolute worst.

Kali's face falls, but I don't feel the least bit bad about it. If she showed up here expecting the fourteen-year-old boy who chased her around and begged her to date him, then she came to the wrong place.

That boy was gutted like a fish—by her.

I'm done with our childhood games.

"Give us a minute," Merry says, closing the door in Kali's face, which would make me laugh if I was capable of feeling any kind of amusement right now.

It might be a small gesture, but it's protective coming from Merry. And her leaving Kali outside as she turns to face me, makes me fall for her just a little bit more in this moment.

"Noah." Her back is to the door and she's bracing herself against it, like whatever's on the other side might find its way through. "Are you okay?"

"No." There's no use lying. Merry would see straight through it, especially since I'm not hiding my disdain.

"Do you want me to ask her to leave?"

She's chewing the inside of her cheek, which means it's one of those rare moments she's uncertain, and I hate that Kali is the reason.

I rake my hair away from my face. "Why is she even here?"

"I don't know."

"What could she possibly want?"

"You'd have to ask her."

"How did she even find me?"

Merry steps forward and grabs my arms with her hands, stopping me in place. I didn't realize I was pacing, but I'm nervous and dizzy.

"How long has it been since you've seen her?" Merry asks.

"Four years."

Merry thinks that over, and I'm sure it's the same thoughts that are going through my head. There's no reason for an ex-girlfriend to show up on your doorstep four years later unless she plans on planting a few more grenades and stepping back to watch the explosion.

"That's a long time." Merry steps in. "What do you want to do here?"

There's only a foot-wide gap between our bodies. She's looking up at me and it makes me want to wrap her in my arms.

Not because she's beautiful—even though she is.

And not because I'm comfortable around her—which I definitely am.

It's that Merry feels like home, like the only place I'm actually accepted as Noah Hayes, the man, not the rock star. She sees into the pits inside myself I've almost forgotten exist because I burned the bridges there years ago.

It doesn't matter if I'm fucking other women while I wait around for her to fall in love with me, or if I'm holding her in my arms fully clothed in bed while she waits for the pain to fade. Merry is unwavering in a way I've never experienced from another person before.

My parents saw a deviant, my church saw a sinner, my ex saw an illusion. But Merry has always seen *me* for exactly who I am and never tried to make me be anything more or less.

It's why I told her the truth today. I want her to have it all. I want her to know *all of it*. And I want to see her face when all is said and done because I honestly trust her to not look at me any differently.

I reach up and brush her dark waves away from her face, not missing that her cherry-red lips part with the sharpest inhale as my fingers graze her cheek.

"Can we rewind to ten minutes ago when we were sitting on the couch, and you were singing to me?" I ask her with a sigh.

If I had to label a perfect moment, that would probably be it.

In the beginning, I used to think I had a real shot at being with Merry, but she turned me down so many times I kind of gave up hope. I was chasing her just to be pushed away. But when we were sitting there talking, it didn't feel like the same game of tug-of-war we've been playing. It wasn't resistance. She let her shield down and was finally letting me in.

Merry's eyebrows crinkle and I almost think she feels it. Like for once the sensation beneath my ribs isn't one sided.

"I'm sorry," Merry says, not actually answering my question. She plants her hand on my chest and my heart beats harder just to feel some comfort.

"What should I do?"

Her expression pinches. "You want my honest opinion?"

"Always," I say, and it makes her smile, which actually has the power to make me smile in this moment.

"Talk. To. Her." She pats my chest with each word. "I get the vibe it might not be pleasant—"

"How'd you come to that conclusion? It wasn't my murderous stare, was it?"

"Something like that." She laughs deep, and it sounds almost genuine, even if I know this has got to be one hell of an uncomfortable moment for her. "But it's been four years. Who knows, maybe she just wants some closure. Either way, I get the feeling you might still have some things to get off your chest. And do you really want to keep carrying them around with you?"

I shake my head.

"Good," she says. She's drawing on her strong side right now, which I appreciate because it's holding me together. At the same time, I kind of want to see her break down and tell me how she *feels*, not just how she thinks. "In the meantime, Cassie said everyone is getting together for a couple of drinks at Sebastian's house, so I'm going to head there and give you some space."

"You don't have to go."

Honestly, the idea of Merry walking out my front door and Kali stepping in sends my brain into a black hole. But I also get it if she doesn't feel like sticking around for a not-so-pleasant reunion between my ex-girlfriend and me.

"You've got this, Noah Hayes." Merry nudges me on the shoulder and it pushes me back a step. "I think it's better if I clear out, anyway. I don't want to make things more awkward. Besides, you'll be fine."

"As long as you believe in me, Mercedes Lopez." She rolls her eyes like she does every time I use her full name.

It's probably a little twisted how much I love her annoyed responses to me, but I can't help it.

"So, you'll be at Sebastian's?" I reach out for her hands and squeeze them in my own.

Merry nods.

"All right, I'll meet you there when I'm finished."

"Or..." Her gaze trails to the closed door behind her. "Let me know if I need to crash over there for the night. I'm sure he and Cassie wouldn't mind."

I tug her arms, and it forces her to take a step toward me, bringing us almost chest to chest. Her chin has to tip up to look me in the face, and I'm so close to her lips I can almost taste her cherry Chapstick.

"I said, I'll meet you there when I'm finished." My tone is firmer this time.

We started something on the couch before Kali showed up and shot it all to hell, but I damn well intend on finishing it.

"Okay," Merry says, pressing her lips tightly together.

I'd like to think it's because she doesn't trust herself not to kiss me, but I know better.

With a deep inhale, Merry takes a step back, and I realize that the chaos I felt in my chest when Kali first showed up at the door, has all but dissipated. Merry might be the embodiment of upheaval when it comes to my emotions, but right here, right now, she settled my feet back on the ground.

"Besides, if she gives you any trouble, just give me the word." Merry grins. "You know I have no problem decking a chick in the face."

"I'm well aware." I laugh, remembering the many fights I've had to pull Merry out of before she ended up with a black eye, or worse.

"You can do this, Noah," she says with a half smile, as she reaches for the doorknob and opens the door.

But as much as I want to believe her, the moment Kali's face comes back into view, I'm really not so sure.

17

Noah

Merry must leave because I hear her boots moving down the hallway before the front door opens and closes. And all I want to do is go after her instead of sitting across from Kali at the table.

"I need some air," I say, walking outside, but Kali just follows me. The slider opens and closes, and when I turn, she's standing there.

I wish I could say she doesn't look almost exactly the same as she did four years ago, but that would be a lie. She looks like pure innocence. The kind of purity that teenage Noah couldn't wait to get a bite of. And back then it wasn't because I wanted to corrupt her. I genuinely thought that a girl like Kali was what I needed. Because even then, the dark thoughts were already swirling, and I wanted to be lost in her goodness.

I never fit into the cookie-cutter life my parents laid out for me. I was the square peg trying to fit into a round hole, and the more they shoved, all it did was chip away at the pieces.

Growing up, nothing felt right—not until I met Kali.

She had a sweet smile, and she tasted like candy. Probably because she was always sucking on lollipops. She made me wait six months before she'd kissed me, and even then, it was chaste and barely a brush of the lips. Eventually, it turned into a little more and a little more, until, by eighteen her lips were wrapped around my dick pretty frequently. But she was a good girl, or so she said. She was saving herself for marriage.

And like the idiot I was, I loved her enough to wait.

Eight. Fucking. Years.

I started recording my first album still a virgin, wearing a stupid promise ring because I honestly thought it would all be worth it. After all, I had the girl. The angel had chosen me, and I wasn't going to give that up.

So, I waited for her—as long as it was going to take. While most guys went for the easy point to score, I've always understood the long game and wasn't afraid to play it.

That is, until Kali broke up with me because she fucked one of my friends. Laid on her back and handed him her fucking virginity. And if that wasn't bad enough, I honestly don't know if she would have even told me if she hadn't gotten pregnant.

She probably would have let me fuck her on our wedding night with the illusion in my head that we were both giving ourselves to each other for the first time.

But it wasn't the waiting that bothered me. It wasn't the sex part that broke my heart. I've more than made up for my years of celibacy in the four years since. It was the fact that I wanted Kali to be my forever, and I would have done anything for her, but she couldn't care less.

Kali lied, while I waited. And, well…

Fuck. Her.

But now here she is, four years later, standing in my backyard looking like the same angel she always masquerades around as. Only now, I've been well acquainted with the devil underneath.

"What do you want?" I sit on one of the lawn chairs and stare her straight in the face.

It's a tactic I've learned from Merry, who refuses to back down when shit is bothering her. She looks it dead on, daring it to do its worst.

Looking into Kali's eyes, the worst already feels like it's here anyway.

"How are you?" Kali asks, sitting in a chair opposite me, and it makes me laugh really fucking hard because that's the first full sentence out of her mouth.

What a joke.

"Fan-fucking-tastic," I tell her, and she winces. I'm not sure she's ever used a profanity in her life, and she's definitely never seen this side of me before.

"You seem different."

I shake my head. "It's been four years, Kal, what did you expect?"

Kali's shoulders sink, and I think for the first time the weight is settling in.

"I don't… I'm not sure," she admits. "Was that your girlfriend?"

Her eyes look back to the house, and I realize she's talking about Merry. It would make sense, after all. She answered my door. She's living here—for the time being.

"It's complicated," I say, for a lot of reasons. I'm not ready to admit what it is or isn't with Merry. But I'm also not prepared to deal with Kali without some kind of barrier between us.

"It's none of your business anyway."

"Complicated," she repeats, but it sounds a little like she's mocking me, and I don't like it.

I was in love with this girl once, wasn't I?

I pictured this day many times after Kali broke me, thinking if I ever came face to face with her again I would second guess myself. Wondering if I'd wish things could have been different. But sitting here in my backyard on this warm, sunny day, I feel nothing.

Or maybe I feel another life. One on the other side of a pile of coke and a death wish. One that stopped whispering after I met a certain dark goddess.

"She's just not what I would picture," Kali says, and it's definitely a jab this time.

I lean forward slightly. "Why? Because you're used to seeing me with people who use their looks to hide who they really are, and she's not afraid to show the truth?"

Kali straightens up, clearly offended, running her fingers over the buttons on her blouse.

Who wears a blouse in the middle of the week anyway?

A white one at that. It's all so pure and innocent—and fake.

"Ben and I are taking some time apart," she says.

"Wonderful." The name of my former best friend on her tongue doesn't sit well with me.

Isn't this the kind of shit you update your real friends with? I don't even follow her on social media, so I'm not sure why she thinks I care.

"Mia isn't taking it well," she says, and it hits my one soft spot. Although I might hate Kali for being a lying bitch, and Ben for being a shit friend, it's not their daughter's fault she was the result of it.

I've only met Mia once, when she was one month old. Back when I was still in denial and trying to keep together whatever it was that was already fractured in front of us. And she was a sweet baby from what I could tell. But she was also proof that Kali didn't give a shit about me. At least, not enough to be faithful.

I like to consider myself a guy who will put up with a lot of shit. From women. From the band. I'm pretty easy going in most settings. But infidelity is black and white, no fucking way in my book. End of story.

When I'm in a relationship, I'm yours and you're mine. I'm committed, one hundred percent. Even if my friends call me a pussy because of it. I don't fuck around on people I care about.

And because of this, the guys in the band have given me a lot of shit over how I'm still chasing Merry. But that's only because they don't get it. Wanting a woman and having one are two different things. She's single and she can do as she pleases, same as me. But if she's ever mine—that's it.

"I'm sorry about Mia." I mean it for Mia's sake. After all, Mia has Kali and Ben as parents, so I really do sympathize.

She nods and a sincere look crosses her face, which makes me realize I've been a dick since she showed up on my doorstep. As much as she brings out the worst in me, it's not who I am, and for the first time since she stepped inside, I feel bad about that.

It's been four years. I shouldn't be giving her the power to get under my skin.

"Thank you." Kali sits up a little taller.

She's pressing her lips between her teeth and it's an odd thing to see because I know it means she's nervous.

You can forget a lot about a person over the years—the exact shade of their eyes, how their body feels against yours. But certain things stick with you whether you like it or not. Like Kali's ticks and twitches when she's uncomfortable, or the octave of her laugh when she's nervous or happy or excited.

Things you wish you could bury, but no matter how far down you put them, they're just waiting for the right moment to come out.

"How did you find me?" I ask her.

"Your mom."

I chuckle, but only because she acts like it's no big deal, when in fact, my parents have never bothered to visit.

"Okay, well can I help you with something? I'm still not sure why you showed up."

Kali's sitting quietly, twisting her fingers in her lap. Clearly some things never change, because I've always had to be the one to drag things out of her.

"I miss you, Noah," she says, looking up at me with tears brimming in her eyes. And even if she doesn't mean the same thing to me anymore, it still gets me to see her in pain, which pisses me off a little.

The woman can take a woodchipper to my heart, and still, it kills me when she cries.

I lean back in my chair and pull my hair back. "I'm not sure what you want me to say to that, Kal."

"I was an idiot." She stands now, walking toward me. She sits in the chair right next to mine and gets so close her knees brush mine.

It's a lot for my body to process. This is the girl who was supposed to be my wife, the girl I was supposed to give my virginity to. And this close, she still manages to send those teenage shockwaves through my system.

"I was pregnant and scared." Kali reaches out and places a hand on my knee. "Being with Ben was a huge mistake, but the damage was done, and I was having his baby, so I thought it was the right thing to do."

She shakes her head, and the curtain of blonde hair catches in the sun.

"It was always supposed to be you and me, Noah." Kali squeezes my knee, and it stirs a lot of unwelcome feelings. "I never wanted to give that up. I *shouldn't* have ever given that up. But it's not too late, we can fix this."

"It's been four years."

"I know."

"You had a kid with someone else." I pause to catch my breath. "When we were together."

"I know, and I can't change that."

I stand up to get a bit of distance. "I'm not asking you to change it. What's done is done."

More is done than she even realizes. That pit of darkness I felt as a child widened when Kali cheated. Inside, I started to become the person I always feared I would be. I filled that fear with anything I could get my hands on. Alcohol, drugs, women. It was an endless void asking to be filled, and when I couldn't handle it anymore, I got tired of trying.

That would have been the end of it if Adrian hadn't found me half dead on the floor of my hotel room.

"I want to give us another try, Noah. I know it's not that simple and it will take time, but I'm not over us." Kali is almost pleading. "I've talked to your mom—"

"Wait." I hold up my hand. "What do you mean you talked to my mom?"

I don't even talk to her, so I'm not sure what the two of them could have to say about me.

"My family still sits by yours at church every week. I see her all the time," Kali says with a pinched expression like I should already be aware of this.

"How cute," I scoff.

She ignores it. "Things didn't work out back then, but maybe that's because it wasn't the right time. We've matured. Grown. We could be good together now."

"We couldn't," I assure her.

"Why?"

"You don't even know me anymore, Kali." I'm trying really hard not to yell. "Wherever you think we'd be picking back up from doesn't exist. In case you haven't noticed,

I'm not that guy anymore. I haven't even been home in a couple of years. My parents don't speak to me. And then there's the band you spent so much time complaining about. In case you forgot, I'm still in it. We're about to go on another tour."

"I can wait," she says with some kind of hope in her eyes that is misplaced. "I know I wasn't understanding about the band back then, but I get it now. I'm willing to make it work for us."

"You're not hearing me. This won't work."

"But why?" she says firmer.

And this time I do yell. "Because I'm in love with someone else."

And there it is—the truth.

Even if I was still that guy she thinks I am. Even if I could forgive. Even if I could forget. None of it matters.

I'm in love with Merry, and I'm stupidly thankful Kali showed up because all she does is confirm what I already knew.

Nothing will change that.

18

Merry

Cassie's eyes are bugging out of her head as she stares at me. She cornered me in the doorway before I had a chance to set down my purse.

"Did I just hear you right?" She shakes her head like it gives her the power to change reality.

"Unless my brain has everything coming out in Spanish, yep." I step around her and toss my purse onto the nearest piece of furniture.

"Noah's ex is at his house right now?" She looks a little pale in the face, and I wonder if that's supposed to be my reaction. But then again, I don't react to things as intensely as Cassie, so it shouldn't surprise me.

I pat her on the shoulder. "You heard me right."

"What?" Cassie shakes her head again, making more pink tendrils come loose from the messy bun on her head. "How? Why?"

I shrug. "Beats me."

She follows behind me as I head toward the voices coming from the living room, really wishing I could get out of this conversation, even though I know that won't happen.

It's not that I'm unaffected by the fact that Kali showed up, there's just no point stressing out about it.

This is between Noah and Kali.

Which, come to think of it, does give me a little tug somewhere deep inside. Not because I *like* Noah or am jealous or anything—that would be crazy. But it was something about the look she brought to his eyes. In the span of ten minutes, he went from calm to spiraling. And I don't like thinking about what that means for him now that he's alone with her in his house.

Alone.

Why does that echo somewhere foreign in my chest?

It's his ex.

He's over her, right?

"And you're just fine with it?" Cassie asks again, not letting this shit go.

We round the corner, and I spot the whole band sitting in Sebastian's den. Eloise and Adrian are on one couch, and I wonder if we're ever going to meet his elusive girlfriend. Rome is in a chair with his feet kicked up on the table and he's smoking a joint. Then, there's Sebastian, sitting up taller as he watches Cassie enter.

"Fine with what?" he asks.

Sebastian grabs Cassie's waist, pulling her onto his lap. She squeals but then pushes him off so she can answer his question.

"Noah's ex is at his house right now," she says.

"Who? Kali?" Rome exhales a cloud of smoke.

"That's the one." I point a finger at him.

Rome leans his head back and starts laughing.

"And you met her?" Eloise asks, with a really strange, unreadable pinch between her eyebrows.

I nod. "I answered the door."

"What did you think of the bitch?" Rome chuckles.

Eloise throws a pillow at him. "Stop using that word."

"What, she is."

Eloise crosses her arms over her chest and glares at him. Rome can use the most vulgar language on the planet, and she won't bat an eyelash, but say something offensive about women, you better believe she'll speak up.

"Well, I guess he's not joining us," Rome says.

I almost argue that Noah said he is, and he'll be over once he's done talking to her, but for some reason, I feel suddenly unsure about that, so I keep quiet.

Why was Kali at his house anyway? What could she possibly want after not reaching out for four years? If I had to guess from the look in her eyes, it wasn't an innocent visit. And that shouldn't bother me—but deep down it does.

What if Noah isn't done with Kali? What if he's only been chasing me as a replacement for unrequited feelings for an ex-girlfriend? If she wants him back, would he want to try and make it work?

That's what you wanted, isn't it?

Kali seems like the kind of girl made for a guy like Noah. Sweet, flowery, perfect. She's everything he's probably ever wanted—besides the fact that she cheated on him.

The thought makes me want to punch her in the throat.

But maybe she's changed. She seems like a girl who would pop out lots of babies for him. I can picture her barefoot in a kitchen catering to his every need between tours. That's what he wants, right? And I want that for him. It's the same reason I've shut him down all these months. Because what he needs is very different from what I can give him.

What Kali can give him.

Where does that leave me?

I could come crash with Sebastian. Cassie is headed back to Seattle to pack up more of her things and put them in storage before she joins everyone on the next tour. Staying at his place for the rest of the time wouldn't be so bad. I'd keep to myself, give Sebastian his space. Give Noah room to figure things out.

If Noah is still in love with Kali, I have no choice but to just let that happen. It's not like I have rights to him after I've spent the past seven months telling him to get over me.

My stomach spins, and I don't like the unwelcome feeling flooding in.

"Someone's got a lot on her mind." Cassie drops down beside me on the couch.

I'm not sure how long I've been spacing out, but the band has moved the conversation from Noah's dating life to Rome's, and they're all giving him shit about some stripper he acted like an idiot in front of.

"It's just been a long day."

"Mm-hmm," Cassie hums.

"I'm allowed to be worried about him. He's my friend." I'm not sure what's making me defensive, but I can't help it.

"Of course you're allowed to worry about him," Cassie says, nudging my shoulder. "How was she?"

"Kali?" I laugh. "She showed up looking like Malibu fucking Barbie with a smug grin. She's ridiculous, but I guess if that's what he's into, who am I to judge? But I don't like what him being around her does to him. She acts like it's nothing to show up on his doorstep. But I saw it, he's a mess."

Cassie is nodding at me with the slightest tick of a devious smile on her face.

"No." I shake my head. "Just—no to whatever you're thinking."

"I'm not thinking anything." She raises her hands in defense.

Sebastian slides up behind her on his way to the kitchen and leans over. "Don't let her lie to you. You know exactly what she's thinking."

He lifts an eyebrow, and I really don't like everyone's intensified interest in my relationship with Noah.

Not that it's a *relationship* relationship.

It's a friendship.

We're friends.

"I'm getting a drink." I stand up and follow Sebastian. This group is going to give me a drinking problem if they keep this up.

Cassie follows me and pulls out a bottle of wine from the fridge, while Sebastian grabs water. He's newer to sobriety than Noah is, but it seems to be going well.

When I first met Sebastian, I wasn't sure he had been clean a day in his life. He was the walking embodiment of a drunken, drugged-up rock star mess. Seeing him sober looks good on him.

"Here," Cassie hands me a full glass. "Eloise brought it over."

"That's a generous pour." I lift the wine glass to see it's filled two-thirds of the way.

"Less back and forth." She winks at me, and I laugh.

Cassie might be loosening up now that she's spent some time touring with the band, but she still has this totally sweet, good-girl vibe about her. Which Sebastian seems to eat up because I have to turn away to avoid watching him grope her ass.

As I make my way back into the den, I see everyone standing.

"You're remembering that wrong," Eloise says with her hands on her hips.

"Oh yeah?" Rome inches toward her.

At first, I think I walked into the middle of an argument, but then a smile climbs Rome's cheeks and he stops right in front of her.

"Then let's have a rematch."

Eloise grins. "I guess if you feel like losing again, who am I to deny you."

Adrian seems amused by Eloise standing up to Rome, but Rome just laughs.

"After you, princess," Rome says, waving a hand.

"What's going on?" I ask Adrian as we follow them.

He looks down at me and smiles. "You'll see."

We all make our way to the basement, where Sebastian has a bachelor pad setup that reminds me of Rome's entire house. There's a pool table, recliners. There's even a full bar, although it looks like it hasn't been stocked in a while. And in the far corner, there's a dart board, which Eloise and Rome are currently walking over to.

"Oh no."

"Oh yes." Adrian sits in one of the chairs facing the dart board.

Eloise and Rome are both pretty competitive people. But I've never seen either of them get as fired up as they do when they're playing darts. I'm pretty sure the band is still kicked out of a few bars across the country because of it, and people don't ban the members of Enemy Muse easily.

"Are you sure this is a good idea?" I say to Adrian, taking the seat beside him.

He shakes his head. "I'm not getting in the middle of it."

Watching Adrian around the band is an interesting dynamic. He's only a few years older than the rest of them, but his maturity is light-years ahead. He's the one always stuck talking them out of stupid shit or bitching at them when they've fucked up. If they were all a big fucked up family, he'd be the head of it, keeping the rest in check.

But what I find most surprising is that he doesn't seem to do it for the paycheck like most band managers.

There's a lot more there. He's one of them. He's part of the family.

"Oh Lord." Cassie rolls her eyes as she walks up. Sebastian leans against the wall, making a place for her in his arms.

"Heads or tails, princess," Rome asks Eloise with a quarter in his hand.

He flips it in the air, and she calls tails before he catches it.

"You're up." He grins at her when he looks down at the coin.

An amused grin crosses Eloise's face. Even in leggings and a baggy T-shirt, she's intimidating when she gets a certain look in her eyes, and as she squares off with Rome, I swear she gets taller in an effort to stand up to him. She grabs the bottom of her baggy shirt and ties it in a tight knot, which shows off a sliver of her stomach.

From the corner of my eye, I see Adrian doesn't miss the hint of her skin.

Eloise grabs three darts and lines herself up.

"Hope you brought your wallet," she teases.

The first dart hits near the bullseye, but not quite. The second is a little farther off. But the third hits dead center.

I'm not sure what the scoring system is, but she shoots Rome a smug grin that says she's happy.

"Your turn, Romeo."

Rome rolls his eyes, switching spots with her.

He throws his three darts, and from his proud reaction, he must have done better than her. I really have no idea what I'm watching.

"You'll be in the studio tomorrow night, right?" Adrian turns to me.

"Yep, seven?" I drink a large gulp of wine.

"That works," Adrian says, then his eyes fall over my shoulder. "Hey Noah."

Noah?

I turn my head to see Noah standing a few feet behind my chair, and the whole room falls quiet. Either that or I'm just not hearing them, because things are suddenly feeling a little fuzzy. It might be the wine, or it might be that look in Noah's eyes, but the air is static.

He's here.

"Hey, Adrian," he says, but his eyes are on me.

Focused, determined. And they're saying a whole lot of shit my brain has been revolting against since the day I met him.

19

Noah

My conversation with Kali got awkward fast after I blurted out my feelings for Merry. But at least it had the effect of a bucket of ice water because it woke us both up.

When she finally processed my confession, there was the faintest amount of sadness in her eyes. That is, until she got flustered and suddenly had a lot to say. Although, most of it was a blur because all I wanted to do was get out of there and head to Sebastian's house, knowing that's where Merry was.

I'm not looking forward to the texts I bet I'll receive from Mom over this. Knowing Kali is close with her makes it even more awkward. And just because Mom doesn't speak to me, it doesn't stop her from occasionally reaching out to pass her judgment via text.

"Noah, man," Rome walks up to me and slaps me on the shoulder. "I hear you've got pussy problems."

I have to remind myself I love the guy sometimes, and that he uses this as a barrier for whatever the fuck he's got going on. But the guy is flat-out crude and even I cringe.

"This is why I keep telling you to stop getting all whipped. Fuck 'em and leave 'em," he says, shaking my shoulder. And that's what finally breaks the stare I've had locked on Merry since walking in.

"What the fuck are you even talking about?" I ask him.

He just grins and shoves my shoulder a little before wandering back toward where he appears to be dominating the dartboard.

Sebastian tips his chin at me when our eyes connect, and Cassie is looking me up and down like there are a lot of thoughts going through that blonde and pink head of hers.

I ignore all of them and walk straight up to Merry, who is perched in a chair next to Adrian.

"You hate wine," I say, and she looks from her glass to me, like she's confused by it.

"It's fine." She takes another sip, but her mouth puckers at the taste. "How did it go?"

"Fine." I push my hair back off my face, feeling like I'm crawling out of my skin all of a sudden. All eyes are on me, so Merry definitely told them where I was. "Can we talk?"

Merry's eyes widen in surprise at the question because we both know where this goes—in the circle her and I have been going in for the past seven months. But I'm not looking for another rejection right now, I just need her to stop being so fucking stubborn and listen.

Her cheeks are flushed, and it might be the wine, but there's also a nervous energy radiating from her that's rare, and I take it as an opening.

"Sure." She scans the room until her eyes land on Cassie, and they have some kind of unspoken conversation.

Merry stands up and sets the wine glass down on a table to follow me. The band is dead silent, and I know they're all thinking a lot of different things, but luckily, they don't say any of them.

Not even Rome.

When Merry and I finally make it upstairs, I pause in the hallway that leads to the main corridor of the house and turn to face her.

"What's up?" She tucks her hands in her pockets in a line of defense.

It makes me smile, even though I'm not really in the mood because it's classic Merry—already finding ways to close herself off before we even start talking.

"I talked to Kali." I lean against the wall opposite her when she does the same.

"What did she want?" Merry asks, eyes darting away.

And *that* question from her is what I was hoping for. Because if she didn't actually care, she'd just brush it off and start talking about something else. But the fact that she's wondering means it's bugging her, whether she'll admit it or not.

"She wanted to get back together," I say flatly, crossing my arms over my chest and trying to read her reaction.

It's slight, but her cheeks warm and I spot the cracks in her façade.

"Okay…" Merry draws the word out like she's really thinking it over.

I lift off the wall and it drags her attention back to me. "What do you think of that?"

"What do you mean, what do I think?" She shakes her head and lets out a nervous little laugh that is so unlike her I can't help but love the sound.

"I mean exactly what I said." I take one step toward her. "What do you think of the fact that my ex-girlfriend wants to work things out with me?"

Merry shakes her head again, crossing her arms over her chest this time and tipping her head back. "It's your life Noah, you're allowed to date anyone you want. I don't even know why you're asking me this."

I walk straight up to her and plant a hand on the wall behind her, which forces her eyes back to me.

"You know *exactly* why I'm asking you this."

The forced smile slowly falls from Merry's face and we're standing so close at this point that if she inhales too deeply, we'll be chest to chest.

I've been patient with her.

I've waited for her to get over her shit.

I've watched the way she looks at me sometimes when she doesn't realize I'm watching, and I didn't push it.

She's scared. She wouldn't be who she is if she wasn't. But right now, I need her to get past that limit and I need her to just tell me the truth.

Yes or no.

Stop or go.

I need her to drop the crap and face this with me.

I spent the afternoon with Kali ripping off the Band-Aid. And as painful as it was, after she walked out the door, I finally felt free. And now I need Merry to do the same. I need her to meet me halfway with no bullshit.

"Noah," she says my name the way she has a hundred times. Half a sigh, half a threat.

But she doesn't roll her eyes this time, instead they stay trained on me. And they're lit the fuck up.

"How do you feel about it?" I ask her again, not letting her get out of answering this question. Knowing it's the answer to everything.

"If you feel good about it, then I feel good about it," she says.

I shake my head. "That's not what I asked. I know how I feel already. I told her no."

Merry's posture relaxes the slightest at that, and it pushes me forward.

"My ex showed up today, Merry." I inch closer. "And not just a fuck buddy ex. This was the woman I spent eight years of my life with thinking she was it. She showed up and she wanted to work it out. But I said no to her. And do you know why it wasn't even a fucking question in my head to try again?"

Merry shakes her head, but I grip her chin between my thumb and forefinger to stop her, because it's a lie and she knows it.

"You," I say. Straight up, no avoiding it.

Her lips part and the smallest breath escapes.

"I'm not dancing around this subject with you anymore." I trace her chin with my thumb. "You're it for me, do you realize that? So, I need you to cut the shit right now and skip the excuses, and just tell me, for my own sake, do you want more with me or not? Because you know I do."

Merry swallows hard and her eyes get a little glassy.

"I can't," she says, but it's not a no, and she has to look away right after she says it.

She forgets I know her too well. Because while she has spent all these months pushing me away, I've spent them learning everything there is to know about her and taking everything I could get.

"Yeah, I know you *can't*." I rest my other hand on the wall beside her head so she's caged between my arms. Sometimes it feels like it's the only way to keep her in one place, even if I'm risking her fighting her way out.

"You never can," I say. "And I really don't want to hear whatever your reason for that is today because once again, that's not the fucking question. I'm asking you what do you *want*?"

Merry pulls her lips between her teeth and she's radiating nervous energy. I've called her on her shit, and hopefully this time, she sees I'm not backing down.

"I'm tired of these games." I shake my head. "I'm tired of what you think you can and can't do—which, for the record, is bullshit—because you do whatever you want in any other situation. I just want you to be honest with me and yourself for once. Because I'll wait forever and make a fool out of myself, but I'd rather you just put me out of my misery."

Merry takes in a sharp breath and holds it. Her eyes work me over.

"No bullshit. No defenses. No excuses. Just answer the question, Mercedes. Do. You. Want. This?"

I'm not sure if I'm actually coming apart as the words leave my mouth, but it sure as fuck feels like it.

I'm well aware this makes me pathetic. I have my choice of women, and I could find someone willing to give me whatever I want in a heartbeat. But I really don't care. Because I'd rather beg for the one standing in front of me than have anyone else.

Merry's eyes drift down, and I think this is it.

She's slipping away.

I've pushed too hard, and like the wild thing she is, she'll run scared.

But when she looks back up at me, she doesn't duck out between my arms or fill the silence with more of her excuses. She lifts on her toes to kiss me, and my heart jumps up into my throat to try and meet her lips.

I slide my hands from the wall and dig them into the hair at the back of her head, tasting the cherry Chapstick she's always wearing. And even if I've pictured kissing her puffy lips hundreds of times and imagined how they'd fit against mine, her touch surpasses my imagination.

For as long as I can remember, there's been this black hole sitting inside me. Breathing wider and wider as the years went on. And for the first time in as far back as I can process right now, the emptiness of it is shrinking.

Because Merry is in my arms.

Merry is in *my arms*.

She feels like the home I didn't know existed. A place that fits so well you belong there without having to even think about it. Her body melts in my hands as I run them up and down her sides, toying with the bottom edge of her shirt and the band on her jeans with each pass. Her mouth parts for me and I slip inside, finding the space in this world I was meant to fit in. A place that doesn't feel forced or pretend.

It just feels like us... coming together.

Or maybe, I'm shattering because Merry's body pressed against my skin feels like an explosion going off again and again.

I'm obsessed. She's addictive. I'll never get enough.

I push her against the wall, and she lets out a little moan that tastes so good on my lips. I want to drink every sound she makes. I want to be the person who causes her to make them.

This is it.

She's it.

I pull back, and her mouth seeks mine for a second before she blinks her eyes open and looks up at me. Her lips are red and puffy and ripe. I want to sink my teeth into them and taste nothing else for the rest of my life, but I resist.

"No bullshit?" I say to her with her mouth a fraction away from mine.

Her kiss should be enough. I know she probably wants her kiss to be enough. But I need to hear it, either because I'm selfish or insecure. It doesn't really matter. I need her to say it out loud because my heart can't take another tear down the middle without risking it falling apart entirely.

FOREVER AND EVER

Merry brushes her lips over mine and whispers, "I want you, Noah."

Like a dirty little secret and everything I've needed from the day I met her.

"Then we're leaving," I tell her, taking her hand. And for once, her smart mouth doesn't argue with me.

20

Merry

I'm not the girl who falls head over heels.

I'm not the girl who gets her panties in a twist.

I'm not the girl who swoons over a rock star.

But as Noah plants his lips on mine, I do all three of those things.

We barely make it inside the front door to his house before he slams me against the wall and starts kissing me again. Long, deep kisses I get lost in. The taste of wintergreen on his tongue.

It feels good. But even scarier, it feels *right*.

I'm no virgin, far from it. Sex is my escape. A way for me to not have to deal with deeper feelings. Because if I reduce relationships to purely physical interactions, then I don't have to actually explore anything of substance.

Except, in Noah's hands, it all falls away, and I'm left with the one thing I didn't realize I was scared of since the day I met him—feeling safe, feeling unguarded, feeling like in his hands, I'm where I belong.

One kiss and all the pieces fit right into place.

It's *terrifying*.

There are still things left unsaid between us. Promises I can't make to him. Things Noah needs to know before we go too far down this road, and I end up hurting him. But the fear of saying it out loud and facing his reaction intensifies in this moment. Because I want him, I need him. And I'm not ready for him to reject me.

What if he hears my truths and can't handle them? What if he only loves the girl he thinks I am—the one who can give him the life he's envisioned of a wife, kids, a family? What if once he realizes I can't offer him those things, he decides I'm no good for him?

I never wanted Noah to love me.

I never needed love to complete some unfulfilled portion of my life.

But all that changed with one kiss. One look in his eyes and I was his. One moment and I can't imagine losing him.

I press my palms against Noah's chest and push him away just enough to break the kiss and catch my breath. My head is spinning, and our breaths are racing out our parted lips as we stand pinned against the wall.

Noah's body is flush with mine and I feel him for the first time. All of him. His eyes dragging me under, his arms holding me up, his cock hard as steel pressed against my belly. And I don't just want his body for what it can do for me in this moment. I want it all, everything he'll give. His devotion, his heart, his love.

"Wait," I say between breaths, and he does. Because Noah is the kind of man who is strong but gentle. Demanding but protective.

His pale blue eyes are dark with dilation and all I want is to strip us of everything in between. I want to explore the body I've tried to ignore too many times. I want to see the man I've held off.

I plant my palms on his firm chest and am met with the heat of him. It feels like he's on fire. I feel like I'm on fire. And it's never felt so good to let the flames eat me up.

"What's wrong?" Noah's head ticks to the side in confusion.

I'm falling apart.
I'm falling in love.
I'll break us both.

But I can't tell him any of those things because I'm cruel and selfish. And right now, I need him.

"Nothing." I pull his face to mine again as I start to feel frantic.

Noah peels us off the wall and grips my ass to lift me up as I wrap my legs around his hips. My body begs for so much more and I can't help but grind against him for some friction. I've never wanted someone as much as I do this second.

Still, I almost argue as he carries me to his bedroom because I know it's a dangerous thing for me to fall into his bed. His sheets hold an unspoken permanence, and once inside I'm not sure I'll ever really claw my way back out again.

But I let him take me there because as much as the resistant part of me wants to fight this, I'm tired of the battle. If I'm going to sink into this moment, I'm going to do it fully. I'm going to be consumed by him.

Noah pauses when we reach the bed and he sets me down slowly, my feet finding the ground. He breaks our kiss but keeps our foreheads connected so that we're in the bubble of his blond hair curtaining around us.

"Change your mind?" I ask him with a breathy laugh that I hope doesn't show my fear, because I hope he hasn't.

"No," he says, staring me in the eyes. "But I told you when you first showed up here, that if you ever ended up in my bed, you'd climb in willingly, and I'd wait forever for that day if I had to."

He's reminding me of what he's offering me right now. Because climbing on that mattress means I'm accepting more than sex. He's handing me his heart, and by crossing this line, I'm agreeing to take it.

"I want to fuck you, Merry." His hands run down my back, and it sends a shiver down the full length of my spine. "But that's not what this is. You aren't the halfway point, and if we do this, we aren't waking up tomorrow and going back to whatever this was. It's all in or not at all with you. Take it or leave it."

There are inches between our lips, and even though I feel his lust heavy and hard pressed against my stomach, the pain in Noah's eyes is what's drawing my attention. It reminds me of the first night I arrived, and we stood in his kitchen. I told him he couldn't just fuck me and pretend it didn't matter, and I was right. But now, he's asking me to admit the same.

I bring my hand up to his jaw and hold it, appreciating that he tips his head slightly to offer me his weight, the same way he's offering me his heart. A beating bloody mess he presses against the blades of consequence, waiting for me to either make it whole or decimate it.

He gives fully, and it makes me want to do the same.

I take a step back, and disappointment colors his face as he feels me pull away. But, although I'm sure he probably thinks I'm backing out and leaving, I don't. Instead, I reach for the hem of my shirt and strip it off me slowly, tossing it to the floor beside him and watching his throat bob as his eyes drop to my red lace bra hiding under my layers of black. Reaching for the button on my jeans, I pop it open and drag the zipper down slowly, peeling them off one leg at a time.

Noah watches me without moving, and I've never wanted to be seen more. Because he might pause on my matching lace bra and panty set, but he's seeing everything, inside and out.

Once I'm down to my bra and underwear I take one more step back, then another, slowly climbing onto his bed.

"I want all of this." Those are the most terrifying words I've ever said because there is nothing to protect me from them. I feel them down to my core, and I pray that in handing him my broken parts he won't hurt me.

In this moment I want to tell him everything, I want to bare my soul like he did to me in that hallway. I almost do. But when I open my mouth again, I realize I'm already far too vulnerable on his bed in front of him, and I hold onto what little I have left.

Noah stares at me kneeling on his bed, with a tight jaw and a darkened gaze. It goes beyond desire. He stands taller and embodies something larger as he steps closer. Need running deep.

He looks like he wants to absolutely devour me, and I've never felt sexier.

The corner of Noah's mouth ticks up in a deliciously wicked grin as he reaches for his shirt and strips it up and over his head in one sweep.

I can't help but drop my gaze to his bare chest. Those hard ridges of muscle cascading down his stomach send my mind to the dirtiest places. I've seen him naked before, but this is different. Here, he's handing his body over to me, and God, I want it.

Noah walks toward the bed and wraps a hand up into my hair, pulling my head back to hover his face over mine. His grip is tight, and it tugs the strands on my scalp, but the burn lights me up inside.

"Fuck me," I tell him, pulling against his grip enough to nip at his bottom lip.

I'm absolutely desperate.

He pulls my hair a little harder and smiles down at me. His usually carefree and laid-back demeanor giving way to a dominant side that's been hiding beneath the surface. The power in his stare draining me of my composure and making me want to get down and beg for him.

"Say please." Noah grins, and I'm seeing this whole other side of him that is really fucking hot.

I've never taken commands well from men but coming from his mouth right now he has me soaking wet.

I drag my teeth over my bottom lip and notice his eyes dip to watch me. "Please," I say, smiling sweetly.

He gets this wicked look in his eyes as he absorbs me before him.

"Good girl." He covers my mouth with his, taking what he wants roughly.

I run my fingers over the ridges of his stomach as he deepens our kiss, feeling my body ignite the closer I get to his jeans. Popping them open, I drag them over his hips, and he breaks away just long enough to strip himself naked in front of me.

As he kisses me again, I feel his bare skin on my own, and it sets off something inside. He wraps his hands behind my thighs and picks me up, before spinning around and seating himself on the bed, with me on top of him.

One of his hands winds up to my breast, pinching my nipple through the lace, and it makes me squirm against his rock-hard dick, which he seems to appreciate as he smiles against my mouth.

Noah slides a hand up my throat and holds it firmly, breaking me off his mouth and looking me over.

"You're beautiful," he says, looking me square in the eyes. "And you're mine."

That travels farther than I'm usually comfortable with, but instead of my mind rejecting it, I cling on for its warmth. I hold it and hope it's enough.

"I'm yours."

Realizing now I always have been, whether I wanted it to be the truth or not.

Noah lays back, slowly dragging his hands down my throat, and over my bra. His fingers trace the underside of my breasts, along the wings he tattooed on me. And I wonder if he feels it like I do, how that one is different. While the others are art, his ink marks me as his.

His hands move to my hips, to my thighs, and he gives me a hard tug as he looks up at me.

"I'm going to fuck you, since you asked so nicely," he says with a grin, and I can't help but roll my eyes. "But first, you deserve to be worshiped. So do me a favor and sit on my face."

With that, his hands slide to my panties, and he rips them off my body, leaving me completely exposed to him.

His fingers dig into my hips, and he pulls me further up until I fall forward on all fours and my pussy is hovering over his mouth. As he slides his hands around my ass, our eyes connect for only a second before he's pulling me to him.

I almost come at the first swipe of his tongue running the full length of my pussy. He moves all the way up, and down, before slipping it inside me, eliciting a moan from my lips that sounds feral. I don't look away in shyness as he slides my hips to ride his face, instead I can't take my eyes off him.

The darkness that fills those pale blue eyes deepens as he devours me. He kisses my pussy like he kisses my lips, *with hunger*, like he can't get enough of it. I'm grinding myself on him now, chasing the burning in my core.

Clenching the bedspread, my hips move faster, and he moves his mouth to focus on my clit. It's ecstasy, and I'm drenched as Noah laps it all up.

His eyes watch my mouth, my eyes, my breathing. He's gauging every reaction and adjusting to settle on what makes me feel the best. His firm grip holds me in place when he hits that spot that makes me see stars, and I ride out the first waves that start crashing.

I'm pretty sure I scream his name, but I don't know if it comes out as a word as he tugs the orgasm out of me, not relenting as I start to wiggle and tear at his sheets. He slides my wet pussy over his mouth and takes in every bit I give him like I'm the best thing he's ever tasted.

When I finally collapse, he lets up, lifting my hips so he can slide up my body and lay me over him. I steal a kiss and I can taste myself on his lips and in his mouth.

I love that it's me on his skin. I love that it's me on his tongue. I want to bury myself in that scent.

I settle a little lower and slide my wetness over his hard shaft. His hips lift to grind harder against me.

"Noah," I say, breaking apart ever so slightly, still breathing his exhales.

"Fuck." He pauses like he just realized something, tipping his forehead up to meet mine. "Condoms are in the bathroom."

"Or…" I bite my bottom lip, feeling totally reckless right now because it's Noah, and as much as I've never wanted to be his, that's all I want to be in this moment—fully. "I trust you. I'm good if you are."

Noah's eyes are hard to read as he thinks that over, but I feel his breathing quicken.

"Do you always use protection?" I ask him.

He nods.

"Same. Are you—"

"I'm clean," he says, his arms tightening around me. "I got tested again after the tour, and I haven't been with anyone since."

I feel a small bit of pride with his confession because it means that he hasn't been with anyone since I started staying in his house, even though I know he's gone out to party with Rome on a few occasions, so I'm sure there have been plenty of opportunities.

I slide my slickness over his dick again and feel it twitch to meet me.

"Then fuck me bare. I need to feel you." I brush my lips over his and smile. "Please."

Noah growls deep in his chest at my word choice and flips me around so that I'm on my back and he's on top of me. The weight of him is comforting as he grabs his dick and nudges at my entrance.

"Since you asked so nicely," he says with a wicked grin, then he pushes into me in one thrust, hitting me so far back I see a universe implode behind my eyes.

"Oh, fuck," I moan, pulling my legs around his waist to try and make room for him. Visually, I always knew Noah was huge, but feeling my body stretch around him is a surprising sensation.

His hips start moving slowly at first. One of his hands holds my hip, while the other holds my jaw. As I warm up to the feel of him, I start rocking more and more, and his hips move like a boat over waves.

We fit in every way. How he feels on my skin. How we move as one. He can read me, and I can read him, and I've never been so scared to be this close to somebody because it might be his cock inside me, but what I'm feeling is so much more.

"Merry," Noah says my name as he brushes a kiss on my lips. His eyes tell me there's more hanging on the tip of his tongue, but for whatever reason, he holds back, pressing in for a kiss instead.

My pussy clenches as my orgasm rockets through me. Noah's movements get faster and uneven as he chases that feeling of me tightening around him. And with the waves of my own climax still in motion, Noah empties into me in a myriad of ways I've never allowed a person.

We're slick with sweat as we cling to each other, and as the eruption fades, Noah buries his face in my neck. I hold him tight and close my eyes, feeling our heartbeats thundering frantically in our chests.

I'm yours.
I'm yours.
I'm yours.
I'm terrified.

21

NOAH

I stare at Merry's closed eyes, waiting for them to flutter open, knowing that once they do, her walls might be back in place. I wait to see if she'll regret what happened, and it forms a knot in my throat worrying about it. Because what she says and does sometimes are two different things, and even if I know she felt the same way I did last night, it doesn't mean the skittish parts of her personality won't force those feelings back into hiding with the new day.

She's a difficult person to love.

Sharp and stubborn.

I'd like to think I could have fucked that resistance out of her one of the four times we did it over the course of the night, but she just grows wilder the closer I get to her.

Laying here with her body heat against mine, I feel myself ready to go again. She's a fantasy come to life and being with her is all I thought it would be, and more.

I don't think I could ever get tired of her tight little pussy riding me. Or watching her face as she reacts to every movement. I could spend every day memorizing her naked body, decorated in ink.

My dark goddess.

Last night was transcendent.

Going over to Sebastian's, I hadn't intended on throwing down the gauntlet with her. But after the day I had, I couldn't hold it back anymore. I needed to know what I was still fighting for, even at the risk she'd pull away permanently.

She surprised me with her kiss. Even more so when she climbed onto my bed. I almost pinched myself to see if I was dreaming because there she was, Mercedes Lopez, girl of my dreams, in her cherry red lace bra and panties asking me to have her.

Asking me to fuck her bare.

I've never done that before, and even if it was a little reckless, I saw in her eyes what I was feeling, and I didn't want there to be anything between us. I didn't even ask if she was on birth control before sliding in, which might be stupid. But in all honesty, it wasn't that I forgot, I just didn't care, because with her, I'd be fine with anything.

Merry has me thinking all sorts of dumb shit right now.

I've done a lot of drugs, but nothing compares to this kind of euphoria. The world could end, and I'd be fine with it. I'm not coming down.

Merry shifts as her eyes blink open, and it's my moment of truth as I search them for hesitation or regret. But she smiles, and it lights a fire so deep my soul is in flames.

"Morning," she says, catching me watching her. Not that I look away.

I brush a hair off her cheek, and her skin warms. "Good morning."

"So..." she says, really drawing it out like she's remembering everything wasn't just a dream. She buries her face behind her hand and shakes her head a little. "We really did that."

"We did," I say, and she moves her hand to peek out at me. "You haven't run for the hills yet so I'm taking that as a good sign?"

She rolls her eyes and drops her hand. "Very funny."

"Just saying, I expected you to at least try to claw your way out a little." I poke her in the side and she squirms.

"Me too," she says through a laugh, but then her face gets serious as she tucks her hands under her head and faces me. "Is it bad that I'm not?"

"Fuck no. I meant what I said."

The corner of her mouth ticks. "So did I."

"I'm not doing this halfway."

Merry chews the inside of her cheek, then lets out a long exhale. "I know."

I move closer to her on the bed and her legs part to let me slip one of mine between them. But it's not sexual, even if I am hard as steel lying beside her naked body. It's intimate. Dragging a hand up, I run my fingers along the side of her face. Her makeup is all washed off and it's just her.

Stripped. Messy.

She's never looked more beautiful.

"But I need you to be patient with me." Merry works her bottom lip between her teeth "This is... a lot. And there are still things we need to talk about."

"Merry, you forget I know you." I lean in and kiss her, feeling her lips puffy as they melt against mine.

She pulls back and gives me a pinched expression, but I'm not sure for what. I do know her. I've spent seven months getting to know everything there is to know about her, so maybe it's just a little denial peeking through.

"No expectations, okay?" I say, and she seems the slightest bit relieved.

I trail my hand down her chest and wrap an arm around her waist to pull her perfect body against mine. Leaning in, I trail kisses over her neck, appreciating her moans and groans as she buries her face in the pillow.

"No expectations," she repeats.

"But... I'm not sharing." I plant a kiss where her pulse meets her throat and feel her heart racing. "It's just us. Non-negotiable."

Merry reaches up and grabs the sides of my face in her hands so she can look me in the face. "It's just us."

I blink again, worrying that one of these times everything I'm seeing will be my imagination and disappear. But she's still here, in my arms, in my bed, letting me hold her. She's mine.

Any other woman ceases to be anything because Merry's body is the one that was meant to fit in my arms.

"Are you okay?" she asks, letting my face go. "Yesterday was kind of a whirlwind and you didn't really say much about how things went with Kali."

I groan and roll onto my back. The last person I want to think about with Merry in my bed is my ex. Not that I'm mad at her for bringing it up. I should be glad that she's worried about me.

"It was a little bit of a mind fuck," I admit. "Catching up with her wasn't exactly how I pictured my day."

I turn my head to face Merry and notice the sun shining through the windows, casting light on her Monroe piercing and making her sparkle.

"How did you leave things?"

"Fine, I guess. Although I'm sure it will be to the disappointment of my mother, if she even reaches out."

"Kali talks to her?"

"Apparently. Which is fucking hypocritical considering she won't talk to her own son because of his career choice." I wipe my palm over my face. "I guess Kali getting knocked up by my best friend when we were together is acceptable, but rock music isn't."

"Yikes." Merry shakes her head. "Well, if she comes at you, I'm pretty sure I can take her too."

"Did you just offer to fight my mom for me?" I laugh.

Merry nudges my shoulder. "I'm scrappy, and I give zero fucks who they are. If someone messes with someone I care about, I'll take 'em."

"Such a fighter," I say, rolling on my side to face her and propping my head up under my arm.

"Says the peacekeeper." She lifts an eyebrow.

"Is that what I am?"

Merry nods. "You've got a big heart."

"That you *care* about, apparently."

Merry tips her head forward and leans her forehead against my chest. "Of course, that's what you choose to pick up from this conversation?"

I shrug my shoulder.

"What am I going to do with you?" she asks, planting a hand on my cheek and giving me a quick kiss.

"I don't know." I grin. "But hopefully, whatever it is, we're naked."

That draws a big laugh out of her, and I get lost in it.

"Oh, it will definitely involve us being naked," Merry says, skimming her fingers slowly down my chest until she wraps her hand around my hard cock and pumps it once. My vision blacks out for a second, she feels so good. Her touch, her smell, her skin.

She squeezes a little tighter and moves again, making my dick ache with excitement, and I groan. Not able to take it anymore, I grab her hips and roll her on top of me.

"Stop teasing." I smack her ass with my hand, and she lets out a sexy little yelp as she digs her fingernails into my shoulders.

"Oh, I'm sorry, did you want this?" Merry tries to pass off as sweet and innocent with a sugary smile, but it's dark and sexy as fuck. She slides her slick pussy over my dick with a devilish look in her eyes that makes me almost come undone.

I grip her nice round hips and sink my fingers in, pressing her softness against me. "Fuck yes."

She leans down so her lips are by my ear. "Then ask nicely."

I laugh. "Please make me feel good, Mercedes."

She narrows her eyes at me for using her full name, but there's amusement on her face. Sliding her core against me again, she pauses right where the head of my cock catches at her entrance.

"Since you asked so nicely, Mr. Hayes." And she impales herself on me so fast it takes the air from her chest.

"Fuck."

She sits up and slowly starts circling her hips. She might as well be my damnation because there is absolutely no coming back from being with her. Her beauty, her energy.

Electric.

Reaching up, I trace the wing tattoos beneath her breasts with my fingers, and it brings a smile to her lips.

I love all her ink. The roses on her thighs, the fairytale retellings on her arms, the stars on her hips. But those wings that I put on her, none of the others quite compare to them.

She grabs my wrists and places my hands over her perfect breasts. They're small and soft and fit perfectly in my palms like I was the person meant to hold them. I pinch her nipples and tug until she screams, and she runs a hand down to circle her clit from the excitement of it.

It draws attention to a faint scar on her pelvis I hadn't noticed in the dark of night, and I wonder what the story is behind it.

Of all the things I've learned about Merry over the past seven months, discovering her in bed is a new universe that I'm exploring. Uncovering the secrets that are on her body. Learning how to draw sounds out of her that I want to be the only ears to hear again. Feeling how her pussy squeezes when I grip hard on her ass. Appreciating how she rides me like she genuinely loves it.

Fuck, she's perfect.

Merry leans over me to claim my mouth in a kiss, and all other thoughts cease because all I can do is feel her body on me. Her nipples rub against my chest with excitement. She's drenching my dick with her pleasure. I lose track of whose tongue is in whose mouth, or whose hand is on whose body, and we just melt slowly into one.

As her speed picks up, I know she's close, dragging her body in those circles as she rides my dick and grinds her clit against my pelvis. She wraps her arms around my neck and holds me tighter.

I hold her back, never wanting to let her go.

Her entire body starts to shake in my arms as she tightens around my dick, and I explode into her at the same time as her climax hits. Nothing between us, just her and me.

Merry slows her movements as we both come down from our releases, but she doesn't let go of my neck, she just holds me in this hug with me still inside her. Her breath is hot and quick where she's buried against me, and I rake my fingers through her hair, trying to steady my own.

"Don't break my heart, Noah," she says in almost a whisper. Not looking at me, but not letting go either.

The comment tilts me off balance because I've only ever really thought of my heart as the one on the line with her. But the vulnerability in her voice tells me maybe I had that wrong.

She's scared. Which is a side of her I'm not used to seeing.

And she's not alone. This feeling pushing in my chest is frightening.

"You're safe with me," I whisper, running my hands over her back and waiting for her body to relax. "I've got you."

22

Merry

Noah edges closer to me, and I lap up the heat of his body with my own. When did he start feeling so good? Was this always there between us and I was just blind to it? Because I can't seem to be within ten feet of him without feeling like I'm being struck by lightning.

He leans in, hovering his mouth beside my ear. "How do you expect me to get through practice with you in these fishnets?"

I feel his gaze dart downward, but I stay facing straight ahead, staring at Adrian's front door. Noah's fingers start at the base of my neck and trail all the way down my spine, over my ass, until he's playing with the hem of my skirt and feeling the bumpy fishnets on the backs of my thighs.

"Guess you'll just have to look away." I bump him with my hip, trying really hard to pretend his touch isn't having this strong of an effect on me.

"Not possible." He catches my ass in his hand and squeezes it right as the door opens.

Eloise looks where Noah's hand grips my ass and she smirks at us, while I push him away.

"Well, hello, you two," she says too sweetly.

If me crashing at Noah's house wasn't enough of a red flag, I'm pretty sure us disappearing last night sent up some serious flares. And the way Eloise's eyes dart from me to Noah, it's clear there's no hiding whatever this is. Not that Eloise says anything. She quietly steps back and holds the door open for us with an amused expression on her face.

"Sebastian and Adrian are already in the studio. We're just waiting for Rome to get here." She sighs, looking at Noah. "Please tell me you've heard from him."

"He's not here yet?"

Eloise shakes her head. "He went out last night after you guys left. I don't know if he even got home yet. He's not answering my texts. You may want to talk Adrian off a cliff before he hunts Rome down and strangles him."

"Wonderful." Noah pulls out his phone and steps aside, presumably to try calling Rome himself.

Eloise shakes her head, and I follow her inside to give Noah some space to make his phone call.

Adrian's house is smaller than the rest of the band's houses, but mostly wide-open spaces with lots of windows, so it feels like there's more room to breathe. He built it on the edge of a hill, with the entire back wall made of glass, giving it a tree house effect as you look out to forest stretching for miles.

"You're recording right after us today?" Eloise asks as we head through the house.

"Yeah, late night for me." I nod. "And Adrian, I guess. How does he never burn out?"

"Guy's a machine." Eloise looks over her shoulder and rolls her eyes, even though I'm not sure why she's annoyed by it. "But it shouldn't take us too long unless my brother decides to keep being difficult."

Enemy Muse has a track to lay down today, and Noah's told me earlier it's the one Eloise and Sebastian keep fighting about. From the look on Eloise's face, I'm not sure how well this is going to go.

Noah gave me the option to wait back at his house until they were done to avoid what might be an all-out sibling battle, but I can only sit within the same four walls for so long. So even if I do have to listen to a little fighting, at least at Adrian's house I won't be itching to crawl out of my skin.

Eloise stops at the door to the basement and reaches for the handle.

"Noah and I fucked," I blurt out before she has a chance to open the door.

It's not that Eloise and I are close, we really aren't. But Cassie left to head back to Seattle early this morning, and those words have been bubbling inside me since driving over here.

Eloise pauses with her hand on the door and turns with a smile. "I figured."

"I know. But I just had to say it, because... well... it's Noah. And..." I start running my fingers through my hair and realize my heart is racing. "I think I might be freaking out a little bit."

Eloise looks over my shoulder and my eyes follow. It's still clear. Noah either got a hold of Rome and is hung up on the call or he's trying other numbers to try to reach him.

"Do you regret it?" Her eyes slide back to me, and her face is a little sullen with the question.

There's a protective edge to her tone, and it occurs to me she's worried I'm going to hurt Noah. His feelings have been pretty obvious to everyone, so I'm sure she's concerned about my intentions.

"No."

It's the truth. I don't regret it, but it doesn't make the weight of it any less scary. There are still things Noah and I need to talk about. Big things he might not respond well to, and I don't know how to anticipate his reaction.

This is why I don't normally do relationships, especially those with men who are all in.

"Noah's a good guy," Eloise says with a sympathetic look.

"I know." If only that made things easier.

"And you guys are good together."

"Like sunshine and rain clouds?" I hitch an eyebrow.

"Normally, yeah, I would think that." She laughs. "But in your case, you guys balance each other out."

There's truth to her statement. When I'm around Noah things don't seem as bleak. Possibility starts creeping through. And I don't know if that's a good thing or really dangerous thinking.

But I don't tell her any of those thoughts, settling on a simple, "thank you," instead.

"Anytime." Eloise nudges my arm. "Try not to think too much about it. Just let it be whatever it is."

"You realize we're talking about Noah, right?" I finally smile. "Thinking about it is all he does. I'm pretty sure I have lots of conversations about *all the feelings* in my future."

"I heard that." Noah surprises me at my side.

He wraps an arm over my shoulder and looks down at me with a grin, and Eloise looks pleasantly happy to see it.

"You're lucky I don't care." He shrugs his shoulder. "I'm man enough to be proud of my feelings. After all, one of us has to have the heart in this relationship... Ice Queen."

"Hey." I jab him in the side, trying to ignore the flutters that kicked up at the use of the word *relationship*.

Noah just laughs and doesn't let me wiggle loose as he turns his attention to Eloise. "Rome is already on his way. Don't ask."

She rolls her shoulders back, shaking her head, but doesn't say anything.

I'm used to spending time with the band on tour, where things are wild twenty-four-seven. I always assumed that they chilled out during their off time. Apparently, that's not the case with Rome.

"All right, well we can get started with some of the vocal tracks while we wait for him." Eloise sounds annoyed.

"You and Sebastian worked that out?"

Eloise lifts an eyebrow. "Let's just say he's lucky he's my brother."

Noah shakes his head and laughs. "All right, I'll meet you down there."

She heads down the staircase to the recording studio while Noah hangs back. He pulls a hair tie off his wrist and ties his blond hair off his face, watching me.

"What?" he asks, noticing my expression.

"Nothing," I say, trying to hide a smirk.

There's something about the way he looks right now that has me all twisted up inside. His pale blue eyes are bright with excitement, and it permeates out of him. Then there's the T-shirt that is hugging his chest like he wants me to remember the solid slab of muscles hiding beneath it. Add his jeans, hugging his ass and cock like there's nothing that can contain him, and I'm nearly light-headed.

If I thought Noah was attractive before, the cap to the bottle has been taken off. Because after last night, it's like I'm seeing what I refused to for the past seven months and I can't stop thinking about it.

The thought of him going down there to sweat over his drums makes my brain travel all sorts of places.

"Liar," he calls me out, reaching for my hands and pulling me against his hard chest.

I lift onto my toes, so my mouth is next to his ear. "I was just thinking about what you said about my fishnets," I whisper, grabbing his wrist and sliding his hand up my leg, under the hem of my black leather skirt in the front.

"You should know..." I bring his hand right between my thighs. "I'm not wearing any underwear."

I move his hand and it brushes over my pussy, covered only in the wide holes of my fishnets, which do nothing to hide how wet I am for him.

"Fuck," Noah grunts, cupping me with his hand and squeezing. His other one runs up to my throat and I almost think he's going to slam me against the wall and fuck me right here, but the front door closing in the distance stops him.

"Damn," he says, pulling his hand away and tipping his head back. "You're going to kill me, Mercedes."

He lets out a frustrated sigh, but when he looks back at me, he's smiling.

"Kill you, no." I shake my head. "What would be the fun in that? I'll just torture you a little for the hours of boredom I'm about to endure up here all alone."

He looks at me, and I give him a wicked grin.

"Evil." He leans down and plants a kiss on me that says the opposite.

"Fucking finally," Rome's voice comes up behind us and we break apart. "Maybe now you'll stop bitching about her."

I look over my shoulder and he's standing there with a shit-eating grin on his face as he walks past, slapping Noah on the shoulder as he does.

"Now stop fucking for five seconds and let's record this shit so I can get back to getting wasted."

Noah narrows his eyes, but Rome is already walking down the stairs ignoring him.

"I'm going to wait up here," I tell Noah when he looks back at me. "I've got to finish up some of the lyrics for one of my songs I'm recording tonight."

"Sounds good, babe," he says, leaning in for a quick kiss.

Everything about that—his words, the way it came so naturally—sends my belly spinning.

"Good luck." I wave to him as he heads down the stairs.

Sebastian and Eloise's elevated voices are already making their way up the staircase, telling me Noah's in for a shit session. But he's relaxed as he descends, and it puts me at ease to see him like this.

I head outside to Adrian's back deck to get some air. Writing over the screaming will only take longer, so I drop down onto a lawn chair and appreciate the sounds of the forest.

Pulling out my notebook, I turn to the page that has the song I plan on recording tonight. The more I look at the lyrics, the more of a mess they seem to become. Something about them isn't working, and I can't quite figure it out.

Love is the limit
Love is the limit

I tap my pencil against my notebook and pull out my phone with my other hand, scrolling until I reach the email Adrian sent me with the beat attached to it. I hit play and let it roll in a loop. The same sounds over and over, trying to hear the words and make them sound right.

Stay please
Hold me here for now
Take me
~~Steady~~ Uneasy as we spin around
In this dance
~~We will find~~ Once upon a time was a merry-go-round
~~Wait here~~
~~While roses grow up from the ground~~
a merry-go-round

If love is the limit
How far are you willing to go
If love is the limit
How hard are ~~you~~ we willing to hold
If love is the limit
I was meant to be yours
So, hold on tight
Hold on now
Hold on...
to me

A stray breeze runs through the air and tickles the hair on the back of my neck making me shiver.

~~So, hold on tight~~
~~Hold on now~~
~~Hold on...~~
~~to me~~
I'm yours

The beat ends again and I hit pause, letting the words settle a little bit. If there are limits, I feel well outside of them right now. My growing feelings for Noah are beyond my comfort level, and what he said about his fear of me running for the hills, doesn't feel as crazy as it sounds.

My visceral reaction is to get away, to escape whatever I'm feeling before it's too late. But surprisingly, my feet keep me in place.

When I climbed into his bed last night, I meant what I said. I'm ready to give in to this and see what we can make of it. The trouble is, Noah's limits are still far out on the horizon, way beyond where I'm standing. And I'm not sure how far past my own I'm willing to go to meet him there.

23

MERRY

"Woman, you are going to break my dick with all this sex," Noah says, as he slides his pants on and shakes his head. But the smile on his face is proof that it's not actually a complaint.

"Aww..." I crawl across the bed toward him and kneel when I reach the edge. "Does that mean I'd get to play nurse?"

Noah wraps his arms around my waist and pulls my naked body against him. "You can be whatever you want."

He rakes my hair off my face and kisses me. Even if my lips are sore and every muscle in my body aches, I melt against his mouth and yearn for it.

Being under the same roof as Noah has been a bit of a problem when it comes to my productivity. Because all week, when we aren't at Adrian's recording, we're fucking—in his bed, on the counter, on the couch, in the yard, in the shower, on the table. Give it another week and I don't think there will be a piece of furniture that doesn't remind me of an orgasm.

I'm not sure if we're making up for lost time, but we can't keep our hands off each other.

I push Noah back a step and he frowns.

"In all seriousness though, you're right, none of that. We're getting out of the house and keeping our hands to ourselves for at least eight hours. Recovery time." But I brush my hands down his stomach as I say it, letting them graze over the bulge in his pants.

Noah tips my chin up. "If you don't stop touching my cock, the only recovery your pussy is going to get is when I put you on your knees and stick my dick in your mouth instead."

I'm tempted to keep pushing because there is something really hot about when Noah gets bossy in the bedroom, but he's right. Our bodies need a few hours off, so I pull away and hop off the bed. He smacks my ass as I make my way past him to the bathroom, and I yelp.

Everything he does sets me on fire, and I'm not sure if it's a good thing or totally twisted that I can't get enough.

I've always enjoyed having sex. I'm not shy about fucking and having fun with it. But being with Noah is different—next level. Beyond anything I've felt with any other person. Because it isn't just physical release. It's soul-shattering.

I shower quickly, and Noah is dressed and ready by the time I meet him outside. He gets the motorcycle out of the garage and winks at me as he hands me a helmet. There's something uniquely sexy about Noah's calm and confidence in every situation. His presence relaxes me.

Wrapping myself around him, we take off down the road, and I let my stress melt off me as the wind whips around us. There's nothing but us and the endless feeling of escape as we ride, Colorado trees flying by, sunshine peeking through the branches.

If it were up to me, we'd ride forever.

But when Noah pulls over, the eternal calmness of the road fades in the distance and I'm left again with the unsettling feelings burrowed inside me.

"We should always ride the motorcycle." I pull off my helmet and it feels good to be out of the house, even if it's unusually hot for late July.

He laughs and shakes his head. "What about when it's snowing?" He reaches for my hand, pulling me down a path that winds through the forest.

"Okay, maybe not when it's snowing." I shrug. "But all other times."

"I won't argue with that. Anything to keep your arms wrapped tight around me." Noah looks back at me and winks.

Tiny gestures from him do massive things inside.

I almost pull Noah to me and kiss him right here in the middle of the path, but another couple approaching stops me. This must be a well-known hiking trail because I didn't expect anyone to be out here on such a hot day.

As they walk by, they give us a cordial nod. The woman's stare lingers on Noah and I wonder if she recognizes him. Finally glancing away, she looks down at something strapped to her chest and my eyes follow. She's cradling a sleeping baby.

"I want that," Noah says when the couple disappears behind us. Three words and my stomach sinks because I know where this is going. "Our kids are coming everywhere with us. On hikes, on tour. Everywhere."

"Noah…" I warn.

"Just saying, not right now or anything." He keeps walking, and I'm not sure if he realizes that he's now pulling me behind him. "But in the future, you know—our babies will be the perfect mix of you and me. Wild and happy."

He thinks nothing of his comment when actually it's a knife to my chest.

"Stop." I pull my hand away, getting frustrated because he won't just let this go. "You can't say shit like that, Noah."

"What?" His eyebrows pinch as he turns to face me. "Come on, Merry. You know I say whatever's on my mind, especially when it comes to you. Don't worry, I'm not trying to knock you up… *yet*."

He winks, but while it's playful, the gesture sours my stomach.

"That's not it." I feel my voice catching in my throat.

"Then what is it?" He looks me over, his smile falling. "I thought you were in this. Don't start pushing because of one dumb comment."

I take a step back and run my fingers through my hair. The sun beating down feels scalding, and my heart races.

"You don't understand."

"Then make me." He takes another step forward. "Stop defaulting to a battle and let me in."

"I can't give you what you want, Noah," I yell, surprising us both, and it takes the last of my fight out of me.

Noah stands there still and quiet, as calm as ever. "What do you think I want?"

Tucking my hands in my pockets, I know there's no more running. No more hiding. Noah deserves more than I've ever given him, and he's owed the truth, even if it breaks us before we've really started.

"I can't have kids, okay?" I stare at him and try to hold onto my last ounce of composure. "At least, I probably won't be able to. Ever since I was young, I've struggled with uterine fibroids, and I had to have surgery a few years ago to get them removed. Only, it got messy, and there was a lot of scarring."

I feel the tears brimming in my eyes, and I try with all my might to stop them from falling.

I'm not the girl who feels sorry for herself.

I'm not the girl who cries.

This is my life, there's no use complaining.

I've lived with this since I was fourteen when I started having more intense periods than other girls my age. Except, it wasn't a period. And I wasn't just a girl going through puberty, I was starting what would be a long battle with my body betraying me. Something I learned how to deal with by convincing myself it didn't matter—I didn't care.

Never letting anyone close to the truth, even myself.

"That should have been it, but last year, my doctor confirmed that new ones were growing, and…" I take a deep breath, trying to stop the spinning in my head "…I feel it like I did before. They're going to have to go back in. I don't know when, but probably soon. And even if they can get away with just another surgery to remove them, more can grow. And even if they can save my uterus, the damage is already done. The chance of me ever having kids is so small there's no point thinking about it. So that's the truth, Noah. What you want from me—or from life in general—a wife, kids, a traditional family. I'm not going to be able to give that to you. There won't be any babies that are *the perfect mix of you and me.* It's not going to happen and so you can't just say that like it has no effect."

My heartbeat pulses in my throat. It thunders between my temples. Noah is standing there silently staring at me like he's been shot and is still in shock from the pain.

"It's not that I never wanted to be with you," I admit. If I'm going to let this out, then there's no use holding back now. "I can be a really fun girlfriend. We can have a lot of great sex. But I know eventually, you'll want more, and I didn't want to have to face that day when it would inevitably happen."

Finally, Noah takes a step toward me, but his eyes drop down, all the way to my stomach. He lifts a hand and places it right over the place I'm permanently broken, and I wish the gesture brought me some comfort, but all I can think about is the pain.

"It's not cramping," Noah says, looking back up at me. "When you were hurting, it wasn't cramps?"

I shake my head.

"When's the last time you've been to your doctor?"

"Did you not hear anything I just said?"

"I did." Noah keeps a straight face. "And I don't give a shit about any of it. Now answer my question."

"On our last trip to Seattle." I snuck in a visit before I met up with Cassie and brought her to the unplugged show.

"That's over two months ago," he says, not looking happy. "You almost collapsed at my house in pain. Why haven't you made an appointment?"

"What?" I shake my head. "Why does it matter? I just told you that I'm broken and can't ever give you what you want."

"It matters because I care, Mercedes." My name comes out harsher than I've ever heard it from him. "Don't you get it? I haven't been chasing you around for almost a year to just find someone to knock up someday. I've been chasing you because I've been in love with you. I don't give a crap if you can have kids, or can't, or want to adopt kids, or if you never want them at all. None of that shit means anything anyway if it isn't with you."

He rakes his hair back and lets out a frustrated grunt.

"Yes, I'm a little pissed, okay?" He frowns. "I'm pissed that you kept this from me. I'm pissed that it's the reason you pushed me away for so long when I don't give a fuck about it as long as I can have you. But mostly, I'm pissed because you're clearly not okay and you're not seeing a doctor. So why haven't you made an appointment?"

I try to pull away, but Noah holds my wrist, wrapping his other hand in the back of my neck and forcing me to face him.

There's no running.

There's no escaping.

"I was scared they'd finally say it." My words barely make their way out through stilted breaths. "That they'd have to take what's left. And I'd just be... empty."

His fingers grip into my hair, and he steps closer, bringing us almost chest to chest.

"I was afraid of losing you permanently," I admit.

Because why would a man who can have almost any woman in the world, want a broken one?

"Merry." Noah sighs, holding me in his arms like I'm moments from falling apart. "Before I met you, I was in a place that was so dark, I couldn't see a way out of it. I was drowning. I felt empty in ways that run so deep, I'm still trying to fill them. But you know what I discovered? Sometimes those pieces have to disappear to make us who we are. We have to live with those holes and let them shape us. No matter what they tell you, no matter what you think they can take away from you. They can't. It's up to you to decide what you actually give, and how you make it a part of yourself moving forward. Those are just pieces, but you're the whole. And you're strong, fierce, and incredible."

He brushes a strand off my face and cups my cheeks. Feeling the wetness between my skin and his palms, I realize I've started crying.

"I meant what I said." Noah tips his forehead to mine. "I've got you. I'm not going anywhere. This changes nothing. You're perfect, no matter what happens. Because you're you, and that's all I care about. Whatever life you want to build, wherever you want to build it, with whatever pets or kids or none of it... you decide, all that matters to me is that you let me be in it."

He kisses the tip of my nose.

"I love you," he says, with a slight smile on his lips. "And I promised myself I wasn't going to say it out loud yet because I know how you are and inside those three words probably already made you start to get squeamish. But you need to know that, from me, with no question, that I. Love. You. Mercedes. As is, *always*. I'm not going anywhere as long as you'll have me."

He runs his thumbs along the underside of my eyes and wipes the tears away. And I feel terrible for holding back from him. I feel selfish for keeping this to myself. But mostly, I feel something warm in my chest that I can't explain. Because I believe him.

I wrap my arms around his waist, and his strong arms hug me. We stand there like that as the air starts to chill. We hold each other as the sun starts to set. As the confession grows truth in both of us. And when we finally look into each other's eyes again, there are three words I want to tell him, and I hope someday I have the strength to. But for now, I say nothing, and I kiss him with all I have left.

24

NOAH

MERCEDES LOPEZ IS THE single most infuriating woman on the planet.

She drives me out of my fucking mind.

Nine months—that's how long I've been obsessed with this woman. And she was holding back because of something I could have told her doesn't impact my feelings for her. If she'd just been upfront in the first place we could have avoided all of the push and pull.

I'm not sure why she has this cookie-cutter view of me. Yes, I might have come from the kind of family she envisions, but it's also the reason I know why the façade can be such a load of bullshit. Just because you have both parents doesn't make them unconditionally loving. And just because you have a few siblings doesn't mean you have anything in common with them.

If I wanted the guarantee of a house in the suburbs and a wife in the kitchen, I would have gotten back together with Kali.

I know Merry well enough to not be delusional about the life I'm walking into with her. She's non-traditional. She's unpredictable. She's real. It's why I love her.

But what did surprise me in Merry's confession was how she spoke about a future with me. Truth buried under lies she doesn't recognize. For the first time since I met her, I got the impression the future she talks down on isn't something she doesn't desire because she doesn't want it. It's because she doesn't think she can have it.

Her confession broke something inside me because I felt a pain in her I didn't know existed.

Merry cried.

She doesn't cry—ever.

To hold her in my arms with her eyes leaking might as well have been her heart bleeding all over both of us.

It hurt to know she convinced herself I would reduce her in my mind to anything less than the woman she is just because she can't have children. It's not who I am or who I've ever been.

I meant what I said as we stood there in the forest, I'm in this. I'm not like my parents, my love isn't conditional, and if she thinks this will push me away, she's going to quickly discover how wrong she is.

I finally have her.

Merry is mine.

I'm not letting her go.

But right now, my feelings aren't what's important, because I'm realizing there's a struggle she's kept quiet longer than I've noticed. And now that she's voiced it, it's like something deep inside her cracked open, and I don't want her to spill out all the good in her because of it.

I'm not sure what the right thing to say is in this kind of situation. I've battled my own depression, but it's not the same. Merry seems to be equating her ability to have children to her worth in a relationship, and all I can do is prove that's not the case.

"You need to stop looking at me like that," she says, narrowing her eyes at me from the other side of the couch.

"Like what?" I play dumb, really wishing I wasn't a recovering addict, because all I want right now is something to take the edge off and it's not an option.

Merry kicks me with her foot. "You know *like what*. Like I'm sick or broken or something."

I ignore her comment. "Has the doctor called you back yet?"

I'm not purposely looking at her in whatever way she's interpreting as bad, but right now, it's all I can think about. Merry might need to get surgery again, and depending on the severity of the outcome, it has the potential to be life-changing. Yet, here she is, in Colorado, acting like everything is fine. It's frustrating.

Regardless of how much she wants to brush this off, she almost collapsed the other day. She's not okay, and now that I know what's actually going on, she can't lie to me and pretend everything is fine. If what caused her enough pain she couldn't stand wasn't period cramps, then it's nothing good.

We can't sit around recording albums pretending this isn't happening, even if it means I'm going to piss her off by asking her the same question again and again.

"It was late when I called." Merry shakes her head. "He's probably already left for the night, and he'll call in the morning."

"Adrian will understand if we need to head to Seattle."

That gets me a hard eye roll.

"First of all, I'm sure it's fine, and this can wait until I'm done recording the demo." She narrows her eyes at me. "Second, what do you mean *we*? You have an album to record, one people are actually waiting on and care about. The band needs you. If I have to head up there, I'll go alone. Monica and Carson have a room I can stay in. Besides, even if my parents aren't thrilled with me, they'll be there. I don't need both of us putting our lives on hold."

Try to hold it in.

Try to understand.

Try to not flip the fuck out.

My brain is fuming and it's taking every ounce of control to not yell at her right now for being so dense. She's still treating us like two people in passing, whether she means to or not. And it's infuriating.

"Just tell me when the doctor calls back." I try to flat-out ignore everything she just said, standing up and heading into the kitchen. "You hungry?" I yell over my shoulder.

Maybe we just need some food in our stomachs to take the edge off the grumpiness.

"Yeah, but there's not much in there, I haven't had a chance to go shopping."

I shake my head because as much as she tries to pretend she's not a settle-down kind of girl, she does way too much around my house and it makes me feel guilty. Every time I get back from recording with the band she's cleaning, cooking, or organizing. It might be to keep herself busy, but hopefully, she knows how much I appreciate it.

Digging into one of the drawers, I pull out a stack of menus and head into the living room with them.

"All right, we've got pizza, Chinese, Thai, and Mexican." I hand her the stack.

She quirks an eyebrow. "There's no way any of these deliver this far outside of the city."

"Perks of being a spoiled rock star and having an assistant who works all hours of the night." I shrug.

She shakes her head in disapproval but starts scanning the menus. Once her craving for Mongolian beef kicks in, she no longer cares who we have to inconvenience to make it happen.

I text the food order to my assistant and put the menus back, climbing under the blanket beside her on the couch. She's flipping through movies, and I slide behind her, pulling her back against my chest.

"You're wearing the clear crystal again." I reach for her necklace, spinning the stone between my fingers. "Is all this why?"

Merry shrugs one shoulder and covers my hand in hers. "Maybe. My mom gave it to me before my first surgery.

Obviously new ones grew, so it didn't work perfectly, but I like to think it helped do something."

"I'm sure it did," I say, appreciating this moment. Her showing a vulnerability I know makes her uncomfortable. Feeling her warmth. Having her near me.

My life up until now felt so cold, and I can't imagine going back to that.

"Good thing for modern medicine." She rests her head on my arm and nuzzles her body closer. "You know, for when faith is wasted."

I let out a sigh and rest my forehead against the back of her head, breathing in the scent of her berry shampoo.

"I don't think it's wasted," I say. "Just difficult when it doesn't work out like we expect it to."

"I guess."

"Just because bad things happen, doesn't mean things didn't happen like they were meant to. It's just more difficult to see the light in it."

"That it is." She sighs.

"But I like the stones," I say, once more looking at the crystal she wears around her neck. "I'd like to think they do something."

"I like that it's tangible." Merry shifts until she's on her back, looking up at me. "Faith can feel so far away sometimes. I have a hard time grasping it. So, I try to focus on the here and now. The things I can control. Things I can touch. Makes hope easier to believe in."

I lean over and brush my mouth against hers with a faint kiss, feeling the warmth of her breath from her parted cherry lips.

"Faith can be tricky like that. But I do believe in one thing." I smile against her mouth, slowly swishing my nose back and forth to graze hers, which makes her giggle.

"Oh yeah? What's that?"

"You were meant for me, Mercedes Lopez."

She pushes on my chest playfully and tips her head back in a laugh. The smile is uninhibited and looks nothing like the girl that she usually shows people, so I can't help but soak in it.

"Meant for you huh?" she says between laughs.

I shrug. "You're my soulmate, I knew it the first moment I laid my eyes on you. My dark goddess."

"You just thought I was hot." Merry shakes her head. "Admit it."

"Fuck yeah, you were hot," I say, and it makes her laugh. "But you were also hella fucking scary."

"Scary?"

"I had never met anyone like you. You kind of made my brain explode." I bring my hand up to my temple and make my fingers burst out, but she grabs my hand and pulls it against her chest.

"As much as I appreciate the sentiment, I think that might have been the coke." Her eyebrows furrow.

I flatten my hand against her chest, right over her breasts, where I can feel her heart racing beneath her ribs. Excitement, nervous energy trying to burst free.

"Okay, yes, the coke might have had something to do with the brain exploding part," I admit. "But that's not what I'm talking about. You're just so unapologetic. I'd never met anyone like you before—one hundred percent who you are and not making any apologies for it. There I was thinking I was a fucking god because I'm the drummer for Enemy Muse, and you just kicked your foot up and looked at me like I was the most fucked-up piece of shit. You saw straight through me."

"You weren't a fucked-up piece of shit." She places her hand on my cheek.

I tilt my head and quirk an eyebrow. When she met me, I was naked, wasted, and about to fuck some random groupie I can't even remember. I was two weeks away from rock bottom.

Not my best moment.

"Fine, maybe a little bit." She scrunches her nose like it hurt her to admit it. "But I get that there was a lot more going on. So, let's just say I was unimpressed."

"I appreciate the honesty." I place my hand over my heart. "Even if it stings a little. I mean, I was naked and you're telling me you weren't impressed with..." I rub my hips against her, and she rolls her eyes.

"Did you just dry hump your question?"

"Maybe." I grin.

She groans. "All right, that particular part of you *is* impressive. But I was intent on not fucking around with messed up rock stars, so I tried not to pay attention."

I smile, realizing I'm lucky we've even come as far as we have.

"If it makes you feel better, I don't see you that way anymore," Merry says, her voice softer. "You were working through a lot of shit people put in your head. And I'll be honest, I kind of hate them for doing that to you because you didn't deserve it. I'm proud of you for everything you've done to get to where you are now. I don't think I've ever really told you that. But being sober in this profession is no joke, and you did it. You've never been given credit for your strength. And I hope you know, you are enough, Noah, just as you are."

My chest tightens, and those wounds that live deep stitch up a little with Merry's words.

"You're perfect," I say, holding her face in my hands, and loving the rawness in her eyes right now. No barrier as she stares back at me. "And you're my soulmate."

Merry narrows her eyes.

"I said what I said, no taking it back."

"You sure know all the right things to say to scare a girl off, Noah Hayes." Merry chuckles.

"Uh uh." I wrap my arms tightly around her. "You're not going anywhere. This is forever."

Her hands tangle up around my shoulders and into my hair.

"Promise?"

I bring my lips over hers. "Promise."

And I kiss that word into her with all my heart.

August

25

MERRY

THE CLUB IS ALREADY packed by the time Cassie and Sebastian arrive. Not that it matters when you're partying with Enemy Muse. They have the best VIP booth in the place, and it has plenty of room.

Cassie grins when she spots me, whispering something in Sebastian's ear before sliding into the booth.

"Hey man." Sebastian grabs Noah's shoulder. "Let's get a drink."

Noah nods and follows him into the crowd, but my eyes are fixed on Cassie, who is grinning wide.

"Neither of them drink," I point out to her.

"Water?" She shrugs with forced innocence.

"You're trying to get me alone to grill me," I call her out.

Quinn slides into the booth on my other side and nudges my shoulder. "Of course, we are."

"I'm surrounded by pink hair with no one to save me." I shake my head at them.

The band has some press events this week for the new album, so Quinn is in town to coordinate the photo shoots and interviews. Since everyone was going to be in one place, Cassie timed her trip back from Seattle to *catch up*.

"All right, Ms. Never Going to Happen, dish, now," Cassie says as Sebastian swings back around and hands a drink to her.

Noah starts walking in my direction, but I shake my head at him to keep him away. There may be no saving myself from this inquisition, but it doesn't mean I need to drag him under with me.

"It happened a few weeks ago." I shrug a shoulder and take a sip of my drink.

"Oh, I know when it happened," Cassie says. "And you are lucky I was headed back to Seattle the next morning. That's the only reason you've been able to avoid this conversation as long as you have. So, spill. I don't want your one-word text responses, I want details."

I lift an eyebrow at her.

"Eww, okay, not too many details."

I shake my head and laugh because she can be such a goody two-shoes.

Quinn nudges my shoulder. "I wouldn't mind some of the details." She winks at me, and it makes me burst out laughing.

"I'm sure you wouldn't," I tell her, setting my drink down. "And there's not much to tell that you probably haven't already heard. Noah and I are seeing each other."

"Exclusively?"

"It's Noah." I lift an eyebrow. Regardless of the fuckboy he was before we started whatever it is he and I are doing, he's not a guy who likes sharing—especially where I'm concerned. "Yes, we're exclusive."

"And…" Cassie prods my leg.

"And we're seeing where it goes," I say nonchalantly.

"I call bullshit," Quinn pipes up. "You two have been like asteroids headed straight for each other for almost a year now. You're not fooling anyone with this casual crap."

I look from her to Cassie, and they are both shaking their heads at me.

"I'm not sure what you want me to say. Yes, we're seeing each other. And yes, there are feelings there. But it's still new, technically. It's not like we're getting married or anything."

Although, knowing Noah, he probably already has those thoughts in his head.

It might be early, but things are already more serious than any relationship I've been in. I'm not sure how to define what Noah and I are to each other at this point, but casual is definitely understating things.

It's all headfirst, especially considering what's looming on the horizon.

When my doctor finally called me back, he wanted me to come in for an office visit. But after a long discussion, he decided it would be okay to push that out for a couple of weeks since the aches haven't led to any abnormal bleeding.

Noah isn't thrilled—to say the least. I'm pretty sure he was ready to ship me off on a private plane that day.

Luckily, he didn't put up much of a fight either. I need him to trust me on how I handle this situation and what's best for my body.

Besides, I have things to finish with my demo and depending on how things go with the doctor, I don't know how long I'll be down for. I can't risk it. This is my career. My dream. My body is just going to need to cooperate for the time being.

So yeah, things with Noah haven't been casual like I keep saying. We're working through a lot of shit really early on. But I'm not ready to share all that with Cassie and Quinn. Especially in the middle of a nightclub.

"Okay, I get it," Cassie says, finally sitting back and taking another drink. "I'm done pushing. You seem happy, and it looks good on you."

The corner of my mouth twitches, and I hope I'm not totally giving myself away by blushing.

"I am. We just... work. I don't know how to explain it."

Quinn nudges my arm. "Good. You deserve it."

I smile, but something pangs in my chest, because I don't feel like I deserve it. Especially after I pushed Noah away for so long. He's been so caring and understanding. And I know it's in his nature because Noah is one of those rare people who really does wear his heart on his sleeve and puts himself out there. But it's difficult to accept.

He deserves more than you can give him.

That thought rattles around too loud for my liking.

"What about you?" I say to Quinn, turning the firing squad around on her. "What's up with that guy that tattooed your name on him?"

She rakes her teeth over her bottom lip and tries to bury a grin.

"Oh no, what's that face?" I shove her shoulder lightly. "You're over here grilling me and you're dick-whipped yourself?"

"Is dick-whipped a thing now?" Cassie asks.

"If they get pussy-whipped, then sure." I shrug and turn back to Quinn with a narrowed gaze. "I thought this guy was like a total stalker, what gives?"

"Not a stalker." Quinn holds up her hand. "Just, very... passionate."

"I know those ones." I take a drink as my gaze drifts to where Noah is standing at the edge of a large group of people.

The women among them look a little like sharks circling blood in the water. But when Noah looks over and our eyes lock, I feel something warm in my chest. He could be in the center of the room, surrounded by the most beautiful women in the world, and that look tells me all I need to know.

He's not that guy.

He'd never do that to me.

This is not casual.

I break his stare, trying to reconcile the war happening between my heart and my head.

"I know, you totally get it." Quinn smiles. "But he's a good guy, and I'm not sure what to do with that. I usually fall for assholes who cheat on me and treat me like shit."

"I'm not sure how this is a bad thing." Cassie shakes her head, and I have to agree with her. "Although I guess I did the exact opposite. I always dated the good guys, then I met Sebastian."

"He's good to you." Which is saying a lot since he was a player and a train wreck before they met.

"He's very good to me," Cassie says with a big smile. Her eyes find him and I'm pretty sure they're fucking each other in their heads when their gazes meet. "But that's my point. Sometimes the guy you never go for is exactly who you should be with."

"Maybe," Quinn says, seeming like her mind is somewhere else. "It's fun for now. But we go back on tour in less than three months, and we all know how that is. Even if they are getting more tour buses, it's going to be a cramped mess. And I can't date someone when I'm in a different state every other day."

I scrunch my nose, not really sure how to comfort her. Relationships on tour are hard enough when both people are there. But when one isn't, there's a whole other set of issues. I've heard it time and again from the roadies who have tried it.

The constant question of fidelity. The conflicting schedules. The fact that the band consumes your life, and you don't have room for anyone else.

It makes me wonder what this next tour will be like for me and Noah. If we're still together, and each of the band members is getting their own bus, would I be with him on his? Is that where he wants me?

Is that where *I* want to be?

And what if my demo hits? What happens with us then? Even with Noah's apparent dedication to making this work, I'm not sure how we would see each other if we someday ended up on different tours.

Someday.

I actually just thought of a future with Noah, and it didn't scare me. When did this happen?

"Enjoy it while you can and just see where it goes," Cassie says, always having the right thing to say in situations like this. I'm not the comforting friend. I'm the one who tells you like it is.

"If it's meant to work out, then it will." Cassie reaches across me and plants a hand on Quinn's knee.

"On that note." I place my hand over both of theirs. "Let's fucking dance. We are too young and too hot to be sitting in a club talking about our feelings. I came to party, let's get to it."

They both shake their heads at me and laugh, but I don't care. I grab their hands and drag them up from the table.

"You three look like trouble," Sebastian says, as we walk up to the group.

"The best kind." I wink at him, then I reach out a hand toward Noah. "Dance with me."

It's strange how the little things are what bring a lump to my throat. The fact that I didn't realize the hole inside me from not having him before. And now, instead of watching him disappear with some groupie, he's grabbing my hand and pulling me toward him.

His mouth dips near my ear and he whispers, "Anything for you, beautiful."

It sends goosebumps the full length of my spine.

"Crap, I'm the fifth wheel now," Quinn says as Cassie latches onto Sebastian.

"No, you're not." Eloise comes up beside Quinn and slips her arm through hers. "Let's show them how it's done."

They head into the crowd first and the four of us follow until we settle in an open spot on the dance floor. The beat is vibrating the walls, but I feel calmed by it as I stand in Noah's arms.

Even in heels tonight, he's a good half-foot taller. And with his chin tipped down and his hair falling around his face, I look up at him like we're in our own little bubble.

"You survived the ladies?" Noah grins.

"Barely," I say. "Are the guys that bad?"

"Oh yeah, you know Rome, loves to talk about my relationship status." Noah laughs, and I can't help but smile trying to picture it. "The most I got was, *so you guys are fucking*, and I shut them up with a nod and the middle finger."

"Lucky." I groan.

Noah's hands slip down to my ass and he squeezes right where his fingertips graze the hemline of my very short jumper.

"If we don't leave soon, I'm going to bend you over a bathroom sink," Noah says, grabbing onto my ass harder.

"That's not very sanitary," I say, but he shrugs. "And we just got here."

"Fuck everyone, I'd rather be inside you than talking to them anyway."

"Something we agree on." I lift an eyebrow at him and smile.

Noah's hands move up and he wraps his arms around my waist, pulling me tight to his body, his erection already hard and ready for me.

"Someone wasn't lying." I press myself firmer against him.

He growls as he sways us to the music. "Not lying. Although, as much as I want to drag you home right now, this is better."

"Getting out?"

"Showing you off as mine."

My belly flutters with the intensity of how he says it.

I'm not someone who is generally self-conscious because I rarely think much of myself in general. But, in Noah's eyes, I feel beautiful in a way I never have before. I feel like the dark goddess he says I am.

"It's weird though right?" I say. "I'm so used to watching you disappear with random people and us doing that awkward avoidance thing out in public."

Noah tightens his grip and shakes his head. "It feels right."

His mouth lands on mine like a statement.

Our tongues tangle.

I'm his.

Our bodies sway.

I'm his.

My heart pounds.

I'm his.

We dance for what might be minutes or hours or days. All I know is that I don't want to ever stop.

26

NOAH

SEBASTIAN AND ELOISE STORM in circles around Adrian's living room, and I'm glad I'm not a songwriter for the band because one more opinion on this song and we would never finish this album.

"You're not hearing me," Eloise says, throwing her arms up. "I'm not saying to cut the song altogether, but it isn't working as is."

"It was fine yesterday," Sebastian argues.

"No, I was just too tired to say anything about it yesterday."

Sebastian tips his head back and laughs. "El, you're driving me fucking insane. You've never had this many complaints about one of my songs. And they're not bad, ask Adrian."

He waves a hand toward Adrian, who looks like he wants nothing to do with Sebastian dragging him into this conversation. Eloise glares at them both and I think she's officially going to blow a gasket.

"So that's how it is? You're ganging up on me now?" She crosses her arms and stands tall for battle.

Shit is about to hit the fan, so I finally stand up and decide that even though Rome is going to sit here smoking weed like this doesn't involve him, someone has to play peacekeeper.

"Can we all sit back down?" I ask, moving between Eloise and Sebastian.

They might be siblings—they certainly fight like it—but ultimately this is band shit, and they need to calm the fuck down.

I look back and forth between them and wait until they sit on opposite couches facing each other.

"All right, let's talk about this." I swipe my hair off my face. "El, Sebastian does have a point, what's with all the resistance? Normally you guys are pretty in sync with writing styles."

"Not you too." She glares at me.

"I'm not judging here." I throw up my hands. "I'm just trying to understand where you're coming from. His songs sound good, from what I've heard. And it fits with what you've been working on. Where's the disconnect?"

Eloise rests her elbows on her knees and leans forward to bury her face in her hands.

"I don't know," she says, frustrated.

It's really unlike Eloise to get like this. She's usually the calmest one of us. But for the past couple of months, she's been seriously on edge and not acting like herself. She won't agree with anything Sebastian wants to collaborate with her on, she's been arguing with Adrian about the upcoming tour schedule. If I didn't know her better, I'd think it was rocker pride, but this is Eloise. She always keeps her cool.

Something is off.

"Maybe you just need to get laid," Rome says, leaning back in his chair and taking a long drag of his joint.

That at least gets Eloise to look up again, but it's with a look that makes me think she might murder him.

"Rome, shut the fuck up unless you have something helpful to say," I warn him, before this whole thing goes completely sideways and the band does something like split up before our next tour.

Rome shrugs like he honestly couldn't care less. I'm not sure what's more difficult lately, the fact that Eloise is resistant to everything, or the fact that Rome has all but entirely checked out.

I walk over to Eloise and sit next to her on the couch, placing a hand on her shoulder and feeling how tense she is.

"Talk to us, we're your family, El. If something is going on, or you're unhappy, we need to know what it is, or we can't do anything."

She shakes her head and looks at me.

"I know," she says, sounding much calmer now. "And I'm sorry, I'm not sure why I've been so on edge lately. I just feel nothing—this music, this album—it's not connecting for me. And it's not your fault."

She turns to Sebastian. "It's some of your best work, and maybe that's the problem because while you seem to be one hundred percent vibing, I feel disconnected. And I can't seem to get there. I'm frustrated with myself, and

I'm taking it out on you. Maybe you should just write this album without me."

"No fucking way." Sebastian stands up and walks over to us, sitting on the other side of her.

"Sebastian's right," I say. "Not that I don't have faith in you, bro."

"No offense taken." Sebastian wraps his arm around his sister. "There's a reason Enemy Muse works—a reason we've gotten to where we are today—and it's not just my incredibly handsome face."

Eloise rolls her eyes at him, but his ridiculous comment at least makes her crack the slightest smile.

"We all bring something unique to the band. And it's like we said in the beginning, we do it together or we don't do it at all. Are you done, El?"

The silence in the room is deafening.

Sebastian is right, we're not just a band, we're family, and if one of us burns out, it's not like we can just replace them with a cookie-cutter copy. The band would never be quite the same.

And as much as that has comforted me over the years, because I've been able to depend on this group at the darkest points of my life, right now, it feels a little suffocating.

I've never had attachments that would impact what I bring to the band. But with Merry's health issues and the potential of her going on her own tour in the future, what would I choose at the end of the day?

My family or the girl I'm in love with?

"I'm not done." Eloise sighs, and Sebastian seems relieved about that, even if I'm not sure how I feel right now.

"I'm just uninspired," she continues. "I feel like I'm forcing it and it's just not working. I want to care about what I'm writing again."

"I get that," Sebastian says. "I couldn't write for over a year, remember?"

Hence why it's been so long since Enemy Muse has released a new album.

"If we need to take longer, we can. We'll just recycle old material on tour, right Adrian?"

Adrian nods, but I can't read the look on his face as he stares at Eloise. I would think he'd be irritated that we can't just get over our shit and get the album done, but that seems to be the least of his worries.

"No." Eloise shakes her head and stands up. "We've got this, okay. Let's go over the song again. I'll get there."

I'm not sure if the pep talk is for her or for us, but she nods at Sebastian, seeming intent on pushing through no matter what.

"All right sis." He stands up and walks over to the table where they sit down and start working through lyrics.

"Sorry, guys, it will be a little bit," Eloise says.

Rome opens his mouth to say something, but I cut him off before he can get any stupid shit out that might send her spiraling again. "Take your time. We'll keep busy. Pool?" I look at Adrian and he nods.

Walking over to Rome, I tip my head toward the other room, not giving him an option.

"Fine," he grumbles, and the three of us head into Adrian's den, where there's a large pool table in the center.

Rome pours himself a shot of whiskey from the bar in the corner while Adrian racks the balls.

"How long is this next tour again?" Rome asks, downing his shot. "I'm so fucking tired of this lame-ass city."

"Seven months. November to June," Adrian says. "We'll start stateside, have a short break, and then move overseas. It's a long one."

"Good." Rome lifts his glass in a cheer to no one and then downs a second shot.

Seven months. Why does that bother me so much all of a sudden?

I've always loved being on the road—couldn't get enough. Everything that once felt like it grounded me suddenly has me in suspension.

"You're breaking." Adrian nods at me, and I pick up a pool cue, lining it up. It's a good break, with one ball going in the corner pocket. I make two more shots before missing, and Adrian's up.

"How's El been?" I ask Adrian.

She's staying with him, and if the look on his face said anything earlier, he's as worried about her as the rest of us.

"Okay most days," Adrian says with a shrug, before leaning in to take another shot. "But this past week she's been keeping to herself a lot. I don't see much of her."

"But she's living here?"

If Merry staying at my house made anything clear, it's that you can only avoid a person so much when they are living under your roof. Not that I'm trying to avoid her at all anymore.

"I've been at Becca's apartment a lot, so besides recording time, I haven't seen much of her."

Adrian stands with the pool cue in front of him feigning nonchalance about the mention of his mysterious girlfriend. He's trying to seem indifferent like he always does. God forbid he shows his feelings.

Especially when it comes to Eloise.

Whatever happened or didn't happen between the two of them when he first started managing the band has been kept under lock and key. I don't think they fucked, because if they did, they'd probably be a little less uptight around each other, but whatever it was, they both insist it was nothing.

So, either shit went sour and they pretend they're fine for the rest of the band's sake, or they really don't give a shit—which I don't believe.

"When do we get to meet Becca?" Rome asks with a grin that makes Adrian groan.

"Not anytime soon."

"Sounds pretty serious if you're spending so much time at her place," I say.

Adrian doesn't usually date. He might fuck the occasional groupie, but other than that, he doesn't pay much attention to the women around him. His thing with Becca is the longest he's dated someone in a while, so he must at least like her.

"She's nice," Adrian says, like the wall he is, giving absolutely nothing away.

"Nice?" I raise an eyebrow.

Adrian shrugs.

"I bet she's hot," Rome says, pouring himself another drink. Hopefully Sebastian and Eloise finish up before he's too wasted to hold his guitar. "Why else wouldn't Adrian bring his chick around?"

"Maybe because he thinks you'll be a dick if he does."

"That implies I don't already *know* he'll be a dick," Adrian says, and the smallest smile creeps up on his face.

"Fuck you both." Rome downs his shot. "You guys have fun shacking up with one pussy and I'll enjoy the rest of them."

I remember when that statement would have sounded appealing to me. After Kali broke my heart and I finally lost my virginity to a random groupie who didn't even realize what she did for me, I was intent on never falling in love again. One chick wasn't worth that much fucking heartache.

But then I met Merry, and all that changed. Even if she did put me through hell before I finally got to her, I was never the same. Now it's not even a question of knowing that I'm giving up every other woman on the planet for one.

But looking up at Rome, who is standing there scrolling through his phone, I'm honestly not sure if that's in the cards for him. The kind of shit that makes him not trust people goes deeper than any of the dark shit I've seen. And I feel bad, because even if he talks a lot of shit and pisses a lot of people off, deep down he's the most loyal guy I know. He'll go to the ends of the earth for the few people he cares about.

If only he'd let someone do that for him.

I don't try to convince him of that though, because I know him well enough to know I'd be wasting my breath.

"Have fun with that," I say instead.

At least there's still one guy left in the band to keep the groupies happy.

27

Noah

This is probably the longest it's ever taken us to record an album, and it's almost more painful than when we weren't recording at all. After Sebastian and Eloise finally agreed on the chorus for one of our new songs, Savage Ways, it took another four hours for me and Rome to get in tune with each other on the tempo.

But as torturous as it was at times, it was also cathartic.

Besides Merry, music is the only other thing that brings me sanity. It keeps my heart pumping in my chest. When I'm beating the drums, I might as well be trying to draw blood from them, because music is my faith, my clarity, my religion.

In the studio, I can lose myself for hours—days even. Hammering out the songs again and again. Tweaking, adjusting, seeking perfection.

By the time I finally get home, it's almost two in the morning and I feel like I've been run over and emptied out. But also, the stress I've been carrying for days has melted away.

I find Merry asleep on the couch with the end credits of a movie playing, and I can't help the feeling that blooms inside me at the sight of her. The large furniture dwarfs her tiny body, and she's cuddled under one of the blankets so only her head sticks out. Her hair is up in a bun, with a few rogue waves falling around her makeup-free face.

Her face is relaxed, and she's so soft that she almost looks breakable like this. I wish I could make it so nothing could touch her—nothing could hurt her. All I want to do is keep her safe.

"Are you just going to stand there and watch me sleep?" Merry's eyes are still closed, but she's smiling.

"Maybe." I lean over her on the couch and peel away the blanket so I can replace it with myself. "I like watching you sleep."

"That's not creepy at all." She shifts onto her back and wraps her arms around my shoulders, burying her face against my neck.

"Can't help it," I say, planting a kiss on the side of her head. "It's the one time you actually look sweet and peaceful."

"Ha ha." She pokes my side with a finger, and I can't help but laugh. "I'm always sweet."

I lift my head up to look down at her. "Sweet as vinegar."

She rolls her pretty brown eyes at me.

"But." I lower my lips against hers. "As sour as you can be. You still taste like cherries."

"Oh yeah?" I feel her heart racing in her chest.

"Yeah." I run my tongue along her bottom lip, before taking her in a sleepy kiss.

Unlike when she's amped up and feisty, everything about Merry right now is soft and gentle. Her hands wander over my body like she's exploring them in a dream, and I soak it up.

I lift to kneel between her legs, pulling the waistband of her pajama shorts down as she slips out of her top, laying there naked and exposed in front of me.

Looking down at her, I think maybe it's me who is dreaming. Because I'm not the guy who gets what he wants, even when I do all the right things.

"How was your session?" Merry asks, as I stand to strip off my clothes. She sits up to help, and it's just one of the little ways she takes care of me.

"A mess at first," I admit, as she pulls my pants down. "It's better now though."

"I see that." She grins at my cock as it juts straight out at her.

She moves for me to sit down, but I push her back onto the couch. All I want right now is to rest between her soft tattooed thighs and disappear in her comfort. My fingers stroke down her stomach and I slip two into her. I'm rewarded by the look on her face that tells me I'm curling into all the right corners to drive her insane.

There's nothing that feels as good as making Merry's body wiggle with pleasure under my touch. I'll spend my life learning all the ways she enjoys me doing it.

With my fingers inside her, I circle her clit with my thumb, making her shiver. Her breath quickens against my chest, and I catch her moans with my mouth because I can't help but taste how I'm making her feel. I need every breath. I need every sound.

All of her.

Just as I feel her tighten around me, I slip my fingers out, and thrust my cock in, wanting her climax to wrap around me. Hitting so deep that I set her off with one thrust. Her pussy clenches as a strangled noise escapes her lips.

I drag my hand up her chest and pinch her nipple, before running it up her throat and holding her there so I can look at her gorgeous face and watch her eyes flutter. There's nothing more beautiful on her than when our eyes meet, and I know for certain there's nothing between us.

"Noah..." My name is almost a whisper as she smiles, before something shifts, and hesitation flashes in her eyes. If she was going to say more, she doesn't, kissing me instead.

Her fingers tangle in my hair and she's frantic for my lips as she rides out the final pulses of her climax. Her legs wrap around me, and everything fits right where it belongs. The pieces on the outside, like tongues and limbs. And the pieces I can only account for when I'm around her, like the beating of my heart.

I almost forget to continue thrusting because I'm so lost in the feel of her. But as I pull back and start moving again, her face pinches and the air seems to shift.

Her expression moves from pleasure to discomfort, and everything feels suddenly very tense and... wet.

But not like I'm used to.

I lift further to look down to see everything is red.

"Fuck, Merry." I pull out and climb off her so fast, not sure what I've done. Because with any other chick, I'd think she just got her time of the month, but I know too much and there's so much blood.

Merry's eyes get wide, and she reaches for the blanket to cover herself.

"Oh my God." Her eyes are frantic. "I'm sorry, oh my God, we need to get this off the couch."

"Fuck the couch, are you okay? Did I hurt you?" I reach for the blanket to try and check her, but she holds it close to her chest.

"I'm fine," she says.

But she's paler than before and she won't look me in the eyes.

I reach for her face and cup her cheeks in my hands to force her to look at me. "Mercedes."

Her eyes blink and it's like I'm watching her process it. "I'm sorry."

"You don't have to be sorry; I just need to know if you're okay. I didn't mean to hurt you. Fuck, I didn't even think about that."

"You didn't hurt me. I'm not feeling any pain. If I was... trust me, you'd know." She shakes her head. "I just wasn't expecting this. It's never happened during sex before."

"Is that a bad sign? Do we need to call the doctor?"

"I don't know. Probably..." She trails off.

I hold her arms, and I've never been so equally worried and frustrated. She should have gone back to Seattle when the pain started. I should have made her. Not that Merry listens to me. But fuck, what if waiting made things worse?

"I should clean this up," Merry says, biting her lip.

Letting go of her face, I reach for her blanket and tighten it around her. "Let's get in the shower. I can buy a new couch; I'm not worried about that right now."

"I can use the guest room," she says as she stands and secures the blanket under her arms. "Give us some space to clean up."

"No." I catch her hand before she can turn and pull her against me. "Let me take care of you."

Her eyebrows pinch like she wants to argue. Or maybe she's confused, or embarrassed. But she has no reason to be, and I need her to understand that.

"Okay," she says, letting me lead her across the house and into my bathroom.

I turn up the heat of the shower until it's steaming and ready for her when she comes back from the toilet.

There's blood all over me, and it's something that I honestly would have thought would freak me out—or gross me out—but it's the least of my worries, because all I can think about is what it could mean.

After Merry told me about the severity of her condition. I did a lot of googling. I looked up uterine fibroids, reoccurring cases of them, treatments, surgical scarring. I thought I knew a lot about a woman's body, but apparently, I don't know shit.

From what I could gather and based on what Merry told me about her experience with it, she has some of the more severe symptoms. Depending on the time of the month she'll get intense cramping, even heavy bleeding. And even though they surgically removed the ones they found before; new ones grew back. So, the chances of another surgery fixing it permanently isn't likely.

She's been managing symptoms with her doctor, and doing the least aggressive treatments, but it's a waiting game for them to go back in, and from the look on her face when she told me, she's nervous about what they'll tell her when they do.

Stepping into the shower, it's like Merry can read my mind as I run the soapy luffa over her arms and back.

"It's just a period," she says, although she doesn't sound all that confident. "They're heavier because of what I have."

"Okay," I say, trying to stay calm for her even if I'm freaking out inside.

"It doesn't mean anything."

"Okay," I repeat, moving slowly down her legs to her feet, where pink water swirls down the drain. "You still need to tell your doctor."

She sighs. "I know."

That admission alone worries me even more. Because if she honestly thought nothing of it, she would argue with me.

All she wants to do is finish her demo tape right now, and it's probably really frustrating to have to think about putting that on the back burner, but it doesn't matter. She needs to do what's safest for her body.

I keep all those thoughts to myself as I wash her, no matter how much my tongue hurts from biting it. She doesn't need me lecturing her right now on top of whatever is going on in her head.

After I've washed her whole body, I soap her hair. It's thick and straight in the water, and I love watching her tilt her head back and close her eyes as I massage her scalp. When I'm all finished, she rinses it out and I grab my luffa to work on myself.

"Here," she says, taking it from me.

I try to pull it back. "You don't have to do that. I'm the one taking care of you right now."

But she tugs the luffa from my grasp. "And let me take care of you."

Her eyes narrow, and I drop my arms to my sides in defeat.

It feels good as she rubs the soapy luffa over my body. I've never had anyone wash me before, and it's intimate, standing here, letting her clean me. Not moving as she works her way over my back, my ass, down the backs of my thighs. Then she moves to the front, washing my chest before moving down further. Most of the mess washed off from the spray of the shower, but she doesn't pause or hesitate to clean me of the rest.

We've been dating for only a month, but it already feels like my whole life. I would hand this woman the heart from my chest if she asked for it. I'd share my entire world with her.

I decide right here in the shower, as she sets the luffa down and runs her fingers on my scalp, that I belong to her body and soul from here on out.

"I can help with that," I say, swiping the shampoo out of her hands, noticing that she's struggling with my height to get to me. "Nice try though, shorty."

She giggles and lets me take it, and it's nice to see smiles returning to her face. Because although she's still my grumpy girl with a cheery name, she does smile a lot more recently than she used to, and I like seeing it.

As I rinse my hair out, her hands move over my chest again, tracing the muscles, and I feel like a total jerk when my cock twitches from her touch.

Her gaze drops down, noticing.

"Sorry," I say, trying to think of anything that might take my mind off the water running over her naked body in front of me. "My body has a mind of its own."

"You never got to go." She purses her lips.

"I'm fine. Promise."

The last thing I was worried about was coming after all that happened.

Merry starts sliding her hands down further, but I catch her wrists to stop her.

"Really," I say. "I'll survive."

"Is it because of…" she trails off. "You aren't going to be grossed out, or like—"

I grab her face and kiss her, cutting off her words because it's stupid shit that I don't want to hear.

"No," I say, pulling away, but keeping my hands on her face. "You're the sexiest woman in the whole fucking world, Merry. I honestly feel bad for anyone who has to stand next to you because it's downright cruel to them. Nothing, and I mean *nothing*, can change my mind on that."

"Thank you." Her cheeks light up as confidence returns to her face. She lifts onto her toes to give me a kiss.

"You don't have to thank me." I pull her closer, so her wet body is up against mine. And now I really can't prevent myself from getting hard because it's a natural reaction to this woman. "Thank whatever larger power you believe in because they made you this way."

My words might be corny, but they make her smile.

"Whatever you say," she says. "But I meant thank you for taking care of me. You're too good for me Noah Hayes."

Her hand slips down again and she wraps it around my cock before I can stop her.

She rests her forehead against my chest, and I feel her breath on my skin.

"Just let me thank you," she whispers.

Her hand slides up and down my shaft, and I have to plant a hand on the wall of the shower behind her to hold myself up. I should pull away. I should stop this. It feels wrong and right and bad and good.

But that's everything with Merry and me. Hard fought but worth the wait. And I know that in some fucked up way, her hand on my dick is her answer to the things she can't fix right now. Because sex is how Merry connects. And when there's nothing left to be said, she'd rather let her body do the talking.

I stand with her under the running water of the shower as she jerks me off. And it's not wild or sexy or desperate. But in its own way it's perfect.

I wish I could make her understand what it's like to be helpless because that's how I feel right now—and every minute around her.

I wish I could show her what she does to me in a way that's more than me coming on her stomach as the water washes between us.

I wish we could put off reality and pause in this moment. But I've tried that before, and it never works, so I just hug her harder.

28

MERRY

Noah hasn't said anything since we left the house, and he's not making it a secret how he feels right now.

I talked to my doctor this morning and we agreed to keep the original appointment for next week since I'm not experiencing any pain.

"It's just a period," I say for what feels like the hundredth time. "It's that time of the month anyway, I'm fine."

Noah nods his head, but his eyes are narrow and his jaw is clenched.

"You don't get to be mad at me about this."

He pulls the car to a stop outside Adrian's house.

"You don't get to tell me how I feel about it, Merry," he says flatly.

"It's my body."

"I get that." He tips his head back against the seat. "But that doesn't mean you can expect me to ignore the fact that you're not taking care of it."

I unbuckle and turn in my seat.

"I called the doctor. My appointment is in a week. You have to trust me. I get that this is all new to you, and a lot to handle. But I feel fine." I reach out and place my hand on his thigh and he finally looks at me. "If anything changes, I'll head to Seattle—"

"*We'll* head to Seattle."

I narrow my eyes at him, but now's not the time to add more fuel to this argument.

"I've got a week to finish up this demo. I wanted to do a few more tracks, but I'm fine with finishing up the one song I have left and then doing the rest when I get back."

I squeeze his leg, but he doesn't relax.

"Put yourself in my shoes." I sigh. "You already made your dreams happen, Noah. I haven't, and this is my chance."

"It's not more important than your health."

"It's just a week."

Noah lifts his hand and places it over mine. With a final squeeze, I watch the fight leave his eyes.

"One week," he says, letting me go and getting out of the car.

He walks all the way around to open my door for me, and as ridiculous as I used to find the gesture, it makes my heart squeeze in my chest. I climb out of the car; Noah wraps his arms around my waist before I can get past him. Burying his face in my neck.

"I love you," he whispers.

I feel my throat constrict at his words. Whatever I feel for Noah isn't a short-term kind of thing. A month into this and I already feel like somehow, he's become a part of me. But when I open my mouth, nothing comes out quite yet, so I just hug him harder.

After a long moment, Noah steps back. He slides his hand down my arm to take my hand in his own. We walk in silence to Adrian's door, but the air is thick with things unspoken.

I'm no stranger to people having their opinions about how I handle my health. It's one of the main reasons my parents and I have butted heads over the years. But with Noah, it feels different. The worry I sense makes it clear my feelings aren't the only ones on the line anymore.

He's in this with me, completely. And once more I'm hurting him.

Noah lays on the couch in the control room while I get set up in the recording booth. I don't think either of us slept much last night, but he insisted on tagging along, even knowing he has a long day ahead with the band after this.

I watch him through the glass window as I set my notebook up on the stand. He's on his back with his eyes closed, but I can tell he isn't sleeping. His face is tense and there's the slightest furrow between his eyebrows.

One week.

I just need to get this demo into a usable state, and then the universe can do whatever it wants with me. At least then I'll have something to work with after my surgery.

My only mission now is how to convince Noah to stay in Denver when I head to Seattle to meet with my doctor. He seems intent on following me, but he has a band and obligations. As much as he's willing to toss that aside, I can't be selfish by letting him. Which means, I've got my work cut out for me.

Noah thinks I'm stubborn, but that man is ten times worse. He needs to stay in Denver. He needs to finish up the album. And when the time comes, he needs to head out on tour, whether I join him or not.

The thought alone aches in places I didn't know existed under my ribs.

I don't want to have to give up Noah, and even if I think long-distance relationships while touring are almost guaranteed to fail, I would be willing to try.

Right?

But touring almost always guarantees the end of a relationship. So even if Noah would want to try and make long distance work, we both know what life on the road is really like. I'm not delusional enough to think there aren't constant distractions.

Ones I've kept myself busy with for almost a year now.
And so has he.

Noah might say he loves me now, but after enough time and enough distance, even his commitment would be tested.

I'm fucking pathetic. I don't get insecure over guys. The fact that he even has me thinking this is the reason I've avoided relationships up until now. What has love done to me?

If that's what it is.

"You ready?" Adrian asks.

I look up, realizing I've been zoning out, and see Adrian sitting at the sound board messing with the controls.

"As I'll ever be."

Noah tips his head then and looks at me through the glass. I try to smile, but it feels forced and he doesn't return it.

Someone finally has the power to drain the light from Mr. Sunshine. And it is me.

I flip open my notebook to the page I'm working on. The Road Home is a song I've all but re-written over the past few weeks, and I finally have it to where I want it.

Unlike the majority of the others, this one is more of a ballad, which I don't often write. But Adrian liked how Fairytale showed off my softer side and thought The Road Home should be slowed down as well.

It's an opportunity to show off the range of my voice, and after adjusting the lyrics and changing it up, it's strangely fitting.

Taking a final sip of tea, I put the headphones on my head and take a deep breath.

This is it. One final song to find life in. After this, things could change in so many different ways.

The beat starts up in my headphones, so I close my eyes and start to sing.

"The girl in the mirror saw someone
A dream she was waiting to become
Someone tell her she can be
Even after everything
The vision she was waiting on for so long

Mama hold her tight
Forgive the girl for breaking in the middle of the night
Tell her something, tell her anything
Tell her love can still exist

Follow the yellow brick road
Even when the path gets dark and bleak
Follow the yellow brick road
No matter where it starts to lead
There are truths to find
Fears that thrive
Places deep you'll hide behind
But if you
Follow the yellow brick road
In time, in time, in time
You're home

The girl thought her heart was made of gold
That's how princes, and fairy tales, and stories are always told
But the shine was dulled, we grew old
She's cold, she's cold, she's cold, she's cold

Mama say you're here
Even if the girl has been the burden that you bear
Give her something that makes fear go blind
Show her light, show her a sign

Follow the yellow brick road

Even when the path gets dark and bleak
Follow the yellow brick road
No matter where it starts to lead
There are truths to find
Fears that thrive
Places deep you'll hide behind
But if you
Follow the yellow brick road
In time, in time, in time
You're home

I'm home
Close my eyes
I'm home
Deep inside... inside... inside"

My eyes open, and that's when I realize there are tears trying to get out. I think about the rift with my parents for the past year, and how even if I pretended not to care, the idea of *home* became something of a figment because of it.

I think about Noah, now sitting on the couch staring at me. The selfish way I drain him of all his goodness and somehow, I still feel lost.

I think about the pieces of me that have already been taken, and how those holes might grow in size until I'm not sure if I'll ever be able to fill them.

Dipping my chin down, I wipe my cheeks and close my notebook, taking a deep breath. All I can control is myself in this moment. And I will not break down before I've even fought the battle.

"That was beautiful, Merry," Adrian's voice comes through the headset.

I look up at him and give him a nod. I'll probably still have to sing it twenty more times to get it right and tweak every vocal, but that was the cleanest first try we've laid down and I feel good about that.

"Let's take ten," he says. "I need to make some adjustments and then we'll go back in for just the chorus. Get some water if you need it."

I nod and take off the headset, as the dullest amount of pain festers deep inside me. But I try not to let it show on my face, so Noah doesn't start to worry. Maybe it's denial, or maybe I'm just imagining it.

Noah meets me at the door and plants a quick kiss on my lips as I walk up to him.

"You make the angels jealous," he says, giving me a smile that I've missed on him all morning.

I shake my head. "I don't know about that."

"I do," he says, and he wraps his hands up into the hair at the base of my skull and holds me. "I've never heard anything more beautiful."

Lifting onto my toes, I wrap my arms around his shoulders and give him a deep kiss. If there is light bright enough to bloom what's buried in my darkness, he would be the sun to bring it to existence.

My heart races in my chest, and I want to run away with him, where it's just the two of us. To places where the problems of the world can't reach us.

I want to be his forever.

Untouchable.

Another dull ache strikes me somewhere deep, and I pull away, but it must not show on my face, because Noah is looking down at me and smiling.

"I'm going to use the bathroom." I give him another quick kiss on the lips, before unwinding myself from him.

He hangs back to talk to Adrian as I make my way up the staircase and down the hallway. Throbbing is starting between my temples, and I try to remember how much food and water I've had today because I feel lightheaded all of a sudden.

As I make my way into the bathroom, I lock the door, before walking over to the sink and splashing water on my face. I'm not sure if it's adrenaline from singing, but everything is fuzzy around the edges. Reaching for a towel, a sharp pain stabs through me with such force that I hunch over.

It's unlike anything I've felt before, wrapping all the way around my spine. My body feels like it's heaving from somewhere deep, and I wrap my arms around myself to clutch it, but it does nothing.

"Noah," I say, but it's barely a whisper as I take a step forward.

The sharp stabbing pain runs through me again, so intense my knees buckle, and spots cloud my vision.

What is happening?

My mind is racing, and my heart is pounding in my chest. I can barely think or breathe.

"Noah," I say again, but I don't think it actually comes out. Or I never hear it because my body gives out beneath me and it's just darkness.

29

NOAH

I watch Merry disappear up the stairs with her song still playing in my head. For a girl so hard on the outside, her music shares a lot more of her than I expected. All I want to do when I listen to her sing is go in there and hold her. I want to promise her that everything is going to be better.

If only I believed it.

Merry doesn't talk about her family often, but I know that she is really close with them. Or, at least, she was before she came on tour with us. But their rift isn't like the one I have with mine, it's out of love, not judgment. They worry about her, and it's understandable given the shitstorm around us on a daily basis.

In time, I have no doubt they will be able to reconcile whatever gap exists between them. And I want that for her, especially after hearing her song today.

"You guys all right?" Adrian asks, not looking over his shoulder at me.

I sit down on the couch and tip my head back to stare at the ceiling. "We're good."

It's a half-truth. I don't feel unsettled about Merry and me specifically, it's everything else I can't seem to get a grip on. Things outside my control, that if I could just stop from spinning it would all make sense.

"Whatever you say." Adrian spins around in his chair fully to face me.

I grab the water off the table in front of me and take a long drink. Being exhausted isn't helping my mood, so it's going to be a long fucking day.

"You're in a relationship, so you know how it can be," I say to Adrian.

"Complicated." He half shrugs. This dude is so weird about certain things.

I nod. "And this is Merry we're talking about. The woman does not give a fucking inch. It's infuriating."

Adrian tips his head back and laughs, which is surprising because Adrian doesn't really react to much of anything.

"Noah, you're the kind of guy who can't turn down a challenge." Adrian grins. "But Merry is going to bring even you to your limits. You know I think she's great. She puts up with my shit, and that's saying a lot because I'm not an easy guy to get along with. But she's a steel wall about some things and you're gonna bash your head in if you don't learn how to figure another way around it."

I shake my head because he's right. Going straight at these conversations with Merry is getting me nowhere, and I don't want to lose her, or myself, in the process.

"I love her, man."

Adrian nods his head. "I know. You guys will figure it out."

I think back to when we first got to Denver and Adrian made that offhand comment about how he thought something was going on with her. If only he knew. She's been holding in a lot of shit instead of processing it, and I'm a little afraid what's going to happen when she finally lets it out.

My phone pings and I look down to see my mom has texted me.

"Fuck." I groan, and Adrian looks down at my phone in my hands.

"Don't tell me it's Rome getting into trouble."

I shake my head. "Worse, it's my mother."

Adrian lifts an eyebrow. The whole band knows I'm not close with my family, and that at this point, it's better that way, because all they do is make me feel worse about who I am.

Opening the text, I see some long ramble about Kali coming to visit me. Something in there references Merry, even if not by name. And how she's disappointed I'm living in sin with a "Devil's whore" who is corrupting me.

Somehow, after all this time, she still thinks she has room to judge. And maybe it's that I've let her. I've been quiet while my family brushed me off, crucified me, and abandoned me as their son. I've pretended it had no impact, when really, it ate away at the person I was. It made me doubt who I actually am.

But I'm done with their judgements.

I scroll to the end of her long text and don't bother reading it in full because I don't need to hear what she thinks when she has no desire to be in my life. She might think she can keep me on a string forever, but I'm ready to cut it. The people who really care are here for me, and that's all that matters.

My thumbs are flying over the letters so fast, I feel out of breath from typing.

Noah: I love you Mom, always will. Dad, too. But if you're going to reach out only to berate me and talk down on the woman I love, then I no longer want to hear it. I've been quiet and tried to help you understand my life. But you either aren't willing or can't. When you decide you want to be in my life, the door is open. But until then, I don't want to hear from you. I don't have room inside me for your judgement anymore.

It's ironic to me that Merry thought I pictured a certain cookie-cutter life for myself. Something resembling what I grew up with. Honestly, I'd be fine with the exact opposite as long as it made us both feel content.

I hit send on my text and breathe a sigh of relief. I've been carrying around the weight of my family's opinions for years, letting it chip me away to nothing. I'm not doing it anymore.

"What does your mom want?" Adrian asks. "Something about the ex?"

"If only exes could stay in the past."

He gets a strange look on his face, and I'm not sure what that is all about.

"It's fine though, I'm not letting my mom get to me anymore," I say, then change the subject. "How's Merry's demo looking?"

"Good. She's got a killer sound, as you heard."

I nod.

"I'll pass it along to a few contacts, but I have no doubt she'll get some bites on it. And I'm not sure if she told you, but I offered to manage her."

"No shit?" She hadn't mentioned it, but every time we're around each other lately it feels like there's a lot going on.

"Who would have thought I'd be in this business?" Adrian chuckles, and I can't help but agree.

It's not like he went to school for it. After eight years in the military, he got out and was working at a bar back home where he connected with Sebastian.

Adrian had to learn the industry as he went. He had no experience. We asked him to be our band manager because we could rely on him and we knew he'd have our backs. One thing led to another and here we are now.

"You're a force," I tell him because I'm not sure how we'd do it without him.

"Hopefully the band doesn't mind me taking on more talent. I know you guys have been it for me up to this point, but I think I need to start branching out a bit."

I shake my head. "They'll get it, especially for Merry," I say, looking at the doorway. "How long has she been in there anyway?"

It feels like she's been gone a long time now. Too long. Something bad settles in my gut, but Adrian shrugs.

I stand up and walk to the doorway, looking up the staircase.

"Merry," I yell loud enough that she should be able to hear me from down here, but there's no response.

"What's up?" Adrian stands, probably sensing my mood shift.

But I don't answer his question because I'm too busy heading up the stairs to find her. How long has she been gone now?

Five minutes?

Ten?

"Merry." I knock when I reach the door to the bathroom. My fist hits the door harder than should be necessary, but she doesn't respond.

I try the handle, but it's locked.

"Fuck," I say, banging on the door again. "Merry, open the door."

Adrian is right next to me now, looking at me confused.

"Sorry man," I say, barely giving him a glance before slamming my body into the door to get it open. I'll pay for this shit later, right now it's the least of my concerns.

The door frame cracks on the third shove, splitting enough that I can push the door open. I'm rushing inside so fast I barely have time to process Merry lying on the bathroom floor.

"Shit." I hurry to her side and lift her head to set it in my lap. Her eyes are closed and she's really pale but breathing. Looking down between her legs I see blood soaking through her jeans and that's when I start to freak out.

"Adrian," I say, but when I look up, he's already got his phone out and is talking to someone on the other end, giving them his address.

"Everything okay?" Eloise comes around the corner before she freezes in place. "Oh my God!"

I remember when I hit rock bottom. It was at the bottom of a pile of coke, a bottle of whiskey, and a baggie of pills. I could feel my life in my hands in that moment, like a substance that was slipping away. I honestly thought that was as bad as things could possibly get.

But right here, right now, with Merry in my arms, I realize I didn't know shit because this is what it really feels like when you're losing something, and all I want to do is hold on.

Picking her up in my arms, I start carrying her out of the bathroom.

"An ambulance is on its way," Adrian says. "We probably shouldn't move her."

"We're too far out." I turn with something that must look like desperation on my face because it stops him. "Get us to the hospital."

Adrian nods, not arguing.

Eloise piles into his SUV with us. I'm in the backseat with Merry, and I do my best to buckle her in, but she's kind of twisted with her head in my lap.

"What's going on, Noah?" Eloise turns to look at me. "What happened?"

"She went to the bathroom and—" I cut myself off because I don't really know what the fuck happened, just that this can't be good.

Merry moves and I look down to see her eyes blinking open.

"Noah," she says, but it's a rasp.

"Hey." I brush her hair off her face and stroke the side of her cheek. "It's okay. I've got you. We're going to go see the doctor."

I run my hand over her forehead, down her cheek, repeating the same pattern again and again.

"What happened?" Her gaze darts around the car, her eyebrows furrowing.

"You were in the bathroom, and you never came back."

"Oh, right." Her hand drifts down her stomach and settles really low. "I was in pain."

I try really hard not to react to that because knowing she's in pain again, while also bleeding, can't be good. Reaching down, I rest my hand over hers.

"Does it still hurt?"

She shakes her head the slightest. "Not right now, no. But I thought it was a cramp, and then—it just got so much worse. I tried to call for you, but I don't think I did."

That stabs like a knife to the chest. While I was bullshitting with Adrian, she was calling out to me.

"I—" she starts, but her face winces.

"Relax," I say, brushing my thumb over the back of her hand. "There's plenty of time to run that smart mouth of yours later."

My comment at least makes her smile, which I appreciate right now. I love the fire that flickers bright in her even when she's tired and fading in the backseat. There's a fight in Merry that never fades.

"Adrian and Eloise are taking us to the hospital, and we'll get this all figured out."

That's when Merry turns her head and sees them up-front, like it's sinking in where she is. Adrian tips his head, facing front, but Eloise reaches her arm back behind her and squeezes Merry's shoulder.

"We've got you, Merry," Eloise says, without looking, but in the side mirror I see tears on Eloise's cheeks, and I realize it's hitting everyone in different ways.

They don't even know what's happening. Not that I do either, I guess.

"Noah," Merry whispers, turning back to me and burying her face against my stomach. It's never felt so good just to hold her in my arms and hear my name on her lips. "I'm sorry."

"You have nothing to be sorry for." I brush the side of her face with the back of my hand. "I love you. Everything is going to be okay. It's all going to be okay."

I'm not sure how many times I say it, or if it's for her or myself, but I repeat it over and over like I can manifest it into existence. I pray it's possible.

As I hold her tighter, I look up and catch Adrian's gaze in the rear-view mirror. For a man who rarely reveals anything, he looks worried, and it's unsettling.

Everything needs to be okay. Whatever is wrong, we'll fix it.

30

MERRY

My eyes feel heavy and impossible to open. I hear things happening around me: people talking, machines beeping. They move me as I drift in and out of the darkness. I hold onto Noah's words through all of it, even though I know I'm no longer in the car hearing them.

It's all going to be okay.

I hope he's right.

It's quiet now, but the light on the other side of my eyelids starts to wake me up, and it's almost impossible to move my body. I'm not sure how I'm sore from doing nothing, but everything hurts. Finally blinking my eyes open, I'm met with the sharp light of the sun streaking in through a window, and it takes me a minute to adjust.

Looking around, there are white walls and machines everywhere. This must be the hospital, which is a good sign because it means I made it. But then that fear inside creeps back up because I still don't know what happened.

"I know."

I hear Noah's voice, and it sounds at a distance. But when I turn my head, I realize he's standing right by the bed, turned away from me, and talking to someone on the phone. I try to lift my hand to reach out to him, but it's heavy, and I can't find the energy.

"She's been in and out," I hear him say to the person on the other end of the line. "The doctor hasn't told me much of anything."

He pauses and I faintly hear another voice I can't make out.

"They're waiting on her to wake up. But yes, I know. She told me."

There's another beat of silence while he listens to whatever the other person says. His shoulders are tense, and his hair is tied back in a bun on his head. I can't see his face, but his voice sounds tired and gravelly.

"Of course. I'll keep you updated. And I'll have her call you when she's up and feeling okay."

More silence, that feels like it drags on longer this time.

"You're welcome." Noah hangs up the phone.

His arm falls to his side and he looks up at the ceiling, taking a long breath. I'm not sure what's stressing him. But the weight he's carrying is heavy enough that I feel it in my own bones.

Lifting my hand up again, I reach out for his and brush the backs of our fingers together.

"Merry." He spins around so fast, it makes me jump, which he seems to notice. "Sorry, you're just awake."

A nervous smile brightens his face as he looks me over. He runs his hands over my cheeks like he's feeling for proof of life, before leaning in to give me a kiss.

"Hey." I smile against his mouth.

"Fuck. Don't scare me like that again," he says.

I tip my chin up to kiss his lips, drinking up their warmth. "I'll try not to."

He sets himself on the edge of my bed and holds both my hands in his tightly.

"Where's Adrian and Eloise? Or did I imagine that?"

Noah shakes his head. "No, they were here—or are here. They're in the waiting room with the rest of the band."

"No," I say, slowly shaking my head. "They don't have to do that."

"They know they don't have to, Merry." He gives me a stern look and I know there's no point arguing. I might normally be uncomfortable forming the type of attachments I have with Noah and his band, but it's too late now.

"You know you're safe here, right?" Noah says with a concerned look on his face.

"I know, it's a hospital." I'm not sure what he's getting at.

"I'm not talking about the hospital," he says. "I'm talking about with us, with our friends. You don't have to always be on the defense. It's okay to let others in and to let them take care of you sometimes."

I want to believe that. And even more so, I want to allow it to happen. But there's something that's always lived deep that resists the hands reaching for me when I'm drowning, and I can't help but cling to that.

"What did the doctor say?" I ask, changing the subject.

Noah's jaw tenses, and I know he wants me to be open and raw with him right now, but I'm not like him. Being exposed doesn't come naturally to me.

"Nothing yet." Noah shakes his head.

"But you told them?"

"I explained the best I could, and they said they'd reach out to your doctor in Seattle to get more information."

I look at the door, wishing they would come in already. I hate waiting and not knowing. Rip off the Band-Aid already and just tell me I need surgery.

"When you're feeling up to it, call your sister," Noah says, drawing my attention back to him.

"You talked to Monica?" I realize she must be who he was on the phone with.

"Hopefully you don't mind that I went through your phone to get her number, but I figured you would want your family to know. And I wasn't so sure about calling your parents—because, you know."

"She'll update them."

It means a lot that he reached out to Monica, but I'm sure my family's in a tailspin now worrying about what happened. Mom and Dad bugged me about having another surgery before I first joined the band on tour. But I was still hoping that more natural remedies would work, and the fibroids would shrink. The last surgery already did enough damage, I didn't want to risk worse.

Maybe they were right. Not that I'm in the mood to say that to my parents.

Noah's eyes skim my body, and he has a tense look on his face that matches how I'm feeling inside.

"Ms. Lopez," the doctor says, coming into the room. "You're awake."

Noah jumps up and stands next to the bed, but doesn't let go of my hand, which is really sweet and comforts me in a way I'm not sure he realizes.

The doctor walks around the other side of the bed to take a look at the readings on the machines, looking from them to her clipboard, before turning to me.

"I'm Dr. Cameron. How are you feeling?"

She's strangely warm for a doctor. I'm used to the ones I've dealt with in Seattle who were cold and clinical. Maybe it's the way the sun from the window catches on her honey brown hair, or maybe it's the richness of her eyes, but she's surprisingly comforting.

"Okay, I think. There's still some cramping." I move my free hand down my stomach, and I feel Noah tighten his grasp on my other one. "Do you know what happened?"

Dr. Cameron's eyes dart from me to Noah, and then back again. "Would you like to talk in private or—"

"He can stay," I say. "He's my boyfriend."

I'm not sure I've used that word out loud to describe Noah before, but it's what he is. I wish today wasn't the first time admitting that because there's an uneasy feeling behind it, when I should be happy.

"Of course," Dr. Cameron says, skimming her clipboard again, before tucking it against her chest and looking back at me. "Dr. Winters updated me on your fibroids, and I understand you've been going to him for treatment. It appears there has been some growth since the scans he took last year."

I nod. It's nothing I wasn't expecting. The hormone treatments were only doing so much, but all roads led back here eventually.

"I've sent Dr. Winters my scans, but I'm confident he's going to want to see you to discuss your options considering the size and the amount of bleeding." She gives me a sympathetic look, but it doesn't sit well because I know doctors deliver bad news all day and this is rehearsed for her. "Ms. Lopez, there's something else."

She peels the clipboard from her chest to look my chart over once more, and I get a bad feeling deep in my gut. I know she already knows what it says, which means there's another reason she's pausing.

The minute stretches on for what feels like hours before Dr. Cameron is looking back up at me.

"Did you know you were pregnant?" she says.

The earth must shift because those words slow down as they come out of her mouth and float out into the air between us.

"Pregnant?" Noah repeats it, and that's when I remember he's standing right there holding my hand. Only now, his palm is sweaty, and when I look up at him there's panic clouding his face.

Dr. Cameron nods. "I'm sorry to say that you lost the baby."

Lost the baby?

Right then a pain shoots through me, but I don't know if it's physical or imagined, just that it reaches every nerve ending.

"No, that can't be right," I say, but the words come out rushed and panicked as I shake my head. "I can't have kids. Or, at least, the chance is so small it's basically non-existent, Dr. Winters said the fibroids and the scarring..."

I trail off because I don't really know what I'm saying, just that everything coming out of her mouth doesn't make any sense.

Dr. Cameron looks like she's about to reach out a hand but then pulls back.

"You're right, it would be very unlikely," she says. "And it looks like it was very early from your HCG levels, no more than a few weeks. But the existing fibroids combined with the scarring increased the risk. You had a miscarriage."

I look down now, where there was so much blood. And pain, and stabbing. I thought it was my condition getting worse when really...

My heart clenches.

"I'll give you some space. We can discuss this more when you've had some time to process. And Dr. Winters will be coordinating your transfer to Seattle."

Dr. Cameron leaves the room and I realize she wasn't warm or comforting at all. She was a grim reaper wielding a scythe. One she used to slice through the last ounce of hope I had left.

"Pregnant?" I say again, to myself, but I feel Noah's grip tighten.

I look up at him and his eyes are as empty as mine feel. Like this can't be happening right now. I'm not able to get pregnant, that's why I wasn't worried about not using protection with him. Even if I used it with every other person I've been with.

I did this, I let it happen. Noah and I actually created the one thing that I never thought I would be able to offer him. And now it's just…

Gone.

I was pregnant. I *got* pregnant. But still, my body couldn't hold it.

The ache inside me comes from so many places I don't know what's my body and what's my mind. But it all hurts, and at the same time, I feel numb.

"Noah," I say, and his eyes snap back into focus. "I—"

What do I say to him?

Sorry, I thought we were safe.

Sorry I've brought us this pain.

Sorry I found a way to break what we already can't have further.

I say nothing.

There are no words as the tears brim in my eyes and the overwhelming burden starts to spill out of me. It's run out of room and has nowhere else to go. So, it spills, and it spills, and it pours down my face. And I'm shaking so violently I don't even realize it when Noah sits on the bed and wraps his arms around me, because nothing feels comforting anymore.

Not even him.

Noah was right, the doctors can only take so much because my body will apparently take care of the rest.

31

NOAH

At some point in the afternoon, Merry falls asleep crying. I lay next to her in bed, my body willing me to sleep too, but the thoughts in my head won't allow it.

Pregnant.

Merry was pregnant with our baby, and what we assumed was a period was something I still can't seem to wrap my head around.

I'm not sure how the doctor could stand there and just say that all in one sentence. Like all the parts of it weren't a carefully planted explosion that was blowing our world to bits. I hadn't even had the time to feel the hope before she told us we lost it.

Lost.

That's where I am right now. Floating somewhere that isn't here because things are playing out in front of me like a movie scene. Except it's blurry and silent, and the figures I once recognized have taken on new, darker shapes.

Merry wakes up, but she doesn't say anything. At least she doesn't push me away either. She lets me hold her, and I hope that my arms are enough to be her strength when my words and my spirit both fail me.

My phone won't stop ringing because everyone wants to know what's going on. But neither of us answers. Not yet. The universe plays some really evil games and apparently, we're at the center of this one.

We sit in this black hole and see if there are any sides of it we recognize anymore. If there's a door buried somewhere that will let us out.

At some point, the band leaves. Merry finally texts Cassie to give a cliff note summary of what is going on, so they'll stop asking questions. I'm pretty sure she copies and pastes the same text for her sister.

I don't text anyone. My parents don't have a right to know what's going on in my life. The only person I care about is in this room with me, and she's fractured beyond recognition.

Emptiness shouldn't be able to take up space. It's nothing. Yet somehow it does. In the seconds. In the hours. In the room around us. It's all I feel.

"Don't you have practice today—or yesterday?" Merry presses her palm on her forehead. "I'm not sure what day it is."

"We don't," I tell her because either way it's canceled or doesn't matter.

"You guys need to work on your album."

Her expression is hard, even if she looks so soft in her hospital gown with her hair a mess.

"I'm not worried about that right now." Sitting up, I turn to face her on the bed and take her hand.

"You need to be worried about it," Merry continues to argue, and I'm not sure why she woke up so intent on having this conversation. "You've only got a couple of months until you go back on tour, and you have to finish the album so you can record some of the music videos—"

"I know how it works," I cut her off. "That's not really the top of the list of my concerns right now. How are you feeling?"

"How am I feeling?" she repeats it like she can't believe I asked the question. "Not great."

At least she gave me an honest answer, even if she clearly didn't want to say anything.

"We need to talk about this," I say, but it makes her pull her hand away.

"There's nothing to talk about." She crosses her arms over her chest. "Remember?"

Even if I know she's only being crass as a defense mechanism, the blunt delivery stings. She can hide behind her words but can't bury the look in her eyes, and I know she's hurting too.

"This is all moving really fast," Merry says, and I can feel the distance she's putting between us. "We've barely figured out who we are in this—thing—between us."

"Relationship?" I fill in the blank, feeling myself getting annoyed already with where this is going.

"Sure." She brushes it off. "But this is all too much. You need to go record your album. I need to go to Seattle. You don't need to be dealing with this. There's nothing to deal with anymore apparently anyway."

Although her face is composed, her voice cracking gives her away.

She avoids my gaze. "Maybe once this is all done, we can see where we're at."

"No."

Merry shakes her head and looks at me like she can't believe I dared to argue with her. But fuck this.

"We're not doing that," I say.

"And you get to make all the decisions?"

"When I'm the only one thinking rationally, yes."

She stares at me with narrowed eyes. Part of me really wants to know what she's thinking, and the other part really doesn't. But I won't back down, or take my hand off her leg, or walk away. We're facing this shit, whether she wants to or not.

It's why I know we'll work. One person in every relationship has to be the one to stay and fight for it, and I'll be that for her every time if I have to.

After a long pause, her face softens. "I shouldn't have been able to get pregnant, okay?"

"I know." I've got vertigo from her flipping this conversation around every five seconds.

She takes in a deep breath. "Just because it happened, doesn't change anything. I shouldn't have. And even though I did, it doesn't mean it will happen again."

"I understand that."

Her arms finally unclench around her chest, and she reaches out for my hand. "I wouldn't have asked you to—you know, not wear anything—if I thought for even a minute it was a possibility this would happen. I'm on hormone treatments on top of everything else. It really shouldn't have even been possible."

"I know."

Merry's eyes get watery. "I didn't mean to do this."

That's when it hits me that she feels guilty. On top of everything, Merry thinks she's bringing something on me that she isn't. This isn't her fault.

"We both made that decision, Merry. This isn't on you, at all." I take her hands in mine and hold them in my lap. "Is it hard to process what's all happened? Yes. But would I take it back or change things? No. Because what if it had worked out by some miracle?"

"That's dangerous thinking," Merry warns.

I shrug. "No more dangerous than pining after a girl who swears she'll never give you a chance."

Merry tips her chin down and tries to glare at me, but it's softened by the faintest smile.

"I'm not saying we're ready for our relationship to go there. This is new, and we're still figuring it out. I'm enjoying this part. Fucking all over the house and not giving a shit about who is around to hear it."

That finally makes a full smile break on her face.

"But if anything happened with you, unexpected or not, I'd never take it back. Because it would be with you, Merry. So, if you want to start using protection. Or if you want to put a pause on having sex—"

"I wouldn't go that far." She rolls her eyes.

"That's a relief." I pull her hands to my mouth and kiss the backs of her knuckles. "But what I'm saying is no matter what, I'll understand. You're not backing out of this. If we do it, we do it together. No matter how many times you get stubborn and make me remind you."

Even with her defenses down right now she still feels a little prickly, but I wouldn't want her any other way.

She draws her bottom lip between her teeth, and I realize there's something still bothering her.

"What are you thinking?"

"I heard you out," she says with a long sigh. "But this doesn't just go one way, so now, I need you to hear me."

There's a look Merry has nailed, and it's the one she's giving me right now. A little terrifying, a little abrasive, and a lot sexy.

"All right." I nod.

"I'm going back to Seattle for a bit. At least to see my doctor, but also, probably to have surgery. I need to deal with these fibroids and hopefully it doesn't make things worse."

This is what I've been wanting her to do, so I'm not sure why she thinks I'll argue.

"And you're staying in Denver," she finishes.

I open my mouth to speak but she lifts her hand up to stop me.

"Noah, I appreciate that you want to be there for me. And I *want* you there for me. But we can't ignore every obligation we have for this relationship. My family is there, I've got a support system. But you're needed here with the band. And I'll be back as soon as possible."

"But—"

"Don't you dare argue with me, Noah Hayes," she says, knowing I love it when she calls me by my full name. "I heard you out, and I'm willing to make this work. But I'm not one of those girls who needs you to give up everything to feel validated. So, we need to meet halfway. I'll be back once I'm done with whatever treatment the doctor orders. But don't set your priorities aside just because of me."

She narrows her eyes, and her lashes are so thick her eyes are nearly black. It's surprisingly adorable she's so adamant about this, especially considering she's not actually pushing me away for once.

"Fine," I say, and it gets me a suspicious look in return.

"What do you mean *fine*?"

"I mean, fine." I shrug. "I thought you were saying your piece, so I wasn't supposed to argue with you?"

"That's not—" She shakes her head and wipes her hands over her face. "I wasn't expecting you to do that."

"Well, I am. Is that a problem?"

She's looking at me hard, like she no way believes me but can't figure out why yet.

"So, you're okay with me going to Seattle by myself?" she clarifies.

"Okay with it, no? Willing to accept defeat and let you go up there by yourself, sure."

"And you'll stay in Denver?"

"I'll stay with the band."

I can tell Merry doesn't know what to do with that, and as much as I don't like the idea of her traveling up there alone, if this is what she needs to feel reassured by us, then I know I need to let her go up there by herself.

But I'm also not going to cave in as easily as she thinks I am. So, she can throw out her gauntlet, but I'm an artist. I'm willing to get creative with how I let this play out.

If she's so worried about me not meeting my obligations with Enemy Muse, I'll find a way to make this happen. After all, she doesn't want me to choose between the two, and that just makes me love her more.

All my life I've been made to think that love is this conditional thing, that either you meet the expectations exactly as set or you're a failure. But with Merry, she wants me to achieve everything I want. She wants me to be everything I am. And all it makes me want to do is give her everything she deserves in return.

"You'll record the album?" Her nose crinkles.

I laugh because she's still clarifying like she really doesn't believe any of this. Not that I blame her. "Promise. I'll record the album with the band. I won't let your surgery interfere with recording."

"Why do I feel like there are invisible strings I'm not seeing?" She narrows her eyes and I just grin.

Leaning forward, I brush my lips over hers and smile. "Guess you'll just have to wait and see."

But as she opens her mouth to argue, I kiss her, and it feels like a little of our pain melts away. Her arms wrap around my neck, and I thank her with my lips for being exactly who she is. Because although to her, this kiss might be some kind of temporary goodbye, at no point did Merry seem to hear exactly what I was promising.

I said forever, and I meant it.

32

Merry

Seattle rain is my favorite. It hangs out like an old friend waiting for you to return. While most people probably prefer the sunshine, I love watching the water slap against the pavement. Hearing the earth roll with thunder as it tries to cleanse itself.

The cool air is still somehow warming. The sound comforting. It's the beat I wrote my first song to. And as much as I wanted to escape, Seattle is still my home.

Unfortunately, that doesn't stop me from missing Noah. I almost caved at the airport and told him to forget everything I said. Suddenly, I really wanted to be that girl who asks a guy to give it all up for her. But that's not us, and I can't let him do it. So, I got on the plane, even if I was a little surprised he let it happen.

By the time I arrive at my sister's doorstep, I'm exhausted and ready to sleep for a week. If only that were an option.

I went to the doctor straight from the airport and he told me exactly what I expected—I need surgery. Soon.

He didn't hesitate before scheduling it, and now the official countdown has begun.

If I wait it out any longer, I risk the fibroids continuing to grow and cause problems. And as much as the alternative treatments have helped keep the surgery at bay, they aren't shrinking, so I don't have much of a choice.

All I can do now is hope for the best. Pray they get in and out with minimal scarring, and even more so, that they can save my uterus.

The door to Monica's apartment swings open and she's standing there in a bright yellow feathery sweater.

"What the fuck did you do to Big Bird?" I ask her.

Monica crosses her arms over her chest and glares at me. "Good to see you too Morticia."

"Ooh, I like that." I grin and it makes her laugh.

"Good to see you, sis." Monica reaches for me as I step inside and wraps me in a hug.

Even with a seven-year age gap between us, there's no one on the planet I'm closer to than my sister.

When we were younger, I was the annoying little kid who followed her around and bugged her. But as we both grew up, she's been the one person in my family who has accepted me as is. She might give me the side eye or not always understand it, but she doesn't judge either. And I'm thankful to have her on my side.

Stepping back, she brushes her wild curls off her face and gives me a big smile. "I hope you're hungry, Carson got a little carried away with the pasta."

At the mention of his name, she gets those swoony eyes she has whenever she's thinking about him.

"Oh geez, Mon, keep it in your pants while I'm here." I lift an eyebrow, and she swats at me. "But seriously—he can cook?"

"He can," Carson says, walking into the room, drying his hands on a towel.

His eyes immediately land on Monica, and I can't help but roll mine in return, because being around the two of them is vomit-inducing. They met in kindergarten and were basically childhood sweethearts—although Monica swears they never actually dated until they were older.

But just because I was a kid, didn't mean I was blind. These two have been looking at each other like they are now for as long as I can remember.

"Carson." I walk over to him and give him a hug. "Thanks for having me here."

He gives me a hug back, before moving to Monica's side and wrapping an arm around her. His height makes her look miniature in comparison, and I wonder if that's what I look like standing next to Noah.

Come to think of it, why did both of us Lopez sisters fall for blond-haired men with pretty-boy faces? Although Carson does have a bit more scruff on his jaw than Noah, so it makes him appear a tad rougher around the edges.

"You know you're welcome here anytime," Carson says. "I'll hide in my office if needed."

"Bring on the chick flicks and wine coolers then." I nudge Monica on the arm, teasing her because she's always been so girly from her drinks to her taste in movies. "I like the new place, by the way."

I look around, taking in their new space. The living room is large and open with vaulted ceilings. Wide windows look over the city and frame the lights below. This apartment is triple the size of her last place, and stunning.

"Someone's smutty books must be selling." I wink at my sister.

"Mercedes, you better not be reading my books." Monica's cheeks get red, while Carson just laughs.

Monica spent years writing sweetie-pie romance, but in the past year she released a spicier series, and of course I read it. Especially because I know it embarrasses her. After all, I'm her sister, it's my job to tease her any way I can.

"Don't worry, you can't shock me. I've done way worse than anything you've written." I wink again, and that makes her glare at me really hard. "Let me know if you need any pointers for the next book."

Monica slaps her hands over her eyes and shakes her head, burying it against Carson's chest. "Please make her stop talking."

He gives her a kiss on the head and smiles, brushing her curls off her face. She looks up at him and my heart warms from the look he gives her. Unconditional, filled with love. Exactly like she deserves. Carson leans in, giving her a chaste kiss on the lips before turning to head back to the kitchen.

"Try not to torture your sister while I finish the pasta." He looks over his shoulder at me and shakes his head.

"I'll try," I yell. "But it's just so much fun."

Monica glares in my direction, walking past me to grab my suitcase. "Let's get this to your room."

"Please say it's on the opposite end of the apartment from yours, I'm happy you found love and all, but gross."

"Says the sister shacking up with rock stars." She lifts an eyebrow.

"Rock star, singular." I follow her down the hall and into a large guest room with a king-size bed in the middle. Both of their books must be selling well because this place is incredible.

"I was joking," Monica says. "But really, you and Noah? Finally?"

I shrug and sit down on the bed. "Yeah, he's…"

But I can't seem to finish that sentence because it hurts right now remembering how far away he is. I'm so used to traveling the globe alone with no attachments, that I didn't realize what it would mean to miss someone. It's an emptiness I've never experienced.

"This is serious." Monica sits on the bed beside me, and she must recognize something in my eyes.

I nod. "There's something I didn't tell you when I texted."

My throat tightens and I can't look at her, because if I do, I'm not sure I'll be able to get the words out.

"Noah and I started dating a little after I went to Denver, and it's been good," I say. "He's good to me."

"He better be." Monica puts on her best stern big sister face, and it manages to drag a smile out of me.

"He is." I sigh. "But there's something else—why I was in the hospital. I didn't text you everything."

Monica places her hand over mine and squeezes. "What's going on?"

I let out a deep breath and hope it will carry the weight I'm feeling away with it, but it doesn't.

"I was pregnant." I finally blurt the words out, and beside me, I feel Monica's entire body stiffen. "But I lost the baby because—well you know. It was early, I didn't even know. It shouldn't have even been able to happen. Apparently, my body agreed."

"Merry…" Monica wraps her arm around my shoulders.

"It's fine," I say, even though deep inside I crack open wider with that statement. "I never wanted kids anyway. Or a family, or any of that crap. I wanted to be a rock star. All I care about is my music."

But with every statement it feels like a lie I didn't see coming. Resting my head on Monica's shoulder, I try really hard to hold in the battle I'm losing.

"I never wanted this," I say. "I wasn't supposed to be able to have it."

Monica runs her hand over the side of my head, wrapping an arm around my back. I will myself to keep it together and fail. Somewhere deep, I shatter.

"Maybe you just never allowed yourself to want it, Merry." Monica traces the side of my head with her fingers, and as they brush my cheek I feel the tears as they start falling. "But even if you honestly didn't want it, or even if you still don't, it doesn't diminish the loss you're feeling. I know you're tough, but you're allowed to hurt. You're allowed to feel it."

With those words a sob escapes my throat. Because the pain inside is unbearable. Something I can't put into words.

From the moment I found out I was pregnant, everything I thought I knew for years was tested. What I didn't want, what I *couldn't* want, changed. Noah and I made it happen, by some miracle, and the loss of knowing it still didn't change the end result breaks me.

I've never let myself picture a certain life because it was easier that way. Yes, I know there are many ways a person can have a family, and at some point, maybe surrogacy or adoption would have crossed my mind. But to get to that point, it would require me to face a loss I wasn't ready to grieve just yet—not birthing kids of my own. And being only twenty-three, I wasn't ready to face it.

I wasn't ready to face this moment right here. The fact that maybe I do want things bigger than myself in my life. Maybe I do want more with Noah down the road. Except, if I allow myself to want those things, I have to admit they'll look different for us.

So right now, I cry those fears and that loss into my sister's shoulder. I spill my tears out like they're secrets I've been holding back. And she holds me knowing she can't really understand, but it's a comfort anyway.

We sit like that for what feels like forever. Time starts to disappear. At some point, I hear movement at the bedroom door, and I'm sure dinner is done, cold and put away. But Carson doesn't interrupt or say anything. He leaves us alone as I sob in my sister's arms and feel everything I haven't allowed myself.

Finally, I wipe my face and Monica sits on the bed facing me. There's something cathartic about crying it out—releasing what's deep inside and feeling it all. It's painful, but my body no longer feels frozen in place.

The hurt exists, but my heart beats through it.

"I'm here for you, Merry," Monica says, holding my hands in her own.

"I know."

"And you're welcome to stay as long as you want." She pats my hands.

"I appreciate it." I tip my head to the side and look at her. "But don't worry, I'll only be here as long as I need to. Wouldn't want to cramp your newlywed style."

Monica blushes and shakes her head. She's so easily embarrassed about sex for a woman who writes filthy smut.

A knock comes from the doorway and we both look up. I expect to see Carson standing there ready to claim his blushing bride, but that's not the face staring back at me.

"Noah?"

I try to process why he's in my doorway in Seattle and not Denver like he's supposed to be.

"The one and only, babe." Noah shoots me a blinding grin, standing there looking way too good in a damp wet black T-shirt and ripped faded gray jeans.

"So, this is Noah." Monica scans him head to toe and then turns to me with a wink, pretending she doesn't already know. His face is plastered everywhere, and I know she's been to their concert because I gave her the tickets. "The boyfriend?"

"That's up for debate at the moment." I stand up and walk over to where he's in the doorway, nudging him on the arm. "You promised."

He catches my wrist and pulls me against him. "Yes, I did. And before it turns into a fight club in here, let me explain."

"Oh, I like this guy for you," Monica says, and I look over my shoulder to find her grinning.

"That makes one of us." I narrow my eyes and train my expression back on him. "Explain."

"I promised I would let you come to Seattle by yourself, and I did. Said goodbye at the airport and everything."

"Okay but—"

"And the band," he cuts me off and holds me tighter. "Is not putting anything on hold. I promised you I'd stay with the band and continue recording the album. So, I brought them with me."

"To Seattle?" What is he even saying right now?

Noah nods. "Yes, to Seattle. It's not like it took that much convincing since Cassie is here right now and Sebastian can't stand not being around her."

"Where are you recording?"

"Adrian knows a guy." Noah shrugs, like *no big deal, I just picked up my band and my career and moved cities with them for you.*

"You—" I shake my head, trying to process the shock, frustration, and excitement. I'm tempted to be mad at him for twisting my words around and still not doing what I asked. But he's relentless, and it's one of the infuriating things I somehow love about him.

It's been easy for me to push people away because I'm stubborn and strong-willed. But Noah doesn't let me hide behind excuses. He forces me to face things that scare me. And he brings out the side of me I didn't know existed.

"You kept your promise," I breathe out.

"I did."

"Albeit, creatively," I remind him.

He smirks but doesn't look the least bit guilty.

"Thank you." I lift so I can kiss him. My fingers tangle in his hair, and I want to devour the devotion that he pours out for me. I want to drink the love straight from his lips. I want him to tear down the life I've seen myself building and replace it with dreams I've never imagined.

I want to make this work, to meet each other halfway. I want to believe in things I never thought existed.

Pulling away, I look up at him. Those pale blue eyes bright and piercing straight through me.

"I love you, Noah Hayes," I say—finally—out of breath and tired of fighting what I've been feeling inside. "I love you so damn much."

Noah smiles, and it makes my heart constrict harder in my chest. He leans in, a breath away from my lips.

"Fucking finally," he says, kissing me so deeply I forget why I ever fought this.

33

NOAH

Merry glares at me, but her smile is all I'm paying attention to.

"You promised you guys wouldn't put recording on hold for my surgery." She's trying really hard to be stern right now, and it's adorable.

"We didn't." I wrap my arms around her waist. "We just happen to be taking today and tomorrow off, and then we'll be back in the studio."

"Mm-hmm," she hums.

But I dip my face down to hers to capture her lips before her pretty little mouth can argue with me anymore. Sinking my teeth into her bottom lip and making her wiggle in my arms.

"Noah Hayes." She swats at me playfully.

"You two gonna go somewhere and fuck all day or are you gonna come hang out and have a beer?" Rome stops in front of us with his arms crossed over his chest.

"Neither?" I say to him and Merry starts laughing.

Fucking Rome. I swear the guy is in his own world half the time.

"I can't drink the day before surgery," Merry reminds him.

Not to mention that I don't drink *at all*. Lately he acts as if he has no idea what's going on with anyone other than himself.

"More for the rest of us." Rome shrugs and he turns to head back to where the group has settled on the beach.

It's a nice day for late August. Cooler in Seattle than summers in California, and there's a breeze coming off the bay. The salty air feels good.

"Guess we should join the party," Merry says, but she nuzzles against my chest instead of pulling away. "I can't believe everyone is here."

Dipping my nose to the top of her head, I breathe in her berry scent. "Believe it," I tell her.

Finally, she pulls away and grabs my hand, dragging me down the beach when I'd rather just stand there ignoring everyone and holding her. But this is her party, so I don't grumble... too much.

Merry splits off from me when we get to the group to go chat with Cassie and Eloise, and I make my way over to where the guys are sitting and set myself down in the middle of them.

"How you holding up, man," Sebastian asks, handing me a water bottle.

"On the outside? Great." I laugh, but I can't help that it comes out nervous.

All I can think about is Merry going in for surgery tomorrow. The thought alone eating away at me.

It's been a whirlwind since we got to town a week ago with the doctors' appointments, one after the other. Luckily, they were a lot more optimistic about it than Merry seemed to think they would be. Her doctor is going to do a myomectomy like she's had done before, but with any luck, it will go better and there won't be as much scarring.

Either way, even after the surgery, the chances of her getting pregnant again are slim, if not nonexistent. But that's a bridge we'll cross when we come to it.

It's been a lot to take in. But surprisingly, the conversations with the doctors haven't been the hardest part of this trip. Nothing could top dinner with Merry's parents.

There was definitely still tension, even though Monica and Carson tried their best to act as buffers. Carson's a laid-back guy so it made me feel like maybe I wouldn't be totally out of place in her family, but her dad spent most of dinner giving me a warning with his eyes from the other side of the table.

Her mom was warm, at least. Apart from the comments she made on more than one occasion about my long hair and Merry's growing tattoo collection.

I was just glad to see them all in the same room together making progress. Merry needs her family right now, and even if they don't understand her lifestyle choices, I'm happy they're doing the right thing by being there for her.

It's more than I've ever been able to say about my own family.

"It's just a lot," I tell the guys.

The sound of waves crashing is calming, reminding me of all the times as a kid I spent playing at the beach. Back when my dad still gave a shit about the son he was raising. We would play catch and chase waves. A time when things were lighter.

"It's a lot of shit for a new relationship," Adrian says, breaking the silence.

"It's not that—although yeah, I guess by normal standards it is." I shake my head. "But with Merry, I don't know, it feels like we've been together forever already. I just wish there was more I could do."

Leaning back, I rest my hands in the sand.

"I can't believe she's been keeping all that in for so long. Even Cassie didn't know," Sebastian says.

"I get it," Rome says, taking a drink of his beer. His eyes are fixed on the horizon. "Some shit is easier to keep inside. Because once you let it out—" Rome waves his beer bottle out in front of him but doesn't finish his sentence, and it makes me wonder what's living inside, tormenting him.

"She's just going through so much shit." I lean forward again. "And I'm sitting here unaffected."

"Not exactly unaffected," Sebastian says with a solemn look on his face.

He's right, but I'm still having a hard time thinking about what Merry and I lost. There doesn't feel like a right way to grieve something that you didn't know existed in the first place. It's a loss unlike anything I've dealt with before. A hole I'm not sure will ever fill.

"I still can't believe she was—" Adrian stops, dropping his chin and shaking his head. With him and Eloise being there when she collapsed at his house, he has an understanding deeper than the others, even though we've shared Merry's pregnancy news with the rest of the band.

"You and me both," I say.

Adrian reaches out and slaps a sandy palm on the back of my shoulder. "We're here for you though. You need anything, we've got you."

"I appreciate that, all Merry can seem to worry about right now is that she's cutting into the band's recording time."

Adrian lifts an eyebrow at me and Sebastian laughs.

"You're shitting me?" Adrian says.

I shake my head. "Nope."

"Fucking Merry." Rome chuckles.

"I think it gives her something to focus on that isn't herself, so I can't blame her." I shrug. "After all, if anything is to blame for all the album delays, it's this dipshit over here."

I shove Sebastian's arm and he topples sideways in the sand laughing.

"Fuck you, man," he says, sitting up and shoving me back, which sends my water flying at Adrian.

"You guys are worse than children." Adrian shakes the water and sand off himself.

Rome's just sitting there laughing so I throw some sand at him.

"Hey," he says. "That got in my beer."

"Good," I tell him. "You drink way too fucking much anyway."

Rome rolls his eyes and hops up to grab a new drink.

"All right, who's causing trouble?" Merry pops up beside me. She sits down between my legs with her back to my chest and I take in a deep breath.

Cassie sits on Sebastian's lap and Eloise sets herself down next to them.

"Noah started it." Sebastian points at me.

Merry looks over her shoulder and quirks an eyebrow.

"He deserved it." I shrug. Hearing the back and forth play out in my head, Adrian's right, we really do sound like children. I'm not sure how that guy puts up with us.

Merry sighs deeply, and I feel the whole weight of it leave her chest. With my arms wrapped around her, I want to feel every inhale and exhale. I want to forget about surgery and the album and everything else we're obligated to. I want to plant us in the sand and stay here.

Everyone moves on to their own conversations. Eloise gets wrapped up in an argument with Rome while Adrian plays mediator, and Sebastian and Cassie are in their own little world. But my attention is on Merry and her warmth against me.

The sound of waves crashing.

The salt in the air.

"This is the beach where Cassie spread her brother's ashes," Merry says, tipping her head back against my shoulder.

I look over at Cassie and Sebastian and notice how quiet they are as they stare out at the bay, and I wonder how being here affects them.

"It's pretty, right?" Merry says.

I nod. "It's perfect."

She sighs, and the gentleness in that noise sends my heart to funny places.

Places I can already see in my head. A future that it's probably way too early for me to be thinking about. Marrying her, loving her. Growing old and watching how she changes with age. Being the only one who really knows her. The sounds she makes when she's happy or upset. The things that bring her joy. The things that break her heart.

All of it.

"I want tomorrow to be over with already," Merry says.

I look down and see that her eyes are closed as she rests the back of her head against my chest.

"Soon enough." I kiss her temple.

"Are you going to stay the whole time?"

"I wouldn't leave."

We've already had this conversation, so I know she's just asking for confirmation.

"Your parents are going to be there it sounds like."

"Yes." She sighs. "Things went okay at dinner, right? They seem like they're okay?"

Merry likes to pretend that she's tough and unaffected by her strained relationship with them, but there are moments like this she shows me the parts that aren't as secure as she'd like.

"They seem worried about you," I tell her honestly, breathing in the scent of her shampoo.

"Only because I'm shacking up with a deviant." Her eyes open and she grins at me.

"Hey." I squeeze her tighter. "It takes one to know one."

That makes her laugh, and I swear the wind carries it all around me.

"I want to go back to Denver," Merry says.

"Wow." I feign shock.

She nudges me with her elbow, but I don't let her wiggle away. "What?"

"You can't stand Denver." I laugh. "What did you say... it's too quiet and boring?"

Merry purses her lips. "Maybe I'm learning how to slow down."

"That's dangerous." I lean in, with my lips against her ear. "You slow down, and I'll definitely catch you for good."

I run my tongue along the ridge of her ear, and it sends a shiver through her whole body.

"Not fair," she says with a groan. "You know I can't have sex with you right now."

"I know," I say, peppering kisses behind her ear and down her neck. "You've got to learn to enjoy the anticipation. It makes getting what you want so much better."

"Says the guy who would know a thing or two about that." She groans as I make my way back up her neck.

"Exactly." I lift my head and look down at her. "But you know what, Mercedes Lopez?"

"What, Noah Hayes?" she mocks me.

I lean down and kiss her temple.

"You were worth the wait."

She smiles and I swear it brightens up the darkening sky around us. "You're so ridiculous."

"Mm-hmm," I agree with her, "and you love it."

Merry rolls her eyes, but she settles into my arms and stays there. "I wouldn't think too much of that. I've never been known for making the best decisions."

I tickle her and she laughs.

"Admit it," I say, "Or I won't stop."

She's laughing so hard that everyone is looking over at us now, but I don't let up until she finally manages to swat me away.

"Fine, fine," she shrieks, turning her body so she's sideways sitting between my legs, with hers draped over one of mine.

She wraps her arms around my neck and leans in so she's nose to nose with me, her breath still quick from laughing.

"I love it, and I love you." She smiles. "Happy now?"

"I don't know." I give her a kiss. "Say it again. And again, and again."

But she just laughs, which I love even more. Because she finds me absolutely ridiculous, but she loves me anyway.

34

MERRY

My eyes peel open, but everything is foggy. The room is filled with a bright light, and if I didn't know any better, I'd think maybe I should follow it. But it doesn't take me long to realize I'm waking up in my hospital room, and the procedure is over, even if I'm not sure how long I've been sleeping.

I try to move, but everything is heavy as I blink myself awake. I'm pretty sure I should probably be in pain right now, but it's all dulled by whatever medication they're pumping into me.

Slowly I start waking up, and that's when I notice my mom and dad are sitting on the couch in the hospital room.

"Mom," I say, but it comes out sounding like there's a frog in my throat.

She jumps up and hurries over to my bedside, grabbing my hand. Her hands are warm, and I run my thumb over the wrinkles that have started forming in the last few years on the back of them.

Although she tried to pretend all morning she wasn't worried, I know her too well. Her brown hair is in a tight bun and there are dark circles under her eyes, reflecting the stress from today back at me.

"Hola, Mija," she says with a careful smile, as she looks me up and down trying to read my facial expressions. "Don't try to move too much. The doctor said you need to rest."

"Did it go okay?" I can't help but be worried after what happened last time.

Mom nods. "It went wonderful, don't worry. It took a little longer than expected, but Dr. Winters took his time and said that everything went according to plan. There should be minimal scarring."

She pats the back of my hand and gives me a warm smile.

"Good," I tip my head back, feeling relief that makes me realize how stressed I've been. The weight I've been feeling inside physically and mentally feels like it's lifted, and for the first time in a year I take a deep breath.

"Where's Noah?" I ask her, surprised he isn't in the room right now, and hoping my dad didn't scare him off.

"He went to grab us water," Mom says. "He thought we might be thirsty."

She gives me a little smirk that shows me she's coming around to him. After all, if anyone is proof that it's impossible to deny Noah's charms, it's me. He'll win them over in time.

Mom looks over her shoulder at Dad, who is standing now, looking at me with a straight face.

"I'll go find Noah." Mom leans down to give me a kiss on the cheek and whispers, "Play nice while I'm gone, Mija."

I grumble, not sure why she's worried about me. I'm the one chained to my hospital bed by IVs and wires right now, so if anyone has the advantage, it's him. Mom pulls back and gives Dad a look over her shoulder that says something similar before leaving.

"Hey, Dad," I say when Mom disappears, resting my head back and closing my eyes for a minute. It still feels like a lot of work to stay awake right now.

Machines hum, filling the silence of the room. Everything from my eyelids to my toes feels heavy.

The bed sinks and I open my eyes to find my dad sitting on the edge of it beside me. He looks a lot like Grandpa when he's stressed, even more so these past couple of years now that there's a sprinkle of gray hair starting at his temples. He has the same dark, hard stare Grandpa always wore, but Dad's is softened by his rounder face and softer features.

"You look good." Dad's gaze moves down, taking me in.

With him sitting here, I miss how close he and I used to be. Growing up, Monica was close with Mom because she was a lot like her—down to earth and outwardly loving.

I was a daddy's girl. He understood Monica and I weren't close in age, so he found ways to make up for it. Every day after work, he'd find me. We would run around, play catch, go on walks, or take trips to the bay.

I've always been more like him—adventurous, wild, difficult to love. We don't trust as easily, even if we're passionate and impulsive. But with all our similarities, we're also headstrong and set in our ways. And while it made us close when I was younger, as the years went on it formed a rift.

"Sounds like things went well," I say, trying to fill the room with something other than our tension.

Dad nods, and I reach out for his hand. His eyes look down as my fingers rest on the back of it, and he covers it with his other hand.

"I worry about you," he says.

"I know, Dad."

"You run off with this band, and next time I see you is like this." His mouth forms a hard line.

I shake my head. "That's an exaggeration. I saw you a couple of nights ago for dinner. And I saw you last time I was in town."

"You know what I mean," he says, stubborn as always.

It makes me feel a little bad for what Noah must have to deal with when trying to get me to budge on something. While my dad's bullheadedness is frustrating, I know it's also a reflection of my own.

"How have they been treating you?" Dad asks, giving the smallest inch, and I'm relieved to hear it.

"Good. It's not like you think."

It might be, actually, but I don't need to throw gasoline on this fire, especially when he has nothing to worry about. I hold my own on tour, and he forgets that I'm fully capable of doing so.

"It's just, you had one year left—"

"I know." This conversation has only had one result in the past year, and that's one giant circle that leaves us both irritated. "But music is my dream. Remember?"

He nods, although he doesn't look happy about it.

"You remember that summer you set up the stage for me in the backyard?" I say, and it breaks his façade for a second. "I spent the entire summer out there singing at the top of my lungs. I'm sure the neighbors loved it."

Dad's frown cracks and the smallest smile crosses his lips. "You sung beautifully, if they didn't love it, then that's on them."

I smile. "I know you're not happy with me dropping out of school, but you have to understand, I'm doing what I'm meant to. If anything, all this..." I wave to the hospital room... "is a reminder. I'm not going to waste my time doing things that don't make me happy. Monica didn't when she started writing books, and I won't either."

"My daughters." He sighs. "Always such free spirits."

I tip my head and we look at each other. Even if we might always be on opposite sides of the fence, for the first time in a year, it feels like we're seeing the other side, and I'm hopeful about that.

"That summer I built you the stage in the backyard, your mom and I would sit out on the back porch until it got dark listening to you sing." Dad rubs the back of my hand with his thumb. "You were begging to be free up there, in your own world. And even if your sister spent years giving me a headache worrying about her and Carson, I knew you were the daughter that was really going to test me."

I scrunch my face because there really is no arguing. Testing my parents might as well have been my favorite hobby as a teenager. The moment they told me to do anything, I did the exact opposite.

"I'm sorry."

He shakes his head. "You wouldn't be my Mercedes if you didn't."

Dad looks down at my arm and probably notices I've filled it with a few more tattoos since the last time I was in town.

"Those are new." His eyes fall on the tattoo of a mirror with the reflection of a drooping rose in it.

"You hate it."

He tips his head to the side and then smiles. "I don't understand it."

That makes me laugh, and a cautious smile climbs his face. I rest my other hand over his and we squeeze each other's fingers. I forgot how good it feels to be home until this moment, where my family is once again a place I belong.

"Thank you for being here."

Dad pats my head. "Mercedes, I will go to the ends of the earth for you and your sister. Even if it will destroy me."

That makes me smile.

"Now..." Dad sits up a little bit taller, still not letting go of one of my hands. "Tell me about this Noah. How terribly are you torturing him?"

"Hey, *he's* the rock star. You're not worried about me?" I cross my arms over my chest.

"I know my daughter too well." He smirks.

I roll my eyes but don't argue because there's really no point when I know Noah's actually the sweetheart out of the two of us.

"It seems like he takes care of you." Dad's face relaxes and I finally feel the tension between us melting away. "I may not like his little band, but I can't fault him for being good to my daughter."

"First of all, his *little band* is the number one rock band in the world." I lift an eyebrow at him. "And second, you're right, I should probably torture him a little less."

Dad leans in with a smile. "Oh no, you feel free to torture him a little. Remind him what he's working for."

He winks at me, and I laugh. Whether my dad comes around with Noah or not, it doesn't mean he'll go easy on him. After all, Monica knew Carson almost her whole life and Dad still makes him work for his approval.

"Speaking of the boyfriend." Dad narrows his eyes as he spots Mom and Noah walking toward the room through the open door.

"Play nice." I pat him on the arm.

"For you, Mija." He leans down and kisses my forehead, "I will make him work his ass off."

I start laughing so hard that it hurts all over.

"I'll take these smiles as a good sign," Mom says, walking into the room.

Dad stands to meet her near the door and Noah walks over to my bedside smiling.

God, he looks so good with that grin, that it warms all the way to my heart.

"Hey, beautiful." He leans over to give me a chaste kiss on the forehead, probably because my parents are standing right there. Because the Noah I know would climb in bed with me and kiss me so hard I'd be panting in a matter of seconds if we were alone.

"Hey, yourself." I reach for his hand. It feels like it's been weeks since I've held it, even though I know it was only this morning.

Noah sits beside me on the bed, and I lean against him. For as much of a fight as I put up for him to stay in Denver, I'm thankful right now that he didn't. There's no one else I'd rather wake up to than him, sitting there looking at me like he wouldn't let anything bad happen.

Mom gives us a warm look, but Dad just glares at Noah, and I can't help but smirk in return. It's better to have a room of people in your corner looking out for your best interest, than not.

"We'll give you some space," Mom says.

Dad doesn't take his eyes off Noah. "But we'll be back."

They disappear and Noah finally settles down next to me. He lays on the bed and turns to face me, balancing on the edge so I don't have to shift. When he lifts his arm for me, I let him slip it under my head and I curl against his chest.

"You never mentioned how terrifying your father is." Noah chuckles.

"Didn't I?" I grin.

He brushes a strand of hair off my face and looks down at me. "It's good to see you smiling though."

"I think we came to a mutual understanding."

"Good." Noah kisses my forehead again.

"They said it went well."

Noah nods. "They did. You relieved?"

"Yes. Not that it means I won't have to deal with it again the future, but at least for now."

Noah's hand rests on my arm and his fingers are tapping away like they always do. He probably doesn't even notice, yet, I find such comfort in it.

"And if that's so, we'll deal with it," Noah says, resting his head on top of mine and holding me.

I feel my eyes getting heavy again, comforted by the fact that whether I wanted Noah here or not, I'm glad he is. Noah would be by my side through anything.

"Stay with me." I nuzzle against his chest, feeling myself already drifting.

"Always," Noah says, planting a kiss on my forehead. "I wouldn't be anywhere else."

I take a deep breath and feel like I'm absorbing him in that inhale. Wintergreen and warm laundry. Comfort. Calm. Peace.

"Move in with me," Noah says, sounding almost nervous.

I look up at him and his eyes are burrowing into me like he's trying to plant the answer he wants in my brain.

"To your house in Denver?"

Noah nods. "I know we're on tour most of the time anyway, but I told you I'm in this. You're the person I want to come home to—to make a home with. Whatever that looks like. And who knows where things are going to go from here with your demo, or my next album. But wherever it takes us, I want to be in this together."

There's a wrinkle between his eyebrows and he's rambling, which is adorable. He looks genuinely scared of me running in this moment, not that I could with all the IVs in me. But also, I don't want to. Not anymore.

"Okay," I smile, and his face relaxes. "Let's do this."

"Yeah?"

I nod. "I'm in."

Noah leans down and kisses me so hard it takes my breath away. Pausing only to say, "I love you."

"I love you too," I mumble as he parts my mouth with his tongue.

And I'm finally ready to accept all that comes with it.

35

MERRY

SIX WEEKS LATER

I HAVEN'T CALLED A place home since I was a kid living with my parents. After that, I moved to the dorms at college, and from there, I was either on tour buses, in hotel rooms, or crashing on couches.

It isn't until I use the key Noah made me to his house in Denver that I feel like I belong somewhere again.

The house is quiet when I walk inside. Noah mentioned that he would still be at Adrian's finishing up a song when I arrived, but I'm still bummed because I miss him.

The band stayed in Seattle as long as possible after my surgery, but they had a few things that were easier to record in Denver, so Noah reluctantly returned two weeks before I was able to.

Technically, I could have, but I decided to wait out the full six weeks at my sisters so I wouldn't have to go back and forth for post-op appointments.

Even though it was tough being apart, it was nice to have that alone time with my sister again. Growing up, there were too many years between us. But in these past six weeks it feels like Monica and I had a chance to connect in ways we couldn't at younger ages.

Carson might have had to act as mediator a few times, but for the most part, it was surprisingly nice lazing around the house while Monica worked on her books. We binged Hallmark movies, ate take-out, and laughed. It was freeing.

I bring my suitcase into the bedroom and see Noah left a present for me on the bed.

Of course, he did.

The man is so ridiculously thoughtful. Between the flowers he had delivered every few days he was gone, and the daily phone calls, it's safe to say I'm finally starting to adjust to receiving this level of affection.

After rolling my suitcase into the closet, I sit down on the bed and place the small black box in my lap. It weighs nothing and I can't imagine what he could have hidden in here, but when I open the lid, I see a simple piece of paper with a drawing on it.

Lifting it up, I see he's drawn a winding brick road with twisted trees and vines on either side. At the end of the path, is the silhouette of a girl holding a heart in the palms of her hands. It's dark, beautiful, and strangely familiar.

"You got my gift." I jump at Noah's voice and look up to see him standing in the doorway.

I hold up the piece of paper. "You drew this?"

He nods.

"It's beautiful."

"Recognize it?" he asks.

My eyebrows pull tight as I scan the paper, looking for any hint. I shake my head. "No, sorry, but I love it."

Noah crosses the room grinning. "Flip it over."

I do, and on the back of the paper, he's scribbled something.

Follow the yellow brick road
Even when the path gets dark and bleak
Follow the yellow brick road
No matter where it starts to lead
There are truths to find
Fears that thrive
Places deep you'll hide behind
But if you
Follow the yellow brick road
In time, in time, in time
You're home

It's my song, The Road Home.

I turn the paper over again and look at the girl at the end of the path and see it now. My words brought to life in his drawing. The girl has made it past the thorns and through the forest, and she's standing at the other side, with a heart in her hands.

She's home.

"Noah," I say, tears brimming in my eyes. "It's a dick thing to do to make me cry when I just got here."

I swat the paper at him playfully as he sinks down next to me on the bed, but he ignores it.

"Do you like it?"

Setting the paper back in the box, I put it on the bedside table. I turn to wrap my arms around his shoulders, and he quickly pulls me into his lap, so I'm straddling him.

"I love it."

"You said you've been looking for the right fairytale to finish your right arm, I thought you should finish it with your own." He smiles.

"That's so cheesy. Did you practice that speech while I was gone?"

Noah shrugs.

"Well…" I lean in. "Cheesy or not, I love it."

Noah wraps his arms tighter around my body and it feels like I'm home in this moment. His pale blue eyes are fixed on mine, and I lean in to press my lips to his. It feels like it's been forever since we've been like this.

After surgery, there was a lot of healing. And even if he stayed at Monica's house with me, it wasn't a pretty recovery. I was in a lot of pain, and he was understanding through all of it.

I've missed being lost against his lips and in his arms. I open my mouth for him to slip his tongue in and I sink deeper into it, trying to make up for every moment we've missed.

Noah's fingers clench on the back of my shirt, and I know he feels the tension like I do, thick enough we could cut through it.

I pull away, but he catches my bottom lip between his teeth, and I feel it all the way to my toes.

"I missed you so fucking much," he says, kissing my lip where he just bit it.

I run my fingernails up the back of his hair, scratching the base of his skull and making his body shiver. "I missed you too."

I'm not sure if I'll ever get tired of the way his eyes light up when I say that. Or when I tell him I love him. It makes me wonder if he sees the same thing when he looks in mine, because everything about him consumes me.

"I brought you a present too." I smirk.

"Oh yeah?"

I pull back just enough to reach for the bottom hem of my black T-shirt, and I slowly peel it off, revealing a strappy purple lace bra underneath. Just because I don't like to wear bright clothes, doesn't mean I don't appreciate some jewel-toned lingerie. Especially knowing how much Noah enjoys it.

Noah's eyes rake down my body, and his hand reaches up my stomach, slowly tracing the outline of my wing tattoo, before skating over my breasts.

"Fuck, Merry, you're the most gorgeous woman on the planet." He squeezes my nipple, and the sensation of his fingers clamping tight shoots straight down between my legs.

I lean in so my mouth is near his ear. "The doctor gave me the all-clear."

Noah's grip on me tightens. "You sure?"

I nod.

It's been six long weeks of no sex, which has been pure torture. It's not fair to finally be getting the best sex of your life and then have it suddenly taken away. My body has been aching in frustration, so I can only imagine how hard it's been on him.

Noah leans in, ready to devour me, but I bring my finger up to his lips to stop him.

"One more thing," I say, and he narrows his eyes at me like if I don't hurry it up, he'll eat me alive. "The bra was only half of the present. It's a matching set."

Noah grabs my wrist and moves my hand.

"That's it." He grabs my hips and flips us around, so my back is on the bed.

He unbuttons my jeans and slides them off, standing back so that he can appreciate the view.

"You like your present?" I tease him, propping up on my elbows and shifting my knees over to one side so he can get a peek at my bare ass in this barely-there thong.

He tips his head and takes me in from my breasts to my ass, running his hand along the bulge forming in his pants.

"You know I do." He bites his bottom lip. "That's a sexy little outfit."

"They're also crotchless." I shrug and narrow my gaze. "I was feeling naughty."

"Oh yeah?" He strips his shirt off, showing off his sculpted chest, and I don't know how I've made it six weeks without his body all over me.

Noah leans forward on the bed and reaches for the hair at the base of my skull, wrapping his fingers through it. But right when I think he's about to kiss me, he tugs my hair just a little and stops me inches from his lips.

"You wanna be a bad girl?" He smirks, and his eyes drop to my mouth. "Then get on your knees."

Noah releases my hair and stands up, undoing the button on his pants. But he doesn't move for the zipper.

His stare darkens as he watches me slide off the bed and get down on my knees in front of him. It's intoxicating looking at him standing over me, with his muscles on display in the dim light of the bedroom.

I reach for his zipper and slide it down slowly, torturing both of us with anticipation as each click of the teeth unclenches. Sliding his pants and underwear down his legs, I feel myself getting wetter by the second. I run my hands back up his legs, over his muscular thighs, taking in every ripple of his rock-hard body as I move around and feel his firm ass in my grip.

He lets me explore him, with his dick hard and ready inches from my mouth. I drag my hands around the front of him, over his stomach, appreciating every ripple of his abs. He's perfect in all the ways I can see standing in front of me like a Greek god, and all the ways only I know about.

When I finally move down and wrap my hand around the base of his cock, the slightest tug pulls a bead of cum from the tip, and I lick it off slow enough to savor how it tastes on my tongue, and how it makes his entire body shiver.

Noah wraps his hand into my hair, holding me firm with his fist. His other hand grabs onto my chin and his thumb peels my mouth open. I run my tongue over it to taste him.

"Don't play with me right now, Mercedes. I've missed this," he says, placing the tip of his cock on my tongue. "Suck it like the naughty girl you are."

Then he shoves himself in until he hits the back of my throat and makes me gag. He uses his hold on the back of my head to fuck my mouth, and I get lost in the feeling of his dick sliding between my lips. He's rough enough that I know I'll feel him in the back of my throat tomorrow, and I love it.

I want him to claim me, to have me, to use me. I want to show him all the things he shows me in return. Unconditional love and true acceptance. He makes me feel like the woman of his dreams, and I want to be that for him.

Reaching up, I grab onto his thighs and brace myself. His thrusts make me teary, but I don't want him to stop. He's watching me take his cock in my mouth, and I can see the effect I'm having on him in his eyes. The intensity hits me so hard I feel pressure building between my legs for him.

He's close, his entire body stiffens, and his jaw clenches. But instead of coming down my throat, he pulls me off him by my hair and lifts me up onto the bed.

"Fuck," he says, climbing over me, and pushing my knees apart. "Your mouth is perfection."

Noah kisses me hard, dipping his tongue into my mouth. I don't know what we're searching for, but I feel frantic to find it.

"You feel so good," I tell him. "How long has it been?"

"Too. Fucking. Long."

Then he starts trailing kisses down me, until he captures one of my nipples in his mouth. He twists the other one in his fingers as he clamps his teeth down on me, and it vibrates all the way to my core.

Lifting my hips, I feel the head of his dick toying with me. He hovers his hips down just enough to coat himself in my wetness, before pulling back and leaving me with an unsatisfied moan.

I grab the sheets in frustration. "Noah, please."

That word gets his attention, and he pulls his mouth from my nipple with a pop.

"You know how I love when you ask nicely."

His dark stare makes me shiver as he grabs my body and flips me over onto my stomach, tugging my hips up until my ass is in the air and he's kneeling behind me. His hand moves down my spine, kneading my ass, before settling between my legs where I'm begging for him.

I groan as he slips a finger in.

"Is this okay?" he asks, and I realize he's being gentle.

Looking back over my shoulder I'm met with a genuine look of concern.

"Yes." I watch him intently as he slips in another finger.

I stretch around him, and it's been so long it's like my body has forgotten what it's like for him to be inside me. But with one touch, he's awakened every nerve.

"Yes," I say again, with a moan this time as he moves his fingers in and out.

I'm soaking his hand, I'm so excited, and when he pulls his hand away and gets into place, I feel my whole body on edge with anticipation.

Unlike when he fucked my mouth, he nudges in slowly. Inch by torturous inch until he's fully inside me and I feel like my body has been brought home.

"Still okay?"

I shift my hips to press them against him and he groans.

"Yes," I say. "Fuck me, Noah. I need you."

His hips start to move, slow at first as my body adjusts. He's stretching me to my limits, and I love the sensation. Slowly, he starts to quicken his pace, moving faster and faster until the sound of my ass slapping against his pelvis fills the room.

He reaches down and grabs the sides of my arms, pulling me up so he can press my back to his chest. He widens his knees and thrusts in slow, torturous circles. His hand wraps around my throat, and I turn my face to his, so I can meet his mouth with my tongue.

It's intimate and possessive, and I love everything about it.

"I love you," he says with his mouth hovering over my own.

His hips circle and I feel every ridge of his dick as it hits me in a magical place that leads to every corner of my body.

"I love you too."

His grip tightens and his pace quickens. He holds me against him, and we might as well melt into one person because as he comes inside me and I tumble over the ledge, I fall for him all over again.

Epilogue

Noah

One Year Later

My fingers trace over my fresh tattoo. It's a solid black ring and I can still feel the buzzing as the needle dragged along my skin. Although this tattoo has mostly healed, the sensation of it is still there, vibrating through me like Merry does.

Finally, another ring, when it felt like I would be stuck at two forever. Except, this one isn't around my forearm like the others, this one is on my left hand.

For her. For today.

A *big moment.*

When Merry asked me what they represented the day inside the tattoo parlor, that's what I told her. Because I had the other two placed on me at times when I felt everything in my life was about to change. Moments when I knew the time before it and the time after would look like different things. Changing me in irreversible ways.

But nothing compares to this.

Standing on the beach barefoot, wearing dress slacks and a white dress shirt with the top two buttons popped. It's as fancy as Merry was willing to get. While I would have been willing to do the whole church scene with the three-hundred-person reception, she wanted something quieter and more intimate. And ultimately, I'm glad she nixed the big wedding because standing here with the sea breeze cooling this warm day, all that matters is being here in this moment.

I rub the tattoo band on my left ring finger again as I wait for her to make her appearance, and I know this is the one moment in my life that will really transform me. Not that making our relationship official or legal changes anything between us, but it's the commitment. The dedication, in front of our family and friends. A chance to say out loud that my heart belonged to this woman the day I met her, and it always will.

Which is why we're doing this after only being together for a year, and only engaged for two months of it. Most of our family and friends think we're crazy, but the ones that really know us, get it.

After all, it took long enough for me to convince her to date me, so when she said yes to marrying me, I wasn't going to put this off. I've been waiting for this day since she accidentally walked into my dressing room.

Hers are the eyes I want to look into for the rest of my life. Seeing me for all the good and bad and loving me through it.

"You're lookin' a little pale, man. Sure you wanna go through with this?" Rome smirks at me around the back of Sebastian.

Sebastian shoves Rome's shoulder before I get the chance to.

"Shut the fuck up, man," Adrian says from the other side of me.

"Just fucking around with him." Rome grins.

I shake my head. "Someday Rome."

"What... this? For me? No way in hell." He laughs.

Sebastian and Adrian both look at me like I'm crazy for even suggesting it, but I just shrug. I've seen men like Rome fall before. Look at Sebastian.

Rome rolls his shirt sleeves up his forearms and it shows off more of his tattoos.

"In all seriousness though, I'm happy for you man," Rome says. "Merry's a cool chick."

I know he means it. This might not be the life he sees for himself, but the band has been there through all the shit with me and Merry, and they know there is absolutely no one who makes me happier than my little rain cloud who's soon to be my wife.

"So, when are you and Cassie going to take the plunge?" I ask Sebastian.

He looks at me and grins. "If it were up to me, it would have happened already, but we agreed not to talk about it until after the world tour."

"It's after the world tour now," I remind him.

A shit-eating grin stretches his face, and he slaps me on the back of the shoulder. "That it is, my brother."

From the look in his eyes, I get the feeling it won't be long before we're at another one of these, and I'm happy for him.

I look out at all the faces around us. It's a small ceremony of people, and it's perfect. Everyone we care about. Friends and family, even if my family is noticeably absent.

Merry tried to reach out to them when we got engaged, but there was no use. My parents decided a long time ago that if I didn't want to fit into their life in a very particular way then they didn't need me, and they are committed to that decision. For the first time in my life, that's okay. All the family I need is right here.

People who supported us through everything. People who picked up their lives during Merry's surgery and moved to Washington for a full month so that I could be near her. People who advocated for her demo when she got back to Denver. People who believe in us both as a couple and professionally.

Adrian managed to land Merry a spot opening for Four Clovers on their latest tour. And although it was a dream come true for her, it was a test for us. Halfway through the world tour, Merry had to head to LA to meet up with them, and even if I spent every free moment going back and forth, once the band was overseas, we ended up spending a lot of time apart. But we made it work, like I knew we would.

I'll do whatever I have to, and I know she'll do the same.

I spot Merry's mom walking out from the reception tent, where Merry and her bridal party have been hiding.

She walks up the aisle, giving me a nod to let me know we're ready, which forms a knot in my throat.

This is it. The moment I've spent my life waiting for.

While you always hear stories about little girls planning their weddings in their heads as kids, no one talks about us guys who do it. Just because we have dicks doesn't mean we can't be romantic and sweet and want all this stupid cute shit.

So call me lame, call me whatever you want. I'm marrying the girl of my dreams, so fuck everyone's judgment.

Eloise is the first one down the aisle, followed by Cassie and then Monica. They look like a line of angels walking toward us in their simple white bridesmaid dresses. The silk shines against the setting sun and a halo of warm light surrounds them.

It's interesting to me how three women can all be wearing the same thing and look so different. Eloise with her sandy brown hair in a tight ponytail and her half-sleeve of tattoos. Cassie with her bubble-gum-pink-tipped blonde hair and barely any makeup. And then there's Merry's sister Monica, with her curly hair that can't seem to be contained even when she ties it in a bun on her head, wearing a necklace with a lemon-yellow gemstone hanging from it that looks a lot like the kind their mom makes for them.

There's a pause as the three of them line up across from the guys at the altar and then the music changes. Merry refused to let them play the wedding march or anything traditional, so Only One by Yellowcard starts instead, and I feel the air shift.

I'm not sure if the wind quiets or the world pauses, but it all fades away as Merry steps out between the sheath of white curtains.

My dark goddess.

Merry stands with her arm looped through her dad's and she's wearing a black lace strapless wedding dress that hugs her tightly around the chest, before flowing out at the waist. A thick braid acts as a headband for her hair, and waves flow over her shoulders and down her back.

My heart might as well stop in my chest because my entire world is walking in slow motion toward me, and I want to run out and meet her halfway.

But I don't. I wait what feels like hours for her to make her way down the aisle, with her bare feet and tattoos on display. She's a fucking vision.

Her dad unwinds her hand when they reach us, and I take his hand and shake it.

"Be good to my girl," he says, slapping his other hand over our clasped handshake.

"I will, sir."

He nods, before giving Merry a kiss on the cheek. She waits until he's seated by her mom before stepping forward.

Merry stands in front of me at the altar and I lean in to whisper in her ear. "It's not fair to the rest of the world for you to be so beautiful."

I brush the faintest kiss on her cheek and then pull back as Sebastian clears his throat, reminding me we're not alone.

"You don't look so bad yourself," Merry says with a narrowed gaze that travels the full length of me. She bites her bottom lip, and I can't wait to mess up her cherry-red lipstick later.

"Should we get started?" Adrian asks.

He offered to officiate when Merry started ranting about non-denominational ceremonies.

I nod because I've never been more ready for anything.

"I want to thank you all for coming here today to celebrate the love between Noah Samuel Hayes and Mercedes Adelita Garcia Lopez. Marriage is a commitment. It is a devotion to the person who stands in front of you. A promise to honor them, support them, and love them, through all struggles and successes. It is a relationship built as much on faith as it is hard work. And as someone who has the pleasure of knowing Noah and Merry well, I have no doubt they will honor these vows to each other."

Adrian's not usually a man of many words, so I'm a little surprised to hear true sentiment in his voice.

"Noah and Merry have written vows they would like to recite to each other." Adrian nods at me. "Noah."

I hold Merry's hands in mine and look down into her dark eyes.

"Mercedes Lopez," I say with a grin, and she rolls her eyes. She still hates it when I call her by her full name, which makes it that much more fun. "I loved you from the moment I met you. And, while that's usually just a line people say, for me, it's the truth. I haven't always believed in destiny or fate. But whatever put you in my path that day was something bigger than us. Because you not only saved me, but you also saw me, through and through. You changed me. And I'm a better man because of you."

Merry's grip tightens and tears brim in her eyes.

"Merry," Adrian says, and she nods.

She looks down, and when her big brown eyes meet mine again a tear falls from them.

"Noah," she says with a smile. "I didn't see you coming."

Her words choke in her throat, and she stumbles a little on her words, so I pull her close and whisper in her ear.

"It's okay, I've got you."

She squeezes my hands and gains her composure.

"I'm not good at this. And not just love, but relationships in general. More than a few times I've failed at us because of it. But you don't quit."

Her statement gets more than a few laughs from the crowd because it's no secret I had to chase her endlessly until she gave in.

"Thank you for never giving up on us," she says with a smile. "Because I'm never going to give up on us. I'm yours, always."

I reach over to wipe the tear from her cheek, and she smiles at my touch as I hold her hands once more in my own.

"I love you," I say.

"I love you."

We hold stares as Adrian steps forward again and nods.

"For hundreds of years, couples have exchanged rings as a token of their vows to each other. The ring is an unbroken, never-ending circle that represents the commitment of love that is forever. Can we have the rings?"

I turn and Sebastian hands me the ruby infinity band I had made for Merry, while Monica hands her the solid black tungsten band for me.

"Noah, do you accept this ring from Merry as a token of her love and faithfulness to your vows?"

"I do," I say, looking into Merry's eyes and holding back that knot that won't break loose from in the back of my throat. She slips my ring over the permanent one tattooed on my finger.

Then I take Merry's hand and hold it up, rubbing my thumb over the solid black tattoo ring that already circles her finger as well. I thought the wings would always be my favorite tattoo on her. And they were until she asked me to tattoo this band on her left hand.

"Merry, do you accept this ring from Noah as a token of his love and faithfulness to your vows?" Adrian asks her.

Merry narrows her eyes at me and smirks the slightest, making me sweat for a second on purpose, which I plan on making her pay for later.

Finally, she smiles wide, with tears brimming on her bottom lashes. "I do."

I slip the ring over her tattooed band and kiss the back of her hand. Her skin is so warm I want to kiss her all over.

The sun is setting on the horizon behind her, and she looks more beautiful than any painting by any artist as she stands there in her black dress.

"Noah and Merry, you have pronounced your love and commitment to each other in front of your friends, family, and each other through the promises you have just made," Adrian says. "It is with these in mind, I now pronounce you husband and wife. Noah, you may kiss your bride."

I stop hearing anything Adrian says after the word kiss because I'm already grabbing Merry by the waist and the back of the neck and dipping her down so I can kiss my wife for the first time.

"Noah," she says with a little squeal as I dip her lower. "My family is here."

"Oh, I'm aware," I say, hovering just over her mouth. "And that's the only reason I haven't ripped this dress off your hot little body yet."

She grins and wraps her arms around my neck to kiss me deeper.

There are hoots and hollers from the crowd as our friends and family go wild. It's the best audience screams I've heard in my life.

Breaking the kiss, I pull us both back up to standing and hold her firmly against my chest.

"I love you, Mrs. Hayes." I smile at her.

"I love you too, Mr. Hayes," she says back, lifting on her toes to steal a kiss.

My love. My wife. My everything.

BOOKS BY EVA SIMMONS

Seattle Singles

Miss Matched
(Matchmaker meets Billionaire)

Miss Behaved
(Second Chance, Friends to Lovers)

Miss Understood
(Enemies to Lovers, Fake Relationship)

Enemy Muse (Rock Star Romance)

Heart Break Her
(Celebrity Crush)

Forever and Ever
(Opposites Attract)

Heart of a Rebel
(Second Chance)

Worth the Trouble
(Forbidden Love)

Find a complete book list at www.evasimmons.com

- amazon.com/Eva-Simmons/e/B07MMX2MLB?ref_=dbs_p_ebk_r00_abau_000000
- facebook.com/AuthorEvaSimmons/
- goodreads.com/author/show/16225312.Eva_Simmons
- bookbub.com/profile/eva-simmons
- instagram.com/evasimmonsbooks/
- tiktok.com/@evasimmonsbooks
- twitter.com/evasimmonsbooks

Acknowledgments

Love isn't always pretty. It isn't always kind. It's never easy. But it's worth it, even through the messy parts.

Many of you might be reading this hoping for an epilogue where Noah and Merry have a baby... I'm going to be brutally honest with you, they don't. At least, not in the traditional way. But what is tradition anyway? We build families in many ways—through blood, friendship, adoption, circumstance. The same way Enemy Muse built a family through music, Noah and Merry will create theirs in a way that is right for them.

Happy endings aren't always *all* happy. And in this case, I felt it was important to show that.

Noah and Merry broke my heart. But they are also one of my favorite couples I've written because they are honest, messy, and filled with love.

Noah and Merry have an incredible support system surrounding them. And like them, I couldn't do this without mine.

An enormous thank you to my husband, Chris, for being my greatest support as I write this series. Thank you for being there to help out when these books take up all my free time. Thank you for being there through every setback, every struggle, and every bit of success. There's no one else I'd rather have by my side on this journey. Now, please send me more mood music so I can write another book and do this all over again. Love you.

To my boys, I love you both with all my heart. I hope you always remember to follow your dreams, and that it's never too late to chase them.

Mom, I remember telling you I'd never write a surprise pregnancy story right before sending you this book. And while this story isn't necessarily that, sorry for breaking your heart with this one. As I sit here, I'm at a loss for words, because there aren't enough to capture how thankful I am for you and your endless support. To my left, I see the little note you left on the chalkboard last time you were in town, and it's just one of the many little things you do that means more than you'll ever know. I love you and couldn't have done this without you.

Mikki, I'm pretty sure we covered the good/funny/inappropriate versions of what I might write here over Facetime just now. So here's the blank space we talked about for you to fill in with what's already been said_____. Joking aside, thank you for just being you. For being the person I can sit in a room with and not need words to fill the space. For being the best sister on the planet. For sharing pizza, laughs, and life with me. You cheered this story on before I put a single word to paper. This one's for you.

Alba, I've lost count of the years we've been friends, but I'll always remember the night I knew we'd be friends for life. We sat on a green couch and talked like we'd known each other forever. We've had thousands of conversations since, but I still clearly remember that one. To call you a friend is not enough. You're family to me. I love you and am so thankful to have you in my life.

To my beta readers, you come through every time. This one was no different. Thank you for seeing the story in the chaos and for loving the characters enough to make sure I do them justice.

Kat, you're a dream come true as an editor. You're a true collaborator, and I appreciate you well beyond the incredible work you do cleaning up my messy books. This series has been a roller coaster to write and I appreciate you being on this ride with me—especially in the case of this story. You are truly the best.

Ellison, thank you for your eagle eyes on this one. My writing can be a little poetic and all over the place, and I'm thankful to have you on my team to clean up the details I inevitably miss.

My wonderful author friends—starting this journey is lonely. Publishing is so much more than writing, and we all walk in blind. I'm so thankful to have found a community of writers who lift others up, share ideas, and spread the love.

A special thank you Rafa Catala for a beautiful cover image. And to David for being the perfect Noah.

To my ARC readers and Street Team, I considered just filling an entire page with *thank you's* but decided that still wouldn't be enough. Your reviews, shout outs, posts, messages, videos... they fill my heart. Thank you for being the voice shouting from the roof top in a big and noisy publishing industry. Thank you for the support, the energy, and the love. I couldn't do it without you.

Finally, A BIG HUG AND THANK YOU to my readers. You breathe life into these characters and books. Your reviews, messages, and shout-outs mean the world to me. I can't possibly put into words the special place you hold in my heart. Thank you, thank you, thank you! I hope you loved this book as much as I loved writing it. And I can't wait to share more stories with you soon.

About the Author

Eva Simmons writes hot, heartbreaking romance with complex heroines, and broken, dirty-talking bad boys who fall hard for them.

When Eva isn't dreaming up new worlds or devouring every book she can get her hands on, she can be found spending time with her family, painting a fresh canvas, or playing an elf in World of Warcraft.

Eva is currently living out her own happily ever after in Nevada with her family.

Printed in Great Britain
by Amazon